MOONLIGHT DRUID

A NEW ADULT URBAN FANTASY NOVEL

M.D. MASSEY

MODERN DIGITAL PUBLISHING

1

I stood in front of the Pack clubhouse with the alpha, Samson. The entire Pack had surrounded me, and something told me they weren't here for a Tupperware party.

The alpha looked me in the eye and sighed. "If you want my help, that means you have to join the Pack, just like any other prospect."

I'd come to him for help in learning to control my ríastrad, the curse that caused me to shift into an enraged, deadly creature out of legend. Since I was stuck with the curse, I wanted to learn how to control its effects so I could use it as a weapon. I was stronger, faster, and much more resistant to pain and injury in my other form. But more importantly, the only time I had access to the magic of Balor's Eye was when I shifted into my Hyde-side. The Eye's magic would be my ace in the hole when I confronted Fuamnach, the fae sorceress who'd cursed me, and her accomplice, the Dark Druid.

One was responsible for the death of my former girlfriend, Jesse. The other was responsible for the death of my father. I owed them both a hell of a lot of pain and misery. If getting justice for Jesse and Dad meant I had to face down a pack of werewolves, so be it.

Samson's eyes narrowed as he explained what was about to happen. "Every prospect starts the same way. I'd tell you this is going to hurt me more than it's going to hurt you, but that'd be a lie." Samson nodded to someone behind me, and that's when I triggered my cantrips.

Cantrips were relatively weak spells that performed a specific function, such as providing light, lighting a candle, or silencing footsteps. Since things hadn't gone so well the last time I'd met up with the Dark Druid, I'd spent time preparing myself in case I ran into him again. His magic was well beyond mine, and the only thing that had saved me from certain death was my ríastrad, and a great deal of help from Balor's Eye. The Eye's magic was powerful, as in god-killer powerful. Back in the day, Balor had used it to wipe out entire armies. If I could use the Eye's magic, I'd wipe the floor with the Dark Druid and Fuam-nach. But until I could control my change, its magic remained beyond my reach.

Which was why I'd set up these spells, working them into the weaves that held my wards. They were designed to save my ass in case I needed to become scarce in a hurry. One triggered a flashbang cantrip I could project from my hands. It was rela-tively simple magic, but useful just the same. The second cast a see-me-not spell on me; rather, it triggered the see-me-not spell I'd woven into my overcoat. And the third temporarily hardened the protection wards I now constantly wore in the form of an amulet and bracelet. Each provided me with some resistance to spells and physical attacks, just enough to save me from one of the Dark Druid's attacks.

But not from a full on beat down from a werewolf pack.

I knew the first attack would come from behind, so I pointed my right hand to the side and my left behind my back as the cantrips released. This would ensure that the flashbang spell blinded and deafened whoever was behind me. That would allow me to momentarily concentrate on defending my left flank. Or so I hoped. The see-me-not spell would only work on those wolves who broke eye contact with me, which was why the spell chain began with the flashbang.

The spell triggered with an explosive boom and enough light to blind the sensitive eyes of the wolves, even in daylight. As I heard gasps from the wolves to my rear and right, I rolled toward Samson and came up in a crouch to face the wolves who hadn't been affected. One was already closing with me—a large bruiser of a guy with deeply tanned skin, long dark hair, and a horse-shoe mustache. He could have been a Danny Trejo double if it weren't for his size. I spun and swept his legs out from under him, and heel-kicked him across the jaw.

Lights out, I thought. At least, for a few seconds. Werewolves healed fast.

I shuffled quickly to place the downed wolf between me and the rest of the Pack. I'd blinded two-thirds of them with my first spell, but the other ten or so were closing in fast. A rough-looking female with prison tats and short dark hair came around the Danny Trejo look-alike, crouched in a boxer's stance and looking like she knew how to throw a punch. I faked a jab and side-kicked her in the knee—not hard enough to snap it, but enough to give her a limp so she couldn't pursue.

"Fuck, Samson!" she yelled. "This kid fights dirty."

I backed away from her, still attempting to keep Danny Trejo between me and the rapidly closing group. The female wolf limped away from me, but the wolves I'd blinded had formed a tight half-circle, blocking my escape. I circled away from the group, looking to engage a wolf who broke away to flank me.

Maybe fifteen seconds had elapsed from the time I'd triggered my spell. I gave myself another twenty seconds, tops, before they bum-rushed me. As I calculated my next move, someone pulled Danny Trejo out of the ring, distracting me.

I glanced away momentarily, then turned my attention back to my attackers. My eyes snapped around just in time to see a long, slender leg ending in a steel-toed boot, coming right at my face. Not at regular speed, but werewolf speed. And it didn't look like this she-wolf was going to pull it.

That was the last thing I remembered before the boot connected with my jaw. *Lights out again. Shit.*

I woke to bright lights and lots of noise. I vaguely registered the thump and whine of loud, hard rock music blasting from somewhere nearby. The sound drove a spike through my temple. My jaw hurt like hell, I had an epic headache, and I wanted to puke.

Concussion. Definitely a concussion.

A voice shouted from close by. "Hey, everybody, the druid's awake!"

I sat up, nice and easy, to the roar of several dozen biker werewolves cheering my return to the land of the living. It made my head pound even worse. I rubbed my jaw, moving it around to make sure it wasn't broken. I'd be eating soup for a day or two, but my mouth still worked. My protective spells had done their job, but only just.

I felt someone slap me on the shoulder, and turned to acknowledge them. Sledge, the club's sergeant-at-arms, shoved a glass in my hand. The contents looked like beer, with stuff floating in it.

"Here, kid, drink this. Samson bought it off a witch we hire sometimes. Said it'd help you heal."

I sniffed the drink and gagged.

"No idea what's in it, but trust me, you want to drink it. Your face looks like it got into a fight with a Brahma bull—and lost. Drink up."

Fighting back a wave of nausea, I slugged down the drink. It was beer, but whatever witch's brew they'd poured into it made it taste like swamp water and piss. Not that I knew what either tasted like, but if I had to guess, this was it. There were solid chunks in the liquid, and I had to force a few of the slimier particles down, breathing heavily through my nose as I finished the glass off.

A chill passed through me, and the dull ache in my head turned into a sharp, stabbing pain that started at my jaw and radiated to the back of my head. The pain intensified until I was ready to scream with agony. Then, as suddenly as it had appeared, it faded away until my discomfort was nothing more than background noise. I felt my jaw pop and readjust, and feeling seeped back into the left side of my face—first in a wave of pain, then with a rush of relief as the soreness and swelling also receded. I tongued a loose molar that I hadn't noticed previously, and felt as it sunk back into its socket, settling firmly into place.

I popped my neck and took a deep breath, then surveyed the scene. I was sitting on a pool table, and there was a bloody stain in the felt where my head had rested a moment before. We were inside the Pack's clubhouse, and they were partying like there was no tomorrow. Werewolves loved to raise hell, and this Pack's parties were legendary, or so I'd heard. I got a few nods as Pack members strode past, but most pointedly ignored my presence.

"You guys jump everybody into the Pack?"

Sledge shrugged. "If they have the beast, they get a beating. Always been that way. That's the first step to being accepted into the Pack. Gotta see how a 'thrope fights. Fastest way to find out if they're going to be a liability or not."

"So—"

"How'd you do? Meh, I was surprised you lasted as long as you did, but some of the Pack thinks you cheated. A few stood up for you, 'cuz you can't even shift yet. So, you were fighting at a major disadvantage. Had to use what tools you had to protect yourself, and you did. Plus, you didn't go overboard. You could've collapsed Trina's knee, but you didn't. And Guerra might have had a headache earlier, but you could've hurt him a lot worse. So, I'd say you did alright."

I rubbed my jaw. "Did you get the plates off that truck that hit me?"

He chuckled. "Yeah, that was Samson's daughter. Likes to play rough. You'll meet her later."

I cracked my neck again and surveyed the club. Dozens of werewolves and humans filled the place, drinking, brawling, making out, and generally having a good time. "You know, I didn't expect this sort of welcome when I asked for Samson's help."

The huge werewolf smirked. "Bet you didn't expect to be brought into the Pack, either. Well, it's only temporary—but I'll let Samson explain his reasons for that." A dark look came over his face. "It was—not a popular decision."

I got the impression Sledge was telling me to watch my back. "Thanks for letting me know."

His face relaxed, and he grinned. "Hey, I owe you, anyway. I won six hundred bucks betting against everyone who said you wouldn't last five seconds. Figured you'd hold your own."

I'd fought Sledge on a sort of dare a while back, when I'd helped Bells with an investigation for the Cold Iron Circle. I was glad he wasn't the type to hold a grudge. I couldn't say the same for the Circle, though. They were self-appointed protectors who stepped in whenever a supernatural creature threatened the local human population. Belladonna's boss at the Circle didn't like me much, because in his eyes, my curse made me as much of a threat as the fae. Maybe worse.

Still, Bells was my girlfriend and a loyal friend, so I didn't hold it against her.

He grabbed two beers off a tray as a barmaid passed by, and shoved one in my hand. "Enjoy the party, prospect. Cause after tonight, you're going to be earning your keep around here."

I had no idea what that meant, but I expected it wouldn't involve selling Girl Scout cookies. But now wasn't the time for concern. If getting Samson's help meant I had to join the Pack, then I needed to blend in and play the part. I slammed down the beer and did my best to join in the fun.

I SOON GOT the impression that my presence wasn't exactly welcomed by the Pack. After getting the cold shoulder a few times, I took a seat at the bar. Before long, I heard someone calling for me from a table in the corner.

"Hey, druid! Yeah, you, the guy who fights dirty. Come over here."

It was the woman I'd knee-capped earlier, the one Sledge had called Trina. She had an up-to-no-good smile on her face, a bottle of beer in one hand, and her arm draped around some skinny redhead ten years her junior.

I sighed and walked over. The redhead looked me up and down—not in a sexual way, but perhaps to size me up as competition. Trina was still grinning ear to ear as I approached the table.

"Oh, don't look so damned butt-hurt. I'm just giving you shit, prospect. Pull up a seat."

I shrugged and sat down. "Sorry about the knee."

She waved my comment away. "Don't mention it. Barely did

any damage—doesn't even hurt now. Truth is, you did alright. Whole purpose of the exercise is to see if you're game, and if you'll do anything chickenshit. You passed on both counts. If the rest of these assholes don't see it that way, fuck 'em."

"Thanks."

She set her beer down and stuck her hand out. "Name's Trina."

"Colin." I shook her hand. "Sledge told me who you were earlier."

She stuck her lip out slightly and nodded. "And I know who you are, so we're even. Doesn't mean we shouldn't be polite. Hell, we're bikers and shifters, not animals." She grinned at her own joke. "Shit for, Colin, smile! You're among friends here, more or less."

The redhead gave me a sideways glance and stifled a short laugh. Trina raised an eyebrow and rolled her eyes, outside of the redhead's view. "Babe, I need a fresh beer. Bring one for Colin too, a'right?"

The redhead frowned slightly, then got up and headed for the bar. Trina nodded her chin at the girl's back. "Don't mind Suze—she's just protective of me. Thinks if you and I hang out, it won't go well for me with the other wolves." She leaned in and took a swig of her beer. "Got news for her, though, I'm already none too popular here. Some folks don't like a female wearing the Pack's colors. But like I said, fuck 'em."

"How's that work, exactly? I thought women were treated like property in outlaw biker clubs."

"Pfft. Please. I ain't no one's property. Naw, what you're refer-ring to are the 'property of' patches that the old ladies wear in some MC's. Yeah, that's old-school stuff, but really it just means 'hands off' to other clubs. But here, if you're a 'thrope and you pass the trials, you get full member status."

I nodded slowly. "There's a lot about this I don't know. What do you mean, 'trials'?"

Trina sat back in her chair and kicked her feet up on the table. "That's for Samson to explain. Probably should've done it before you got jumped in, but he's the alpha, so it's his decision about what he tells new prospects. But I'm curious—you're not a 'thrope, so what in the hell are you?"

I shrugged. "Complicated."

Trina's eyes narrowed, then she gave a short, tight-lipped chuckle. "I bet. Your choice if you don't want to say. Got no problem with that."

I shrugged. "I guess it's no secret. I got cursed by a Tuatha sorceress, and whenever I'm badly injured, I change into something else. Something old and fae. It's—not friendly. At all."

"Ah, so Samson agreed to help you learn to control it. I see. Must be why half the Pack is pissed at him."

"They don't want me here."

She tilted her head. "Well, it's not that. It's that you're not the typical shifter. Don't get me wrong. Packs sometimes take in strays, even those who aren't lycans. Most 'thropes are wolves, but each local pack has the responsibility to look after all the 'thropes in their territory, non-wolves included. They keep loners from killing indiscriminately, see to the widows and orphans, that sort of thing. So, when we get a 'thrope who isn't a wolf, and who hasn't been taught control yet, either we find someone of their kind to train them, or we do it ourselves. It's not common, mind you, but it happens.

"But you—you're something else entirely. Can't say I've ever heard of a Pack taking in a shapeshifter who wasn't a 'thrope. Samson'll take a lot of heat for this. So, either he likes you a lot, or he owes someone a favor, big time." Trina swigged the last dregs of her beer and winked at me. "Either way, this is going to be interesting."

I digested what she'd told me for a moment. "I had no idea it was going to be like this when I asked for Samson's help. In truth, he offered his help to me first. But I didn't know I was going to put him at odds with his Pack by accepting the offer."

She sniffed. "No backing out now, kid. Once you accept the offer to become Pack, the only way out is finishing the trials. Or..."

"Or?"

She grimaced slightly, as if she'd said too much. "Or that's it. That's all I can say. Talk to Samson if you want to know more."

I noticed us getting some stares from around the room, and heard a few comments that were none too friendly. I decided to extricate myself from her presence before she took too much heat.

"Thanks, Trina. I appreciate you sticking your neck out to make me feel welcome."

"I got the same shit when I joined up. Gut it out, 'cause after you pass your trials they can't say crap."

I nodded and stood. "See you 'round."

She chuckled. "Oh yeah, you will. Welcome to your new home away from home, prospect." She spread her arms wide, and laughed.

I was starting to have serious reservations about asking Samson for help.

SAMSON CALLED me into the clubhouse office a short while later. He was joined by Sonny, the Pack beta, and Sledge. Samson sat on the other side of a poker table, leaned back with his legs kicked up, so his face was just barely outside the light cast by the overhead lamp. As I walked in the room I interrupted a discussion between the alpha and his second-in-command.

"I still think it's a bad idea, Samson. He's not like us." Sonny glared at the alpha, barely disguising his contempt.

"He stays, and that's that." The alpha paused as I walked in. "Speak of the devil. C'mon in, kid. Have a seat." Sonny and Sledge remained standing. Sonny moved behind and to the right of his alpha, and Sledge moved to his left, leaning against the wall where he could keep an eye on all the windows and exits.

Sledge was huge, intimidating, and had a bushy red beard and mustache that would put any lumberjack to shame. None of that neatly trimmed hipster crap would do for Sledge. His beard was a wild mane, and he had hair on his arms to match. It was easy to see why he was in charge of the Pack's enforcers, because he looked the part. And he could back it up.

Sonny, on the other hand, was an odd choice for second in command. He wasn't tall—maybe five-nine on a good day—and he was rangy in a way that only hardcore alcoholics and endurance athletes could manage. For some reason, he chose to forego the large amount of facial hair favored by most of the Pack, and sported a soul patch with a piercing in the middle, a shaved head, and earrings like a pirate. Based on his tattoos, he'd done hard time. But he seemed to be more of a fixer than a fighter. Anywhere there was a bet to be had or money to be made, Sonny would be in the middle of it.

Samson, though—one look at him and you knew why he was the alpha. He had a wild beard like Sledge, but shaved his head like Sonny. He was lean and wiry, with the same rodeo cowboy build as my mentor Finnegas and the musculature of a man in his prime. But it was his presence that was intimidating, not his build or appearance. When you were near him, you felt something—power, authority, call it what you will—and you *knew* he was in charge.

The last time I'd been around him, I'd felt the urge to fight him. This time, I just felt calm. Like I knew he had things under control. *Pack ties*, I thought. *Interesting.*

I wasn't sure if I found it comforting, or disturbing. I'd never been much of a joiner, after all. I took a seat across from him and decided to let this scene play out.

Samson nursed his whiskey, swirling the liquid in his glass. I noticed he took it neat. I wondered if he kept the good stuff back here, because the selection behind the bar out front was shit. He didn't offer me any, so I supposed it didn't matter.

"It's time to lay down the ground rules. You're a prospect now, so you need to know what's expected. We usually do this before someone commits, but since you're a special case, well—I figured it was best to just get it done and worry about the consequences later."

"You spoke to Finn." I had a hunch that Finnegas had influenced the alpha's decision.

He nodded, his head bobbing slightly in the shadow. "I did. I owe the old man. He called to collect." He tossed back his drink. "But I'd have done it anyway. Druids and werewolves have always worked together. And druids have been in short supply for way too long."

I caught just the slightest hint of disagreement on Sonny's face at Samson's statement. Just a flash of disapproval, then it was gone. He caught my gaze, and flashed a toothy grin at me.

Samson sighed. "Some of the Pack aren't too happy about my decision to bring you in. You'll see why later. Regardless, they have to respect my decision, and they'll see this thing through. But don't expect a warm reception around here."

"I figured as much. Anything else I should know?"

Samson tapped his empty glass in a slow rhythm. "Sonny?"

Sonny sniffed. "Prospects earn their way in. Just because you started the process, it doesn't mean you're Pack. Not until you finish your trials, anyway. Weekends are ours, meaning you show up where we say, when we say. You'll be helping out around the clubhouse, cleaning bikes, and doing any other shit job we give you. That clear?"

"Clear." I expected some hazing, so I was prepared to be treated like the FNG—the "fucking new guy."

Sledge cleared his throat. "There's the matter of his ride."

Sonny rolled his eyes. "Damn it, Sledge. I had a pool going on whether he'd ride up on that European piece of shit."

"What about my ride?"

Sledge smirked. "Can't have no Pack member riding on no scooter. No way, no how. Not even a prospect. So, you need to get a hog, pronto. And no fucking rice rockets or cafe racers, either. It's a chopper or it's nuthin'. American iron all the way. Can you handle that?"

Sonny chuckled. "He lives in a junkyard. If he can't handle building a bike, I'd say he has problems."

Samson exhaled heavily. "You build your bike on your own time. Weekends belong to the Pack. You go where we say. And when I call you to start your training, you drop everything and show up where I tell you. Understood?"

"I understand. But what's the deal with these trials?"

Sonny chuckled. "You'll see, prospect. You'll see."

2

I woke up to the scent of lilac and vanilla, with just a hint of morning breath. I was snuggled up against Bells, spooning her with my arm draped over her slender waist. All in all, it wasn't a bad way to wake up.

I drew away gently to avoid waking her. Bells responded by yanking the sheets off me and rolling back and forth to cocoon herself in them. The air in her bedroom was cold, since she liked to sleep with the heat turned down. I didn't have central air at the junkyard, so I hadn't minded it the night before. But now? The cold air hit my bare skin, raising goosebumps and sending me off the bed to hunt for my jeans and t-shirt.

After a brief search, I located both items and got dressed. After being badly injured while we were tracking down the Dark Druid, Bells was finally out of the hospital. To celebrate, I'd shown up last night with takeout. After mostly making it through dinner, we'd ended up tangled in the sheets, well into the late hours. I thought back to the night before, smiling as I located my socks.

So, that's what I've been missing out on. Maybe I should've come to my senses sooner.

Bells stirred slightly and mumbled something unintelligible. I tiptoed around the bed and leaned in to kiss her forehead. "I have to go work at the junkyard. Did you need something?"

"I said, 'coffee's in the cupboard.'"

"Um, okay. I'll call you later."

"Mm-hmm." She covered her head with the blankets and rolled over, fully staking a claim to most of the real estate on the bed.

So, Bells was not a morning person. Good to know. I shrugged and pulled on my boots, then headed to the bathroom for some expedient oral care. Toothpaste, meet finger. Finger, meet mouth. Spit, rinse, and out the door I went. I'd get coffee at Luther's on the way.

I stopped by the front door, at the breakfast bar that separated the kitchen from the living room, and searched the counter for some paper and a pen. I figured it wouldn't hurt to leave a note, on the odd chance Bells wouldn't remember our brief discussion. Yeah, I could have texted, but I thought a handwritten note would be—well, more personal.

So, I'm a romantic. Sue me.

I shuffled through a few bills and letters, hoping to find a notepad. Turning up zilch, I was about to replace them when something sticking out of an envelope caught my eye. It looked like—was that a plane ticket?

I pulled the envelope from the stack and set the rest down on the counter. The corner of a ticket peeked out from a white envelope, addressed to Belladonna Becerra in flowing, handwritten script. The return address was in Santiago de Compostela, Spain, but the sender's name was absent. I pulled the ticket out and examined it.

One way, Austin, Texas to Aeropuerto de Santiago De Compostela, Spain. Departure date, two weeks from today. *Shit.*

"Nosy much?" Belladonna leaned against the hall entrance, in a t-shirt and not much else. Sexy as hell, and looking miffed.

I held up the ticket. "Going somewhere?"

She marched up and snatched the ticket from my fingers. "My mom sent it to me, as soon as she got back to Spain. I was going to tell you." She replaced the ticket in the stack on the counter, then closed her eyes and scratched her head, shaking her hair out.

"Look, I wasn't snooping. I was looking for a piece of paper so I could leave you a note, and it was sticking out of an envelope."

"So you just had to see what it was? And besides, why not just text me?"

That's what I got for trying to be romantic.

"I'm sorry. You're right. I shouldn't have been looking through your things."

She leaned her back against the counter, arms crossed, and looked at me through slitted eyes.

Sure, Colin—go ahead and push your luck. "So, are you going?"

Bells sighed and popped her neck. "It's too damned early to have this discussion. Maybe? I don't know. Why don't you wait until I get some coffee in me, in—oh, five hours or so? Then I can fill you in on all the family bullshit I've been keeping from you since we met."

I walked up to her, pretty much the same way I'd approach a wounded lioness. Slow, calm, and with my hands held up in supplication. "Hey, listen. You don't have to talk to me about anything you don't want to. And if you want to go to Spain to see your family, that's none of my business. I'll be waiting for you when you get back."

I slipped my arms around her waist and nuzzled her forehead with my nose. She held her head down, avoiding my gaze.

"See, that's just—I can't—aw, damn it. You don't understand."

I chuckled softly, and she stiffened. "I'm not laughing at you, Bells. It's just that you're not making any sense."

She pulled away, holding my hands. "Colin, what I'm trying to say is that if I go home, I might never come back."

I blinked a few times before stammering a response. "What do you mean? Like a sabbatical, or something? Is there a sick relative you need to take care of? Forgive me for being slow, but I don't get what you're trying to say."

"It's complicated. And it's way too early to be discussing this stuff now." She closed the distance, then stood up on tiptoe and kissed me on the cheek. "Meet me at the coffeehouse this afternoon, and I'll explain it to you then."

I watched as she walked off to her bedroom. She closed the door behind her without sparing me a glance, leaving me alone and wondering what had just happened.

AFTER I'D FINISHED ALL the work my uncle Ed had assigned me at the junkyard, I decided to spend some time looking for a project bike to help get me in the Pack's good graces. I figured if I had a decent bike, something with a lot of displacement that said "Harley-Davidson" on the side, maybe I wouldn't seem like such an outsider. Then again, it'd probably take more than a sweet bike to get me in the cool kid's club. I figured a few more scars, some serious jail time, and a "L-O-V-E H-A-T-E" tattoo on my knuckles, for starters. Being an outlaw biker was going to be a lot less fun than running away to join the circus.

Hemi had stopped by to chat, and he volunteered to help me move junk while I searched for a suitable candidate. We perused the stacks, deep in the heart of the yard where the good stuff was buried, discussing my current girlfriend woes.

"She said she might be going home, eh? Tough break, that. She'll be back, though—right?"

I shook my head as I tilted a rusted Monte Carlo hood back to reveal what was hidden behind it. "Maybe not. She said something about family bullshit, and that she might not come back, ever. I have no idea what that means. But Sabine said her mom wasn't quite human, and from what I saw, she seems pretty formidable. No telling what kind of stuff Bells is dealing with."

"Speaking of Sabine, what's the deal with her?"

I frowned. "MIA since I hooked up with Bells. And before you ask, yes, I've tried to track her down. She's fae, and she doesn't want to be found. I have no idea where she's disappeared to, and none of the fae will tell me."

"Sure got a way with women, bro."

"Tell me about it."

We hadn't had much luck finding a project bike. Thus far, we'd found a Sportster frame that was salvageable, but Hemi had said it'd be too small for me to ride comfortably. After riding a scooter for a couple of years, I didn't think it'd be an issue. However, the big Maori seemed to think that I needed to look good on whatever I rode. So, I'd deferred to his judgment and kept looking.

Hemi looked behind an old GMC pickup bed and nodded. "Regarding Bells, I know all about that, yeah? Family pressures and all. Ancient curses, leaving home to avoid family infighting, and having to live up to someone else's legacy. What a mess."

I stopped what I was doing and looked at him. "Um, you just dropped a whole load of info, without really providing any details. Is there something you're not telling me?"

"Family business, eh? All I'm saying is that I understand what it's like when your family wants you to do something you don't want to do. Sounds like that's what Belladonna is facing, and you should cut her some slack."

"Guess you're right. By the way, nice use of American slang there, buddy. Next thing you know, I'll have you in cowboy boots and dancing a two-step at the Broken Spoke."

"Been there, done that—without the boots. Gotta say, I don't get how you Texans dance, but your cowgirls sure are gorgeous." Hemi paused and nodded behind me. "We got company."

Uncle Ed came huffing around a row of junked cars. He was a good guy—gruff, but well-liked around the yard. If he had any faults, it was taking in a few too many strays, and eating too much fast food. I worried he'd exert himself around the yard one day and have a heart attack, but I hadn't found a tactful way to suggest he lose weight.

"Phew, sure is warm out here for this time of year. What are you boys looking for, anyway?"

Hemi pointed at me and grinned. "Your nephew wants to join a gang of outlaw bikers, and he needs a chopped-out ride to get in."

Ed nodded, causing his jowls to bounce slightly. "Ah, so you got tired of riding that Vespa. Sure, the Gremlin that Finn left you has its merits, but it's no chick magnet, that's for sure." He rubbed his chin. "Hmmm... I got a guy who wants to trade me an old Softtail for a Chevy Nova. The Nova's worth about a grand to me. If you're interested, I'll make the trade and take it out of your pay."

I sighed with relief. "Ed, you just made the top ten on my uncle of the year list. Maybe even the top five."

He scowled. "Smart ass. I should charge you interest, for that remark." He pulled a rag from his front pocket and wiped his balding head. "Anyway, you got a visitor. He's one of those—how do they say it—little people? Refuses to come inside, and he's been standing at the front gate for a while."

Hemi and I exchanged looks. "Is he wearing a red hat?"

"Yeah, in fact he is. Talks like a Yankee, too. He in a gang or something?"

I chuckled. "Or something. Don't worry, I'm not in trouble. He's probably just here looking for parts for his Olds. He has a sweet restored '72. You'd like it."

Ed rubbed his chin. "Is that so? Ask him if he's looking to get rid of it. I might have a buyer."

I covered my mouth with the back of my hand and whispered to Hemi. "By 'buyer,' he means 'warehouse.' You should see his collection."

Ed smirked. "Hey now, back off. Those cars are my retirement plan."

I smiled. "Like you'd ever let any go. Face it, Uncle Ed. You have a serious addiction."

Ed frowned and waved me off with the rag. "Ah, what do you know?" He grimaced, favoring his right leg as he walked away. He yelled over his shoulder as he headed back to the front office. "I'll make the trade for you. Now, go see what your friend wants, before he starts scaring off customers."

SAL WAS WAITING for me at the front gate. Most run-of-the-mill fae couldn't enter the junkyard, both because of all the iron lying around and because of my wards. That was one of the reasons I chose to live there. Well, that, and I couldn't beat the rent. Uncle Ed let me sleep in a back room in the warehouse. I exchanged work in the yard for room and board, and made a little money on the side besides. After the job I'd just finished for Luther, I could afford to move someplace nicer. But I had the whole yard warded, and I liked the fact that I could sleep in relative peace here, without worrying about some nasty fae with a grudge trying to slit my throat.

At the moment, I didn't have a lot of friends in the fae community. Which was why Sal's appearance in the middle of the day worried me. Never mind that he'd risked revealing himself to mundanes. Something was definitely up.

The red cap's face was lined with worry, and he paced back and forth in front of the gate, wringing his hands all the while. Sal looked a bit like a muscular Danny DeVito, and he talked like a character from Goodfellas. The local red cap clan he belonged to modeled themselves after east coast wise guys, and Sal dressed the part. He wore tailored dress slacks, a light blue silk shirt, a black leather sport coat, and all manner of gold jewelry, including several rings on each hand, and a thick rope necklace and bracelet. About the only thing missing from his ensemble was a gold crucifix; otherwise, he looked the part of a mobbed up goomba perfectly.

And he *was* mobbed up. Red caps, a.k.a. the fear dearg, were a particularly nasty and bloodthirsty brand of fae. Back in the day, they'd been known for waylaying travelers and dyeing their caps with the blood of their victims. These days, the Red Cap Syndicate dealt in drugs, prostitution, and illegal gambling. Sal worked for the local boss, Rocko, who ran his gang out of a club on the South side of Austin. Red caps weren't known to fret, so seeing Sal nervous like this got my hackles up. When he saw me, his expression relaxed slightly, but he continued to wring his hands as I approached.

"I never thought I'd say this, druid, but I'm glad to see you."

Hemi stood at my shoulder, arms crossed. "Why, you looking to start a rugby league? You're about the right size for a ball, eh? Bet I could punt you straight across the field."

Sal barely spared Hemi a glance, ignoring the Maori

warrior's verbal jab. That alone piqued my interest. "What's up, Sal?" I asked.

"Druid, I don't know who else to turn to, because I've exhausted my resources at this point. It's Little Sal. He's gone missing."

I tilted my head and cocked an eyebrow. "Come again?"

Sal paced as he talked. "My boy, Little Sal. He's gone. Can't find him anywhere. The missus put him to bed last night around eight, and I was out at the bar until about three. I came home at my usual time, and about nine this morning I wake up to hear my wife and the girls carrying on like crazy."

"Wait a minute. Someone snatched your kid from his bed? Isn't your house warded against intruders?"

He nodded, his round red nose bobbing in time. "Yeah, and we got one of those fancy alarm systems, too. But the girls say that Little Sal likes to get up early and feed the squirrels. He's—not like the other fae kids in the neighborhood, you know. Little Sal, he's kind of soft-hearted. Has a thing for animals and stuff."

Interesting. Few people would want to mess with the red caps, despite their size—especially not the crew Sal ran with. They feared me, because I'd put them in their place a few times. But the only other person I'd seen them cower to was Maeve, the local fae queen. So, for someone to take one of their kids—well, this had "weird shit" written all over it.

Hemi leaned in slightly. "You think someone grabbed the little anklebiter while he was out feeding the squirrels?"

Sal gesticulated nervously with his hands as he spoke. "It's the only thing we can figure. Well, that, and we found one of his slippers in the yard."

I rubbed my chin and considered his story. Fae were notorious for tricking humans, and while red caps weren't the sharpest knives in the drawer, I wouldn't put it past them to try.

"Sal, considering the circumstances, I *might* be willing to help you. But I'll need your word that this isn't some trick."

He shook his head, eyes pleading with me. "I swear on my hat and beard, druid. This is the honest truth. I need you to help me get my boy back. And I'll pay your fee."

I tapped my thumbnail on my lips as I considered the situation. "I don't charge for abducted children cases. So, this one's on me. You say the last time anyone saw him was last night?"

He nodded. "We searched the neighborhood, and Rocko's had the crew out looking all day."

That meant sixteen hours had passed since the kid had gone missing. This didn't look good. There could be any number of guilty parties at fault. Someone with a grudge against Sal or his boss, another fae crew out to nose in on their territory, or any one of a variety of supernatural baddies that preyed on children. I'd tangled with a few before, and knew that time was of the essence.

"Sal, I'll need to have access to your yard and home." He gave me a sideways look. "I promise, not a word about your extra-curricular activities with 'Allspice,' or whatever her name is. You're my client now, and as much as it pains me to say it, I have a duty to act in your best interests."

"Her name is Cinnamon, and she's as broken up about Sal going missing as anyone. She used to sit with him at the bar when I'd bring the little guy to work with me."

I shared a look with Hemi. "Um, no comment. Listen, I'll be sending the trolls by your place tonight so they can track Little Sal's scent. I'll need that slipper you found, and if you can manage it, I'd like to have a strand or two of his hair for a tracking spell."

Sal took a moment to think it over. Giving a magic user a strand of hair, a drop of blood, or a nail clipping was no small matter. "I trust you, druid. You may be a shit, but you have honor. I'll text my address to you and wait for you at the house."

Sal crossed the street and got in his Olds, goosing the accelerator and peeling out as he left. I tapped a finger on my chin as I watched him drive off. As his taillights faded into the distance, I glanced at Hemi.

"You in on this one, partner?"

"Damn straight. A kid's a kid, right? I've no patience for anyone who harms a child, regardless of their parentage."

"Alright. Meet me back here at five and we'll head over to look at the evidence before it gets dark. I'll have the trolls meet us there after dusk. And Hemi?"

"Yeah?"

"Come armed."

His face broke into a savage grin. "I always do."

3

M y first suspicion about Sal's kid was that Ananda Corp was up to their old tricks, capturing fae for some strange, nefarious, as-yet-unknown reason. I'd never actually met anyone from Ananda Corp, nor had I ever seen their offices —or even so much as a company vehicle—but I knew they were bad news. As far as I could tell, they were a shadow corporation, set up solely for purposes of funding activities that were in direct opposition to Maeve's interests.

A short while back, I'd discovered that Belladonna's former partner, the wizard Crowley, had been working either for or with Ananda. Ananda had been funding CIRCE, which fronted as a cryptid rescue organization, but had actually captured fae and other supernatural creatures to deliver to Crowley. He had then tortured them to secure intelligence on magical artifacts, such as Balor's Eye.

My investigation on their activities had led me to a confrontation with Crowley, who had then turned the Eye's magic on me. Unfortunately for him, his plan had backfired when my alter-ego showed up and beat his pet giant's ass to a pulp. After that, he'd beat feet on me, and since then I'd been waiting for him to resurface and take his revenge. He hadn't yet, but eventually I knew I'd have to face him again.

Crowley's former butt boy and henchman, Elias, had told me he'd shut CIRCE down completely. Once he'd found out someone from Ananda was trying to have him killed, he'd sold everything and skipped town. Whatever. I just needed to make sure that Ananda wasn't back in business.

I drove by CIRCE's former offices, located in a mixed-use neighborhood downtown that mostly housed law offices and nonprofits. CIRCE had formerly occupied a nice, converted two-story home—one that was way too nice for a nonprofit to afford. Rent around that neighborhood wasn't cheap, and the fact they were located there instead of some warehouse in Del Valle indicated they had seriously wealthy backers.

But no more. The place was locked up tight and quiet as church at half-time on Super Bowl Sunday. "For Lease" signs adorned the front yard and windows, and from what I could tell no one had been in or out of the building in some time. That meant Elias was still in the wind. Couldn't say I blamed him, since his former employers wanted him dead. I got back in my car and chewed my thumbnail as I pondered the situation.

By all appearances, Ananda was no longer active in the Austin area, but I wasn't absolutely certain that was the case. Before moving on, I needed to completely eliminate them from my list of suspects. That meant paying a visit to Maeve, the local fae queen. She was the last person I wanted to speak with, because she always found a way to entangle me in her business. Maeve was ancient, even for a fae; how ancient, I had no idea. A few thousand years was my guess, the way Finn spoke of her. Maybe more. And she, like all ancient fae, was a master of manipulating mortals into doing her dirty work.

Right now, I was her favorite human plaything. Until recently, Maeve had possessed ample leverage over me, by way of having a monopoly on my mom's artwork. She'd never outright threatened to ruin my mother's career as an artist, but she'd certainly made it plain that she would if I didn't do her bidding. But recently, she'd voluntarily given her word that she wouldn't use that against me. Why she'd made that promise was a mystery. I felt as though I'd dodged a planet-sized bullet, and loathed the thought of becoming involved in her schemes again.

But nothing said I'd ever escaped her machinations in the first place. It was likely she no longer needed leverage over me, because she'd already manipulated me into doing exactly what she wanted. Despite her overtures of goodwill, I was fairly certain she'd moved me like a chess piece, right where she needed me.

Wherever that might be. I had a feeling it had something to do with the werewolves and gaining control over the Eye... but that was just a wild ass guess.

I sighed, turned the ignition, and drove to her home. It was just a few short miles down the road, and on the way back to the junkyard. Besides, La Creme was right around the corner from her house, and I still had to meet Bells to find out what was up with her crazy life.

Like I had room to talk about drama.

I pulled up in front of Maeve's manse and turned off the car, gripping the wheel of the Gremlin as the throaty roar of the engine and the vibration of the souped-up V-8 rumbled to a halt. That was the thing about muscle cars and motorcycles; they were noisy, and always announced your presence on arrival. I wasn't complaining about finally having decent wheels to drive, but it kind of made me miss my scooter. I wondered if I could trade the Harley for an electric dirt bike after Samson helped me control my ríastrad.

I stepped out of the car and headed up the walk, sparing a glance at the pair of gargoyles that guarded Maeve's yard. They were replacements for two trolls who'd betrayed Maeve. During my last visit, in a spectacular display of drunkenness and bad judgment, I'd picked a fight with them. It hadn't ended well, and I'd escaped becoming pâté only by the barest margin and Maeve's intervention.

I was pretty sure they still held a grudge. Either Lothair or Adelard—I couldn't tell them apart—growled at me and tapped a stone claw against its perch. The other ignored me, but I noted a chip missing from behind the growling gargoyle's ear. Good to know I'd at least left a mark. A smile tugged at the corner of my mouth, and I gave the pair a casual salute.

"Just stopping by to visit with Maeve, boys. Not here to cause trouble," I said under my breath. I knew they could hear me, even though I spoke at a whisper. The one that had growled yawned, and then it resumed its usual static vigil.

I walked up Maeve's front steps, onto the porch that wrapped the front of her beautiful, tastefully restored two-story Victorian. Taking a deep breath to settle my nerves, I raised my hand to knock and announce my presence. But before my knuckles touched the ivory-painted wood of the entry, the door creaked open.

I EXPECTED Maeve's great-granddaughter many times removed to saunter into view, but the foyer was empty. That was unusual, to say the least. On every previous visit, Siobhan had greeted me, escorting me to wherever Maeve might be in her great big shifting maze of a home. But today, I was greeted by silence, and the faint scent of lavender and rain.

I grabbed both sides of the doorframe as I craned my head right and left to view the scene inside. I was careful not to step across the threshold uninvited. No telling what wards and spells

Maeve had protecting her front entrance. I saw nothing but a vaguely familiar parlor and hallway beyond the foyer.

"Hello! Anyone home?"

A pale globe of light popped out from around a corner and floated down the hall toward me. It stopped at the entrance and bobbed up and down a few times, then floated back down the hall. It stopped once more, then bobbed up and down again, more insistently this time.

"I assume you're to take me to Maeve?"

The light bobbed once.

I hesitated. Will-o'-the-wisps were known to be fond of luring travelers into traps, or leading them deep into swamps and forests and leaving them to find their way back again. But I was in Maeve's demesne, and so long as she was this wisp's regent, I doubted I was in much danger—*much* being the operative word. I decided to play along.

"Fine. But if this is a trick, you should know I'm armed."

The faint tinkle of childlike laughter echoed from somewhere nearby, and the will-o'-the-wisp floated down the hall. I sighed and followed close behind. We walked for an unreasonably long period of time, much longer than it had ever taken me to get to Maeve's study or kitchen on any of my previous visits.

I cleared my throat. "Siobhan never brought me this way on my previous visits."

The light paused, and bobbed gently as if to say, "Go figure." It continued, and I had no choice but to follow. Each room and hall we passed was entirely foreign to me, and currently we were in an area full of deep shadows and dark spaces. It was just the sort of place where unseelie creatures from the Underrealms might cross over and decide to have a snack.

Finally, we emerged into a familiar room, which was Maeve's study. She stood leaning over her desk, holding a large scroll open with one hand while examining it carefully under the bright light of an antique lamp. I found it odd that the queen of the Austin fae should be using such mundane means to illuminate her workspace. However, most fae readily adopted whatever modern technology and conveniences caught their fancy. I got the impression they found human craftsmanship to be endearing, if somewhat crude. Maeve seemed to be enamored with Victorian era architecture, art, and furnishings, and the lamp she currently used was no exception. It had been converted from gas to electricity, but still evinced that same regal charm that was a hallmark of the style.

I didn't bother trying to figure out how she'd piped electricity into a house made of constantly shifting rooms and halls. Some mysteries deserved to remain within the purview of the unknown.

Maeve continued to examine the document, and addressed no one in particular as she spoke. "That will be all. Thank you."

The light bobbed once, deeply, and floated out of the room.

"What happened to Siobhan? Did she quit or something?"

She placed a crystal paperweight on the document to hold her place. "My granddaughter is—indisposed at the moment. My apologies if Jack brought you the long way around. It's in his nature to play such tricks on humans."

"Jack—you mean to tell me that's Jack of the Lantern?"

She turned away from her desk and glided to a far corner of her study, where two high-backed chairs sat cater-cornered to each other, divided by a dainty side table. Upon the table sat a lovely tea service set, and steam rose from the teapot. Maeve gestured to a chair, and sat in the one opposite.

"Please, sit." She waited until I took my seat before continuing. "Jack entered my service some time ago, after I found him in thrall to a rather horrid human magician. I—*convinced*—the magician to release him, and Jack felt indebted to me. So, I brought him into my employ."

"Doing what?"

She poured two cups of tea. I left mine on the table. A slight frown flitted across Maeve's face—whether at my refusal of her hospitality or my question, I couldn't be certain. "Oh, this and that. You'd be surprised at how useful a will-o'-the-wisp can be for gathering information. But you didn't come here to discuss my help."

She crossed one knee over the other, needlessly smoothing out her denim ankle pants. Maeve was dressed more Giada than Martha today, and to be honest she looked rather cute—not to mention much more human than she had in our last meeting. While in her presence, I constantly had to remind myself that she wasn't just an attractive, well-heeled soccer mom, but the most dangerous supernatural entity in the city. On my last visit, I'd seen the barest glimpse of the magical power at her command, and it was enough to keep me on my guard, even now.

"True. Although I can't say I'm not curious about what Jack does on his days off." *What does a will-o'-the-wisp do in his spare time, anyway? Golf? Crochet? Performance art?* I waited to see if she'd take the bait. No dice. "Maeve, I need information regarding a case I'm working."

She nodded ever so slightly. "I'm listening."

"Is Ananda Corp still active in the area?"

"You certainly are like a dog on a bone, aren't you, my boy? While I'd rather not comment on Ananda Corporation's activities, they're not behind the fae child's abduction, if that helps you any."

"It does. Why the reticence when it comes to matters related to Ananda Corp?"

"All in good time."

"Plotting the end of the world, Maeve?"

Her lips curled into a tight smile that didn't quite reach her eyes. "Plotting against it. Jack will show you out." She stood and returned to her desk and scroll.

Huh. Maeve had never dismissed me so abruptly before. Typically, she'd toy with me a bit before sending me on my way. On cue, the will-o'-the-wisp floated into the room. It paused a moment, then headed down the hall at a leisurely pace. I gave Maeve a parting glance, then followed the wisp before it left me behind.

Maeve studied her scroll, ignoring me. She called to the wisp just as I departed from the room.

"Jack, do take the direct route this time."

Weird. What the hell had Maeve's panties in a wad? And what had happened to Siobhan?

THE TRIP back was shorter than the one in, yet it was dark by the time I exited Maeve's house. I could only assume that on the way in, the wisp had kept me walking longer than I'd thought. He must've taken me deep, close the Underrealms. Time could get weird in the spaces between our world and theirs, stretching seconds into hours, or compressing hours in the mundane world into seconds. If the wisp had a mind to, I'm sure he could have made the trip back to Maeve's front door last for days.

I made a note to avoid dropping my guard around the creature in the future. Jack of the Lantern was a legendary sprite, known for acts that surpassed the limits of capriciousness and entered the territory of downright cruelty. As I exited Maeve's home, I wondered at just how influential she was, to attract such a legendary creature into her service. It was one thing to have a will-o'-the-wisp working for you, but quite another to have the *original* will-o'-the-wisp answering your door.

I was deep in thought as I exited the house, and I ignored the gargoyles as I trotted down the front walk. I quick-stepped through the leafy arbor that served as the front entrance to the yard, and walked straight into a punch that landed me on the sidewalk. A flurry of soccer kicks delivered by booted feet came at me from all directions. Dazed from the sucker punch, it was all I could do to curl into a ball and cover up to avoid serious damage to my vital areas.

The beating went on for a while, and before they were done, I felt ribs crack and lost consciousness once or twice. Blood poured from my nose, staining the concrete beneath me. It was difficult to breathe, and I felt a sharp pain in my side each time I inhaled. My arms, legs, and back felt like tenderized meat. With each new kick, I felt new waves of agony that made me even more dizzy and nauseous. After an inestimable period of time, the beating stopped.

With great effort, I opened one swollen eye to see a hooded figure leaning over me, with four more around us. Shadows cloaked their faces, but their lean, graceful shapes told me they were probably fae. The one leaning over me grabbed me by my shirt, lifting my upper torso off the sidewalk. He spoke in a lilting countertenor that I might have found pleasing, had he not just danced a jig on my ribs.

"Let this be a lesson to you, druid. You've angered the wrong people, with your traipsing around and poking where you're not welcome. You've been warned. Mind your own business, and stay out of fae matters."

He dropped me to the ground. I complied with gravity and his apparent wishes and stayed there until they faded into the dark. After a few minutes and a considerable amount of bleeding, I rolled to my side and pushed myself to a seated position. I felt bones grind together in my ribs as I did so, and clenched my teeth to avoid screaming. They might have been within hearing range still, and I didn't want to give them the pleasure.

I scooted over to a lamppost so I could stand and get my bearings. After struggling to my feet, I scanned the area with my one functioning eye. One of the gargoyles was sitting on its haunches on the other side of the entrance to Maeve's yard, eyeing me with indifference.

"Thanks for the assist," I mumbled.

The gargoyle snorted, a sound that reminded me of pebbles falling down a rocky slope. Then it walked back into the yard, swishing its stony tail.

I stood there a good long while, until my breathing became labored enough to give me concern. I needed to seek medical attention, or at the very least a few shots of whiskey. Finn was no longer around to patch me up, and I had no idea where he'd run off to or when he'd be back. It was times like these that I wished I'd paid more attention to his classes on healing magic. Finn had always told me I'd need it someday, but I'd just laughed and said I was a better barbarian than I was a cleric. *Ha ha, the jokes on you, Colin.*

If I drove myself to the hospital or the clinic on campus, I'd get a visit from Austin's finest, for sure. After recently being arrested in connection with the murder of a cop, I'd been advised by my legal counsel to avoid future brushes with the police. Besides that, when my mom got the co-pay bill, I'd have to explain all the X-rays and stitches. And while I might regret not having prescription drugs tomorrow, I didn't care to be interrogated by my mom. There was really only one place to go besides the junkyard, so I crawled into the front seat of the Gremlin and drove myself to the Pack's clubhouse.

4

I remembered pulling up in front of the clubhouse and stumbling out of the car, but that was about it. The next thing I knew, I was waking up on a couch in Samson's office, with someone shining a light in my eyes.

I heard a mellow, refined voice speak, with just the slightest hint of a British accent. "He has a pretty serious concussion. Plus some broken ribs. There's a danger he'll puncture a lung if they aren't stabilized. Add to that all the cuts and contusions, and the broken nose. My professional opinion is that he should be in a hospital ER."

I drifted in and out, but I was awake enough to recognize Samson's voice. "He's our responsibility now, and we take care of our own. Gather the Pack."

Sonny's voice cut in, low and urgent. "You think that's a good idea, Samson? Things are already tense around here, what with you bringing a shifter into the Pack who isn't a wolf, much less a 'thrope. Do you think it's going to make things better if you do this?"

Samson's reply was calm, but stern. "I have my reasons. Do as I say, Sonny." I heard someone leave the room, then Samson spoke again. "Keep him stable until the rest of the Pack gets here, Doc. If this kid goes too far over the edge, he'll shift. And that'll be bad for us all."

"Understood. What is he?"

"He's something no one has seen since the days when the Tuatha walked the earth. And he's probably the best chance we have at saving the Pack, along with everything else you know and love. Keep him safe."

"Understood," the Doc said, then Samson's light, sure footsteps faded away as he left us alone.

I heard someone rummaging in a bag, then the Doc spoke. "Colin, I'm going to start an I.V. and give you some painkillers. Nothing serious, but something to take the edge off."

I cracked an eye open. A short, thin man, with deep brown skin and long dark hair pulled into a ponytail, attached an I.V. line to a bag of clear fluid. He reminded me a bit of Fisher Stevens from *Short Circuit*.

"You with the Pack?" I asked.

He nodded as he removed a pin-up calendar from the wall, replacing it with the I.V. bag. "Been living in the area about ten years. When I moved here after medical school, I let Samson know I was sticking around. It's standard operating procedure for 'thropes to notify the local Pack alpha when they move into their territory, even if they aren't wolves.

"Samson took me in, helped me adjust—the works. I don't hang out here at the clubhouse much, because I'm not into the biker thing. But, like a lot of therianthropes who live in the area, when Samson calls I answer." He made a small, circular gesture with his hand, and bowed slightly at the waist. "Dr. Ganesh, at your service."

It hurt to talk, and breathe. "Thanks for the assist," I gasped.

"Don't mention it." He wiped the inside of my arm down

with an alcohol swab, and unsheathed the I.V. needle. "Small poke."

He inserted the needle with expert precision and taped it securely to my arm, adjusting the I.V. drip after everything was in place. He then filled a syringe with a clear liquid, and injected it into the port on the I.V. line.

"A mild analgesic. With your breathing issues, I don't want to give you anything stronger. But it should keep you comfortable until the rest of the Pack arrives."

"Doc, why'd he call in the Pack?"

Dr. Ganesh nodded. "I take it you haven't started your trials and training yet?"

I shook my head.

"Well, training a 'thrope to control their change can be somewhat traumatic, at least the way the Pack does it. In my country, we're taught meditation techniques from an early age, along with breathing exercises and other methods to control the beast. But lycanthropy is rarely hereditary, so 'thropes in the West aren't always raised among clans of their own kind. Typically, the Pack doesn't have years to prepare a new 'thrope to handle the change before it happens. So, they've adopted more—primitive methods. And that, in turn, requires the ability to heal 'thropes who are being trained to control their change."

"Let me get this straight—learning how to control the change requires a 'thrope to be injured beyond their supernatural ability to heal?"

Dr. Ganesh nodded. "Just so, yes."

"Well, this should be interesting."

The doc pulled a chair next to the couch and sat facing me. He took my pulse and blood pressure, and listened to my chest with a stethoscope. "Lungs are clear, and your vitals are stable." He put his stethoscope and blood pressure cuff away in a nylon medical bag. "Now, if you don't mind me asking, I'm curious to learn what you are, and why Samson agreed to take you in."

I shrugged slightly, but it was enough to cause my ribs to scream in protest. "I was cursed by a fae sorceress. Now, I change into something dangerous and inhuman when I'm near the brink of death. It's—not safe for others to be around me when it happens."

He crossed his ankle over his knee, and placed his hands in his lap. "Ah, I see. And I suppose you're curious as to what I am?"

The painkiller must've been kicking in, because I was feeling more talkative. "It had crossed my mind."

"I'm a werecat. More specifically, a weretiger. In my country, we're believed to be sorcerers. Although some of my kind practice magic, it is not the source of our ability to change. We have a reputation for being evil and dangerous to humans, but it is mostly undeserved. The majority of us simply want to lead normal lives among the human population, similar to the Pack."

"Turning into a tiger—that sounds like a neat trick."

"It comes in handy, but I rarely make the change. My kind do not have as great a need to hunt as wolves do. Perhaps it is due to our solitary nature, or the training we receive as children." He paused and adjusted the I.V. line, twitching his nose slightly. "I find it interesting that Samson would bring you into the Pack for training. It seems like a very disruptive decision, to say the least."

"And not a very popular one, I'm finding. I just hope he can help me control my change in short order, so we can part ways before I cause too many problems."

Dr. Ganesh nodded. "One thing's for certain—if Samson agreed to assist you, he'll see it through to the bitter end. He is a man of his word, beyond a doubt."

"Good to know. I just hope I'm worth his troubles."

Dr. Ganesh smiled politely. He cocked his head, reminding

me of a cat listening for signs of prey. "Ah, I believe I hear some of the Pack arriving. I'll be taking my leave now, but I must say it was a pleasure to speak with you, Colin."

It was my turn to smile. "I never told you my name."

"Yes, well—a tiger has its territory, much like the Pack. My grandfather taught me that cats grow old and grizzled through guile and knowledge, more than by brute strength."

"Rest assured, Doc, my presence shouldn't be a challenge or threat to anyone. Truth be told, I just want to be left in peace."

He patted my hand lightly as he stood. "Don't we all, young man. Don't we all. Just in case things don't work out with the Pack's methods, feel free to look me up. I believe I can show you a few things that will help you get a handle on your beast."

He handed me a card, and I tucked it in my pocket. "Thanks, Dr. Ganesh. For everything."

"Don't mention it." He turned toward the door, but paused at the threshold. "And, Colin? Watch your back around here. Some of these wolves would rather have an outsider for lunch than in their Pack."

SAMSON WALKED in shortly after Dr. Ganesh left, flanked by Sonny. Sledge followed, along with a tall, attractive woman in her mid-twenties. She had chestnut hair past her shoulders and the pale brown, nearly yellow eyes of an adult wolf. She looked like a tougher version of Princess Kate, with more muscle—definitely Samson's daughter. Samson walked up to the couch and sat in the chair Dr. Ganesh had left behind. The other three took up positions around him.

Sonny spoke up. "Here's how this works, kid. One of the benefits of being Pack is that we can heal you in emergencies. It ain't easy, it hurts like hell, and it's damned inconvenient for the

Pack to do. We'll be doing it for you on a regular basis while you prep for your trials, but don't get used to it. Supposed to be for pups and emergencies only, because it takes a lot out of the Pack —and Samson, too. Any questions before we start?"

I thought a moment, and nodded. "What if some members of the Pack don't want to participate?"

The woman with the yellow eyes snorted. "Picked up on that, did you? You don't—"

Samson raised a finger, silencing her. "Fallyn, enough."

I ignored her and kept my eyes on Samson. He met me stare for stare. I knew he'd spent a lot of influence to bring me into the Pack. "I lead, and the Pack follows. But let's not make this a habit, any more than is necessary." He looked at Sledge. "Are they ready?"

"Much as they can be. May as well get this over with. Most of us have to work in the morning."

Samson nodded, giving his sergeant-at-arms a sideways glance before placing his hands on my chest. "This is going to suck. Fair warning."

He closed his eyes and his hands first grew warm, then hot, almost uncomfortably so. The heat spread from his hands into my body, until it felt like I was running a high fever. I sweated profusely as the magic moved through my chest and out into my limbs. I felt tissues and bones move back into place as they mended, almost all at once. I screamed as bones knit together, torn flesh healed, and the swelling in my brain receded. The pain was intense, yet brief. I clung to the couch cushions and tensed in agony, screaming with primal urgency until the pain subsided.

Although it only took a minute or so to heal me, it seemed to take a lot out of Samson. After he was done, his hands fell to his sides and he slumped back in the chair. I noticed that the others looked pale and unwell now, the same way a person might look after an all-night bender. But me? I felt great. Better than great, in fact. I felt like I could run a marathon, or wrestle a bear. I felt superhuman.

Sonny staggered to a nearby chair and sat down. "The high'll pass soon, kid. Your body is still healing, and that's just the magic continuing to do its job. You probably want to run some laps or get laid right now, but don't. Just rest and let the magic run its course—else the Pack's efforts will have been wasted."

I sat up and tested my limbs and torso, taking a few deep breaths for good measure. "For what it's worth, thanks."

Samson remained slumped in his chair, looking like he needed the couch instead of me. Sonny mumbled something to the effect of "Sure, kid." Fallyn gave me a dirty look and walked out the door.

Sledge lazily raised a hand to acknowledge my thanks, then he headed out as well. I heard him yell, "It's done, you can all go now," and the sounds of footsteps, grumbling, and motorcycles revving up followed.

I reflected on why the Pack was pissed Samson had offered to help me control my beast. It was plain to see the healing took its toll on everyone. If the training was as brutal as Dr. Ganesh had hinted, they likely wouldn't even want to do it for another wolf... much less a shifter who wasn't even a 'thrope.

Samson took a deep breath and leaned forward, elbows on his knees. "Don't mind Fallyn. She just worries about me, is all."

"She's your daughter, then?"

He chuckled. "Yes." He looked at me with a smile, narrowing his eyes. "So don't be getting any ideas. Besides, she's liable to castrate you if you make a move on her."

I nodded. "Duly noted." I considered my next words carefully. "Samson, I'll back out if it'll make things easier on you."

He shook his head. "Too late. Once you commit, you either learn to control the change, or the Pack kills you. It's purely self-preservation. Can't have a rogue shifter out there with poor control, screwing things up for everyone else."

"Alrighty then. Well, that's settled. I just thought I'd offer, because I know my presence here isn't doing you any favors."

He shrugged. "The Pack doesn't always see things the way I do. I'm the oldest wolf here, by far, so I tend to take the long view on things. They'll come around, in time." He stood, with some effort. "Now, why don't we both get some rest? You and I have a long weekend ahead of us."

"Training?"

He nodded. "And if you think what those fae did to you was bad, just wait. We need to bring you to the brink, so you can learn to control your change. It ain't going to be easy, on any of us. Go rest up, see your girl, and tell her you're going to be gone all weekend."

"Aw, hell. Bells!"

I MESSAGED her as I was leaving the clubhouse. She didn't respond, so I texted Hemi and explained I'd gotten jumped leaving Maeve's. He messaged back saying the trolls had tracked Little Sal's scent to the road, then it had vanished. It looked like he'd been abducted by someone in a car. We agreed to meet in the morning to catch up and devise a plan. I decided to swing by Belladonna's to apologize before I headed home.

Outside, I found that the air had been let out of my tires. *Great.* At least they hadn't been slashed. I did my best to DWSWD, "do what Swayze would do," and chuckled in case anyone was watching. I soon found an air compressor and hose in the Pack's garage and filled my tires back up. Then I headed to Belladonna's, but she wasn't home. I'd pissed her off and then stood her up. I was *so* going to be in the doghouse.

I still felt pretty good after the healing, but I knew I'd better take Sonny's advice and head home. I got back to the junkyard, undressed, and hopped into bed, but I was too wired to sleep. After a few minutes of tossing and turning, I got on the Internet to do some digging, on the odd chance that Little Sal's abduction was related to other abductions.

Sure enough, the local news sites had a few stories of children being abducted. Nothing beyond the ordinary, but enough to merit further interest. Several children had gone missing within the central Texas area over the last six months. Most were foster kids and thought to be runaways, but one had been taken from her front yard in the early morning hours, just like Little Sal. I couldn't chalk it up as coincidence.

After that, I spent some time looking for any new info on Ananda, but came up empty. Then my phone rang; it was Bells. I answered, cringing as I spoke.

"Are you pissed at me?"

"I was, until I got your text. Who jumped you?"

"Bunch of fae. I think they're still hacked that I disrespected their queen."

She laughed. "Making friends everywhere you go. Must be that Irish charm. You want to go looking for them?"

"Naw, I have bigger fish to fry." I filled her in on Little Sal's disappearance.

"Hmm. I'm no fan of the red caps, but taking a kid—even a fae kid? That's messed up. Let me know if you need anything, intel or otherwise."

"Thanks, Bells. And sorry for snooping around your place this morning. I shouldn't have been looking through your mail."

"And I should've told you about the ticket. Apology accepted. You know, I still need to explain all this crazy shit to you, about my family and everything."

I took a second to choose my response carefully. "I'm not going to lose you, Bells. You should know that."

"I hate to tell you this, Colin, but you may not have a choice." She sighed heavily. "Look, it's late and I just got in from work. Can we catch up tomorrow sometime?"

"Sure thing. And Bells?"

"Yes, Colin?"

"I really enjoyed the time we spent together last night."

She didn't respond immediately, and I held my breath as the awkward silence stretched on.

"Me too." She hung up without saying goodbye, and I wondered if I might be losing her after all.

5

The next morning, I met Hemi in front of Sal's place. The red cap lived in what I could only describe as an upscale trailer park, just outside city limits between Austin and Manor, Texas. The area was a mix of office parks and warehouses scattered among older homes, empty lots and fields, and a handful of small farms. Out here, cow pastures and cornfields often bordered new construction, owing to the few holdouts who'd refused to sell their land—despite rising property taxes and real estate values.

The trailer park was strategically situated just a few miles from one of Austin's high crime areas. Rundberg was nothing but fleabag motels, liquor stores, pawn shops, and bodegas. The relative privacy of the locale, combined with easy access to Austin's own vice city, made it the perfect place for a bunch of fae living on the edge of society to hole up. Word around town was that Rocko owned the trailer park and kept it low profile. His tenants consisted of his crew and employees, along with a healthy dollop of low level fae who had neither the means nor the magic for more expensive digs.

The genius of it was, most mundanes wouldn't look twice at

the park. Since it wasn't an eyesore or a cop magnet, it stayed off the radar of mundane society. With a little lawn care and a "No Vacancy" sign to keep curious humans away, Rocko had created a sanctuary for the seedy underbelly of Austin's fae population.

To the untrained and unmagicked eye it looked like any other trailer park, albeit a bit nicer than most. But look a little closer, and what you saw would have any normal human questioning their sanity. Check out the old man in the lawn chair, sipping coffee and smoking Pall Mall reds—was that fur poking out of his worn flannel pajamas? Or that tired-looking blonde in the short skirt, carrying her come-fuck-me pumps—was it just your imagination, or were there scales glimmering under the hem of her mini when she squatted to pick up the paper? And the children who'd just passed you on their bikes, laughing and giggling as they jumped off curbs and over speed bumps—did they have fangs, or was it just your mind playing tricks on you?

These were signs that most mundane humans would overlook, but to Hemi and me they might as well have been broadcasting in bright neon, "Here be monsters." As humans living with one foot in the mundane world and the other in the world of magic and fae, no one had to tell us to watch our backs here. We knew all about the dangers that lived just beneath the surface of everyday life, and we kept an eye out for trouble because of it.

Hemi sipped juice from a plastic bottle as he pointed to a spot on Sal's freshly mowed lawn. The grass was slightly flattened, as if someone had recently been sitting there. "This is where the little bugger was before he disappeared. His sisters said he liked to sit out here and feed the squirrels by hand."

"Sisters?"

"Two, supposed to be watching him. They were the last to see the kid."

The tracking spell had turned out to be a dead end. Wherever they were keeping Sal's kid, the place must have been warded or spelled to block location magic. I ran a hand through my hair and rubbed the back of my neck. Despite the healing I'd received, I'd woken up feeling like I'd been run over. "Does Little Sal sound like the typical red cap to you?"

Hemi yawned. "Eh, I don't know much about North American and European supernaturals, so I can't rightly comment. But from what the family told us last night, he's not what you'd call normal by their standards. Bit of a gentle soul, from what I gathered. Might be why he was targeted. Anyway, over here's where the trail turns cold."

Hemi walked through the neighbor's yard, past some bushes to a street corner where Sal's lane intersected with the main thoroughfare. I looked to the left; the front entrance was just a block away. A weathered, but working, automatic gate and privacy fence protected the park.

"Any other exits or entrances?"

He pointed in the opposite direction from the front gate. "There's a loose section of fence in the back. Kids and teens use it as a shortcut to get to the corner store, to buy snacks and cigarettes and such. Besides a maintenance entrance, that gate is the only way in or out."

"And no cameras, to maintain the privacy of the residents." I looked up and down the street, scanning with my second sight in case there might be something the trolls and Hemi hadn't seen. A variety of formidable magical signatures, some dark and some light, revealed the wards and spells protecting the residences along the block. Every trailer was magicked up, and Sal's was no exception. It made me wonder if it wasn't a mundane who'd snagged the kid after all. No fae or other supernatural creature would've been dumb enough to risk it.

"Let's check out that shortcut. I have a hunch we might find someone down there who saw something."

AT THE END of the street, we found a small park occupied by a group of teens who were too young to drive but old enough to avoid getting caught for truancy. When they saw me, they tossed whatever they'd been smoking and took off running in all directions. However, Hemi had jumped the fence and cut around behind them before I approached. A second later, the big Maori swung a few loose boards away from the fence and squeezed through the hole, carrying a surly-looking teen by the scruff.

The kid looked fifteen or sixteen, but he could have been any age at all. Fae lived long lives, and some grew at an exceedingly slow rate compared to humans. Plus, there was always the issue of glamour, and even I couldn't always see through the disguises the older fae wore. This kid, if he really was a kid, looked human, except for his exceptionally fine facial features and abnormally clear skin. He had a James Dean haircut and a number of brightly inked tattoos. He wore a plain white t-shirt, tucked in with a pack of smokes rolled into one sleeve. His jeans were worn but clean and held up by a wide leather belt, cuffed at the ankles over combat boots polished to a high shine.

I liked him immediately, based on his sense of style alone. He struggled against Hemi's grip, held fast by the collar and his belt.

"Lemme go, you 'roided up freak! No need to be raging about. Wasn't even my weed to begin with." He spoke with a slight lilt that could've been Irish or Welsh, or perhaps something older.

After a few more seconds, he stopped struggling and sulked, hanging in mid-air. "I got no treasure, if that's what you're after. Look around—ain't nobody in Rocko's park got nuthin' but empty pockets and empty stares."

I glanced around for effect. "Doesn't look like all that bad of a place to me. I've seen worse."

He snorted and wiped his nose on a black kerchief tied around his wrist. "Right. Bet you live in one of those nice big houses, out on the west side. Probably got a maid and someone to wipe your arse, too."

"Actually, I live in a junkyard. And Hemi here—Hemi, where do you live, anyway?"

"Me? Garage apartment, off Manchaca. Rent's cheap, and my landlady bakes me cookies. No complaints."

The kid gave me a sly smirk. "You're the druid Sal hired to find his kid." He craned his neck around and looked Hemi in the eye. "Now that you've scrammed me neck all up, you can set me down, arsehole. I won't run."

Hemi just stood there looking bored, acting like he could hold the kid all day. Which he probably could.

The kid looked at me. "Really? You're going to make me talk to you like this? Humiliating." He crossed his arms and sulked harder, if that were possible.

"Hemi, you can put him down." Hemi complied, and the kid took a seat on a nearby swing. He produced a cigarette and lit up.

"Hope you don't mind if I smoke." It was obvious he didn't care if we did, but I answered just the same.

"I don't. I'm Colin. You got a name?"

He took a drag on his cigarette and exhaled through his nose. "I go by Click."

Hemi wrinkled his forehead. "Click? Like clicking a button?"

Click shrugged and looked bored.

"Sorry for the rough treatment, Click, but I figured you guys would think I was a cop and run before I could get any info."

"You were right, obviously." He pointed his cigarette at Hemi.

"You keep strange company. That one's got an interesting parentage, for sure. No mortal would be able to hold me like that."

I cocked an eyebrow at Hemi, who frowned and held his hands up in a "don't ask me" gesture. I filed that info away for another time, and shook my head. "That's his business. What we want to talk about is whether anyone saw who took Little Sal."

The kid held out his hand. "Payment up front."

"Uh-uh, after." I held up a twenty. "Besides, I know you answer to Rocko. If I tell him you're holding out info that might help us find Little Sal, what do you think he'll do?"

Click held up his hands, flicking ash on his jeans. "Alright, alright. I like the kid anyway—everyone does. He's goofy, and acts sort of slow, but nobody messes with him. You don't mess with the blessed. That's our way and we fae stick by it."

He wiped the ash away with his palm, rubbing it into his jeans and eyeing the results. "It was humans that took him. Jeretta saw it. She won't talk to you, but she told me everything. They pulled through in a white work truck, and she thought they was here from the city or something. The men called Little Sal over, maybe to ask him about something—I don't know. She spied 'em from across the street, out the window. A few minutes later, the truck and Little Sal were gone."

"Did she tell anyone?"

"Nope. Thought nothing of it, until later when Sal's sisters came looking for him. Then it was too late. She was afraid Rocko and Sal would be mad about her not doing anything, being as her family's behind on Rocko's rent. So, she didn't say nothing."

I looked at Hemi, and he cocked his head ever so slightly to his left. I noticed a pair of worn pink Chuck Taylors poking out from behind a bit of shrubbery. I shook my head slightly while keeping eye contact with Hemi, and pointedly ignored our eavesdropper.

"You sure Jeretta won't talk to us?"

Click paused as he squeezed one eye shut. "I'm sure. Fact is, she don't talk at all. She's got the sight, and when she does have something to say she just sends us pictures and feelings, mostly." He jumped off the swing and picked up a stick, then scratched something in the dirt at his feet.

"There—that was on the side of the truck." It was a circle with a lightning bolt through it.

"Anything else?"

"Naw, that's all she can remember."

I handed him the bill, and he grabbed it with two fingers, tugging on it gently as I held on. I tilted my head at the shrubbery. "Be sure she gets half."

"Yeah, yeah. Like we don't take care of our own 'round here. Sheesh." I let the bill go and Click made it disappear.

"And Click?"

"Yeah?"

"Sal has my number. If Jeretta remembers anything else at all, or if you see that truck again, have him contact me immediately. I'll make it worth your while."

He nodded, then screwed his mouth sideways as he crushed his cigarette underfoot. "Druid, you think we're going to see Little Sal again?"

"Hopefully, Click. If I can help it."

He nodded. "Make 'em pay, when you find them." Then Click snapped his fingers, and vanished from sight.

———

"Neat trick," Hemi stated. "Wish I could do that."

"Hmmm. He could've ditched us at any time, at least after you let him go. Guess he really does have a soft spot for Sal's kid."

"Or for the cash you flashed him, eh?"

"Maybe. Anyway, he was good for a useful bit of info. That symbol he scratched in the dirt looked familiar. Maybe they were driving an electrician's truck or something. Anyway, I'll ask Bells to help me look into it."

"How's that going, by the way?" Hemi did his best to ask nonchalantly, but his concern was evident.

"About like you'd expect. I'm mucking it up at every turn."

He chuckled and slapped me on the shoulder a little too hard. "Ah, but what you don't know is that's why the girls like you. Being awkward is part of your charm. Keep it up, and she'll be over it in no time."

"That has to be the worst relationship advice I've ever gotten, Hemi. But strangely, it almost makes sense."

"Don't mention it. Now, I have to get to work. You good?"

"I am. Thanks for covering for me."

"Sure. Let me know when you find whoever took the little anklebiter, and I'll help you bust their skulls."

"Will do." Hemi got into his ride, a little souped up rice burner that was half rust and half body work. It made a lot more noise than it had horsepower to back it up. I waved as he drove off, then walked the narrow blacktop lanes of the trailer park for a few minutes, trying to get a feel for how the abduction had gone down. I searched the spot across from Jeretta's trailer, where Click had indicated the boy was abducted, and found a tire tread impression left in a patch of dirt on the shoulder. I snapped a picture, then headed back to my car.

As I turned the corner, I found Detective Klein leaning on the hood of my Gremlin. Klein had decided she had it in for me after her partner died under suspicious circumstances. When someone close to you gets sacrificed to dark forces, and their body is found with all the evidence of said ritual left plainly in view for all to see, it tends to raise questions. And the fact that I'd gotten picked up by patrol officers a few blocks from the scene... well, I didn't blame Klein for thinking I had something to do with it.

Of course, the department chalked it up to Erskine being involved in some strange satanic cult. The truth wasn't far off that mark. He'd been into black magic and had gotten mixed up with the Dark Druid. The Dark Druid's favorite hobby was stealing other people's bodies, possessing them by necromantic means to extend his lifespan indefinitely. He'd planned to do the same to me, but with a little help from Finnegas I'd thwarted his plans.

But Klein wasn't clued in, so she didn't know anything about any of that.

Her harsh, rugged features went from a scowl to an unfriendly smile on seeing me. "Well, well, if it isn't Colin McCool, the most well-connected junkyard employee in Austin. Here I am this morning, following up on a lead in a missing persons case I'm working, and whose car do I see parked in front of the victim's home but yours?"

"Victim? Did a crime occur around here, Detective?"

Her eyes narrowed. "Go ahead, play dumb. I mean, even if you were somehow involved in this case, your high-priced attorney will bail you out, right? Never mind the dirty cops he must have on the payroll."

"Like Erskine, for example?"

She came off the car like a greyhound out of the gate, moving with a surprising amount of speed for a human. She didn't touch me, but she was close enough for me to smell the Tic Tac she was chewing, and the brisket tacos and coffee she'd had for breakfast.

"Let me tell you something, McCool. I knew my partner was dirty—at least, I suspected as much. I was this close to asking my lieutenant for a transfer, because it's hard enough to move up the ranks as a woman without having to cover for some shit-bird partner who's on the take.

"But he didn't deserve what happened to him. Dirty cop or no, whatever he was into, it didn't merit him going down like that. Not on your life. Somehow, I know you're involved, just like I know you have something to do with these missing kids. And when I find out what, I'm going to be on you like dog shit on sneakers."

I did my best to look apologetic. "Look, believe it or not, we're on the same side—"

"Save it, McCool. Whether you think you're some kind of amateur P.I. or a wannabe vigilante, I don't care. If you fuck up my case, or if I find you're connected in any way, I'll throw every charge I can scrounge up at you until I find something that sticks. Understood?"

I nodded. "Understood."

She took a step back. "Stay out of my way, or I *will* make your life a bigger shit show than it is already."

I watched her stalk off to her unmarked vehicle, a late model dark blue sedan that had "cop car" written all over it. She goosed it a little as she sped off, throwing small bits of sand and gravel at me and the Gremlin.

I heard someone snap their fingers to my left, and turned to find Click standing beside me. "I think she's sweet on you, druid."

I snorted. "Anybody talk to her, Click?"

He shook his head. "Nope. Rocko has a strict 'no talking to the fuzz' policy. Besides, nobody reported Little Sal's disappearance. If she was here, it's because she got an anonymous tip—not because anyone got the police involved."

"Let's keep it that way. She's smart, and she knows something weird is going on. The further we can keep that one from the world beneath, the better."

He bobbed his chin at me. "Not a problem. Let me know when you figure out who took Little Sal, alright? Can't say I wasn't fond of the little bugger, and I wouldn't mind getting some payback against whoever took him."

I nodded. "I'll keep that in mind, Click."

"You do that, druid. You do that."

6

Friday morning, I got a text from Sonny.

-Real training begins tonight. Be at the clubhouse by 7 pm.- I had no idea how he'd gotten my number, but the moment I'd been dreading had arrived. I spent the rest of the day preoccupied by thoughts of what I might be in for, and was barely able to focus on work and school. I daydreamed through most of my morning classes, and only realized my last class was over when students started filing out of the lecture hall. I chided myself as I gathered my things. The fall semester was almost over, and I'd be facing finals soon. Now was not the time to be spacing out during lectures.

Of course, I'd decided to go to college back when I was dead set against hunting supernaturals ever again. Sometimes I wondered if it was even worth it, keeping my grades up while I kept the city safe from all manner of arcane threats. But, I didn't expect to be doing this work forever. Eventually I'd want to hang up my sword for good, and I'd need a career to fall back on when that day arrived. So, I kept my nose in the books when I wasn't working hunting jobs or running errands for Maeve.

Back at the junkyard, I rushed through some work, pulling

parts for Ed and checking out a few vehicles that his other mechanics couldn't diagnose. Then I texted Bells to tell her I wouldn't be available tonight or tomorrow, because werewolf stuff. She said she understood, and not to hurt anyone too badly. If only.

After that I tried to nap, but I was still too wired. I spent the rest of the afternoon tuning the Gremlin until Ed came out and found me. He huffed up to me, red-faced from the effort of walking from the office to the yard. Poor guy had me worried. I was really going to have to come up with a spell or something to make him want to get in better shape.

"Colin, c'mon over here. Got something to show you."

I followed him behind the office, where he pulled a tarp off a vaguely motorcycle-shaped something or other. Underneath was a very beat up Harley that looked like it had seen some miles.

"It's an '88 FXR Super Glide. Big displacement, air-cooled V-twin, fairly agile. Frame's a little small for someone your size, but it'll still be a comfortable ride. What do you think?"

I looked it over. The tank had been painted flat black, it had worn leather saddle-bags in back, the seat was ripped, and it carried just enough chrome to look serious—but not enough to be prissy. A lot of it needed a good polish, but the tires had decent tread. If I knew Ed, the engine had good compression and probably only needed a few minor repairs to be roadworthy.

I squatted next to it to get a good look at the underside of the tank. Several small runes were etched into the paint underneath, in the old Anglo-Saxon style. I saw the runes for "ride," "glory," and "horse." Later, I'd see what kind of magic had been woven into them; it'd probably freak Ed out if I went into a trance in front of him. I rubbed a bit of grime off the engine with a rag I pulled from my pocket, and stood.

"It's perfect."

Ed almost smiled, but held it together. "Might need to move the pegs to make it comfortable for a rider your size. And you'll have to learn how to shift gears. But it should come quickly to you."

"I love it, Ed. How much do I owe you?"

He frowned and looked wistfully at the bike. "You can work it off. Shit, and let me ride it now and again. 'Reminds me of the one I loved back then.'"

"You had a hog like this?" I asked.

He chuckled. "Something like that. Let's just say she was built and fun to handle." I looked at him, clueless, and his usual scowl returned. "Ah hell, it's a song. Look it up on your Spot-o-fried or whatever. Let me know when you start working on it—I'd like to tinker with it a bit myself."

"Thanks, Ed, really. It means a lot that you helped me out with this."

"You earn your keep, and then some. Just keep your grades up, and don't kill yourself on the damned thing. Come to think of it, get that girlfriend of yours to give you some tips. And don't paint it up nice just yet, because you're bound to turn it on its side before too long."

I held back a grin and nodded. Ed wasn't known for being the fatherly type. Was he a good guy? Sure. But not the most touchy-feely person. Finally, I had to laugh.

"What?" he asked, as he fiddled with the gear shifter and tested the clutch.

"You sure you don't want to keep it for yourself?"

"Hah, not on your life. I'm too fat and old to be riding on a bike like this. Naw—I'll take a big old bagger over this any day. Something I can fit my prodigious rear on, and ride in comfort and style. This is a young man's bike, that's for damned sure."

He barely looked at me as he spoke. Chances were good he'd pull the plugs, rebuild the carburetor, drain the tank, and polish the rust off it before I'd ever get around to it. I clapped him on the shoulder, startling him.

"I have to go shower. I took another job, working nights and weekends for a friend. He's expecting me in a few."

"Oh, alright." He rubbed his chin. "You don't mind if I mess around with it a bit—see if it'll crank over?"

"Uncle Ed, as far as I'm concerned, it's yours until I work it off. Have at it."

"Alright... but only if you don't mind."

I left him with the bike, chuckling to myself and wondering if I'd ever even get to ride the thing. Something told me Ed would be taking it for a lot of "test rides."

I GOT to the clubhouse thirty minutes early. As soon as I pulled up, one of the enforcers at the door waved me over.

"Prospect! Mitzy needs help at the bar. Go see what she needs."

"Um, Sonny said I needed to be here—"

"I don't give a flying fuck what he said. Just do as you're told." He turned to the other guy, talking about me as if I wasn't there. "Shit, what the hell do they think this is—a resort or something? Fucking prospects these days. Probably doesn't even ride a hog."

I walked past them, reminding myself that I was the FNG. I was going to be treated like shit because of that, and also because I was persona non grata around here. *So be it.* Inside, the place was empty. It was still early, and I figured it would start to fill with Pack members soon. I walked over to the bar and saw no one there, so I looked over the top. A tall redhead in tight jeans, an even tighter babydoll t-shirt, and over-the-knee leather boots with sensible heels squatted at the other end, stocking beer under the counter.

"Guys out front sent me in, told me to help someone named Mitzy."

She barely glanced up. "You must be the new guy. Man, have they got it in for you." She tilted her head toward the back door as she continued filling the cooler with 12-ounce cans and longnecks. "Beer delivery just came in. Leave two cases of each brand stacked by the door, and put the rest beside the walk-in downstairs. Not inside, mind you—it'll freeze."

I did as she asked, and spent the next thirty minutes running various errands for her—wiping down tables, cleaning glasses, and basically barbacking for her until told otherwise. Around the time I was supposed to have shown up, Sonny stuck his head out of the office.

"Prospect! What the hell are you doing out there? I told you to be here fifteen minutes ago. Get your ass in here so we can get started."

Mitzy smiled and shook her head as I walked back to the office, where Sonny and Sledge met me. Sonny gave me a glare. "Next time, don't be late. We're meeting Samson at the hunting grounds. Hope you dressed warm."

The two shared a grin, like some sort of inside joke had passed between them. Then, they headed out a side door, so I followed. Both hopped on their motorcycles and cranked them up. Neither put on a helmet.

Sonny looked at me like he was pissed, probably because I was still standing there. "Don't even ask if you can ride bitch-back, prospect. Go get your fucking car and quit holding us up."

Right, got it. I'm an idiot.

I ran to my car, hopped in, and cranked it up—just as they tore ass out of the parking lot. I did my best to keep up with them, which was easy when they hit the highway and headed north. But right after we hit Round Rock, they exited without any warning, and I sped right past them. I saw the smiles on their faces as they rode down the exit ramp.

"Shit," I said to the steering wheel and no one in particular. I took the next exit and hooked back around, then drove like a bat out of hell down the last road I'd seen them on, heading west down Sam Bass. They were long gone. On a hunch, I took FM 1431 and kept heading west. Eventually, I spotted the telltale lights of two motorcycles in the distance, and followed at a discreet distance to avoid being ditched again.

They drove for quite a while, passing Jonestown and Lago Vista both. We were on the north side of the lake, heading into a sparsely populated area that was home to the largest expanse of undeveloped land around: the Balcones National Wildlife Preserve. They passed the park entrance and drove another few miles, hooking a right on Cow Creek Road.

I was somewhat familiar with the area. It was one of the places Finnegas had taken Jesse and me during our training. The road would make it tricky to follow them without being noticed, because it took quite a few twists and turns as it followed the creek it was named after.

"Screw these guys," I mumbled to myself. I muttered a cantrip as I cut my headlights, and continued following them by relying on my night vision spell to show me the road. Thankfully, we were nearing a full moon, and the sky was clear, so there was plenty of ambient light. A few miles down the road, they turned into a dirt driveway hidden by brush and weeds. I pulled off to the side of the road and waited a minute or two, then followed them down the road with my windows open, listening for the sound of their bikes as I drove.

Less than a minute later, I heard their bikes shut off. I parked the car in the weeds next to the drive and quietly exited the car. Then I stalked through the woods, circling around behind the area where I'd last heard the rumble of their exhaust.

I CREPT THROUGH THE WOODS, far enough away from the road so they wouldn't hear me, but close enough to keep my bearings. Soon, I heard their voices. I figured turning the tables on Sledge and Sonny might get them off my back. Or, maybe it would piss them off worse. I had no idea how all this outlaw biker, wolf pack stuff worked.

Sledge's deep voice cut through the darkness. "You think he'll find his way out here?"

"Naw—well, maybe if he uses that druid magic of his," Sonny replied. "Never can tell with those magic types. I don't trust them as a rule. Can't fucking believe Samson is sponsoring this kid into the Pack."

"He seems alright. Stood like a man when I fought him. Held his own when he got jumped, too."

"Fucking druid tricks, is all." Sonny spat. "He's shit without them. Hell, he's not even a real shifter."

Sledge shrugged. "Seems alright to me, that's all I'm saying."

I slowly duckwalked closer until I saw both wolves in the pale light of the nearly full moon. They were leaning on their bikes, which were parked at the end of a long row of hogs, in front of a modest farmhouse. Behind the house were a few metal buildings, perhaps a barn or stables. There were no lights on inside the house, and all was quiet except for their voices. If the rest of the Pack was here, they had gone elsewhere.

Sonny threw something, and I heard glass shatter a few yards distant. "Yeah, but keep in mind he ain't a 'thrope. That beast inside him ain't natural. It's a fae thing created by Tuatha magic, and you can't trust these fucking Irish fae any further than you can gut them and toss their innards. Hear me?"

"I hear you, but I still say the kid is alright. He at least deserves a chance to prove himself, just like all the rest."

Sonny laughed bitterly. "Like that lizard-man Samson took in a few years back? That asshole nearly killed Crank. Fucking poison fangs and shit. I told Samson you couldn't trust a cold-blooded 'thrope, but he wouldn't listen. Fuck."

Hearing Sonny talk about me like this was a shock. He'd been cool with me until I'd become a prospect, but I'd thought that was just part of the hazing act. It was obvious to me now that he hated my guts. I'd make it a point to watch my back around him from now on.

"What if he don't figure it out? It ain't like he can track our scent like a regular pup would."

Sonny cackled. "Fuck 'em. Normally, I'd send you out after him, but in this case I say let him swing in the wind. He don't show for training, and the Pack'll start thinking he's a coward. Won't be long before we vote against him in a conclave."

"That's cold, man."

"That's keeping the Pack safe. My job is to look out for the Pack's interests, and to balance the scales when Samson loses perspective. He's old, Sledge, and long in the tooth. Old wolves don't always think straight. I'm just looking out for everyone's interests, is all."

Sonny looked down the drive toward the road, scanning the darkness. I ducked behind a tree.

"C'mon, let's grab some more beers, then go tell the Pack he cut and run."

Sledge crossed his arms. "You do what you want, but I ain't saying nuthin' against the kid. He makes his way on his own, or he don't. I ain't gonna do anything chickenshit to him just on account of you not liking him. But I won't go against what you say, either."

Sonny shook his head. "Whatever. Just keep your mouth shut, alright? I'm just doing what's right—what Samson won't. That's all."

"Whatever you say, Sonny."

Sledge headed for the house. Sonny stopped to take a piss, then followed Sledge inside. I waited for a few moments, then crept out of the tree line and up to their bikes. I decided to leave Sledge's hog alone, but I walked up to Sonny's bike and laid a hand on it, preparing to cast a cantrip that would foul his gas.

Someone cleared their throat behind me. "Some wolves would kill you for messing with their ride. Hope you're not doing anything stupid that'll get him killed."

I glanced over my shoulder, and found Fallyn standing a few feet behind me. She wore jeans, desert combat boots, a white tank top under a flannel shirt, and a small backpack slung over one shoulder. *Where did she come from?* I'd never heard her approach. I acted as if I'd known she was there all along.

"No, nothing like that. Just a little payback for getting ditched is all. Fouling his fuel. He'll have to drain the tank and clean the carb."

She shrugged. "It's your funeral if he finds out, but have at it. Sonny's an asshole, and while I'm no fan of yours, his job is to follow Samson's lead and take care of prospects. Not to fuck them over just because he has a thorn in his paw."

"You going to tell them I was out here?" I asked.

She crossed her arms and stared for several seconds. "Nah. I'll tell them I found you driving aimlessly up and down Cow Creek Road. That ought to be enough so you don't look completely incompetent, but not so much as to tip Sonny off. Now, do what you gotta do and let's get out of here before they come back."

"Thanks." I grinned and released the spell. "Have fun cleaning that shit up, asshole," I muttered.

Fallyn shrugged. "Don't thank me—I just do what Samson tells me. Now, wipe that grin off your face, and let's go find the Pack. You have a long night ahead of you."

"About that—anything you can tell me that might help me out? I have no idea what I'm in for, how long it's going to take, or how to prepare myself for it. This feels a hell of a lot like a good old-fashioned hazing to me. It'd be nice to have a little heads up."

She took off at a jog, whispering loud enough for me to hear as she headed for the nearby woods. "Only thing I can say is that Samson's your best hope for learning to control that thing inside you. And, it's gonna be rough."

7

I ran after Fallyn in silence. She didn't offer any conversation, so I figured it'd be best to follow suit. As we sped down rocky paths and barely perceptible game trails, through juniper trees and live oak, I considered whether this had been the best plan after all. It was too late to back out now; I'd made my choice, and I would see it through. I concentrated on following lithe 'thrope as she leapt gracefully over rocks and fallen trees, under overhangs and between branches like a ghost in the night.

She was tall and strong, and looked like she belonged out here. I couldn't help but notice her figure as she ran, because it was impressive—kind of a cross between a fitness model and ballet dancer. After verifying that yes, she had a very lovely ass, I planted my eyes firmly between her shoulder blades as we ran.

"I think I'd rather have you staring at my ass," she stated quietly, never pausing to catch her breath. "The way you're boring holes in my back makes me nervous. Let your vision expand, and take in the whole landscape. When you're being stalked by a predator, tunnel vision will get you killed. Besides that, you miss out on all the best stuff nature has to offer."

She pointed up in a tree, twenty yards to our right. At first, I didn't see anything—then I caught the barest hint of a bobcat's dappled coat. Its tail twitched slightly as we briefly made eye contact, then it was gone.

"Wolves aren't the only nocturnal hunters in these woods," she said, continuing to chug along at a steady pace. As we rounded a large hill, Fallyn slowed to a walk, and held up a hand to indicate that I should do the same.

"Place we're headed is the Shaft. It's an abandoned mine. Some crazy old coot thought he could find gemstones in these hills. After he spent his life digging up limestone and quartz, he died, and his son turned the mine into a fallout bunker. When the Fish and Wildlife Service took the land over and turned it into a refuge, the Pack started coming out here to hunt each month. Now, we use the Shaft for training new Pack members to control their ability to shift."

"And nobody ever catches you guys out here?"

She shrugged. "One of the Pack is a park ranger, and we mostly hunt deer and wild hogs. There are more of both than the land can sustain, so no one notices when a few go missing each month. The other rangers assume it's coyotes, when they come across the remains. We make sure we don't leave a trace of anything that would cause them to think otherwise."

Fallyn stopped and began to disrobe. I stood dumbfounded for a second, then turned my back to her. "Um, a little warning next time would be nice."

She snickered. "You're going to see a lot of naked ass out here, so you may as well get used to it. Wolves don't change while they're wearing clothing—not if they can help it. Gets expensive, going through clothes like that. Plus, it's damned uncomfortable. Hurts enough going through the change as it is. By the way, you're going to have to undress, too."

I kept my back turned to her, raising both hands in the air in protest. "Oh, hell no. Nobody told me I'd have to run around out here in the buff, with a bunch of hairy-ass nudist lycanthropes. Uh-uh."

I heard her stuffing her clothes into her backpack. "Your call, but good luck getting the blood out of your clothes."

I turned my head at that, and got an eyeful. I quickly covered my eyes, which elicited more snickering from the young lycanthrope. "Oh, get over it. I'm about to change anyway. Holy hell, you are such a dweeb."

After a moment of silence, I heard the cracking, crunching, bone-snapping sounds of Fallyn shifting into her werewolf form. I snuck a peek out of curiosity, because I'd never seen a 'thrope shift from start to finish.

It was not pretty. Fallyn's change didn't last long, but watching her skin sprout hair and her hands and feet grow claws—as her bones shifted under her skin and her entire skeleton realigned—was not the most pleasant thing I'd ever witnessed. She shook herself out like a dog as she finished shifting, then crouched in a three-point stance, tongue lolling.

Her werewolf form was awe-inspiring. She wasn't exceptionally large, but she was muscular and well-proportioned. Her face was elongated and very canine, and large teeth gleamed from a mouth that looked like it could take an arm or leg off with one bite. Her eyes glowed softly, golden-yellow as they caught the moonlight. Her coat was thick, a deep shade of reddish-brown, and shimmered slightly in the soft light. Her arms were more or less human-shaped, but her lower limbs now looked almost like they had two knees—the first bent forward like a human's, and the second bent back. She balanced on feet that looked more like paws than human feet, and rested on the knuckles of her right hand, with her left drawn close to her chest. She still had breasts, but they were covered in fur and smaller than in her human form.

She growled and spoke in a much lower, more feral voice.

"Stop looking at my tits and let's get this show on the road. I'd like to get some hunting in before the night is through." Then she took off down the trail, running on all fours at breakneck speed.

I blushed. Deciding to remain fully clothed, I ran after her.

WE CAME around another turn in the path, exiting the trees into a small clearing in front of a cliff. The cliff face supported an iron door, the entrance to the mineshaft. It was open, and the soft glow of LED camping lanterns lit the space beyond. It looked as though the entire Pack had gathered for the first night of my "real" training, whatever that was. More than four dozen wolves milled around outside the entrance to the Shaft, all in their werewolf forms. Surprisingly, they came in all shapes and sizes. Some were large and muscular, others long and lean. Some had dark fur that was nearly black, others light grey or tan —and one was almost entirely white. A few had red and tan coats, but Fallyn was the only completely red-furred wolf in sight.

As I walked out of the trees behind Fallyn, a hush fell over the Pack. One wolf in the back began to howl, then the rest joined in, creating a chorus of cries that would surely be heard for miles around. I figured most people would think the howls came from coyotes, which were abundant in these parts. Not many people would recognize the cries of wolves in this day and age.

Fallyn joined in as she took a place near the entrance to the mine, and the Pack parted as a medium-sized, lean, dangerous-looking werewolf exited from the Shaft. The wolf's coat was black along his back and the top of his head. It faded into silver-gray, and then tan, finally melding into a light tan that was almost white on his abdomen and inner thighs. He was lean and muscular, lithe like Fallyn's werewolf form. He moved with a sinuous grace that practically thrummed with restrained power.

The wolf spoke, and I recognized Samson's voice immediately. Unlike Fallyn, his voice lacked the gravelly properties hers had taken on after she'd shifted. It was very nearly normal, and I found it incredibly disturbing to hear a fully human voice coming from his elongated, canine mouth.

"Tonight, we begin the process of welcoming a new member into our Pack. And while he isn't a wolf, we agree as one to help him learn to control his beast, for the good of the Pack and all who reside within our territory. This is the will of the Alpha, and the will of the Pack."

When the Pack howled in response to Samson's words, I noticed that several wolves in the crowd remained silent. Seeing the division among the Pack made me even more nervous about what was to come.

"Colin, step forward." I did as Samson asked, and walked up as the crowd of werewolves parted before me. I stopped in front of him, locking eyes with his. A hush fell over the wolves around us, and the tension in the air rose noticeably.

Samson growled and whispered to me, although all the wolves could hear what he said. "Lower your eyes, son. It looks like you're challenging me when you hold eye contact for too long."

I dropped my gaze to the ground, and the crowd relaxed. Samson placed a hand on my shoulder. I noted the wickedly sharp, inch-long claws at the end of each of his fingers.

"Colin McCool, are you willing to tame your beast, in order to gain full membership into the Pack?"

I nodded. "I am."

"Are you willing to accept the consequences of failing your trial, with the knowledge that every action you take from this day forward reflects not just on yourself, but also on the entire Pack?"

The crowd had been silent, but I heard a few low growls in the audience. "I accept the consequences of my actions, and my failure." It seemed like the right thing to say.

Samson squeezed my shoulder, piercing my skin with his claws until blood ran down my chest and back. "Even unto death?"

What the fuck? Aw, hell. In for a penny, in for a pound. "Even unto death."

I stood unflinching as Samson dug his claws deeper into my shoulder, causing my blood to flow even more freely. He withdrew his claws and snatched his hand away in a blur, flinging drops of my blood onto the bedrock below us.

"His blood seals us to him, and him to us. So says the Alpha, so says the Pack." The Pack howled as one, some seemingly with delight, while others perhaps joined in to celebrate my impending demise.

"And so it begins. Colin, follow me."

He turned and headed into the Shaft and I followed, noticing that Fallyn and another wolf trailed behind me. Fallyn paused to shut the door, and it clanged against the concrete and iron that framed the opening. I heard someone snap a lock into place on the door outside.

What the hell have I gotten myself into?

I followed on Samson's heels. He led us deep into the mine, down twists and turns barely lit by lanterns placed few and far between. Eventually, we came to a dead end. Samson growled a few words in an unfamiliar language, and the rock wall before us shimmered and disappeared. A chamber sat beyond, dug from the limestone bedrock. Thick chains, ankle shackles, and manacles were bolted into the wall opposite the entrance.

"Take off your shirt, pants, everything," he said. I complied after only a moment's hesitation, and soon stood naked as the day I was born in front of three werewolves, in a mine shaft deep under a hill in the Balcones Canyonland Wildlife Refuge. He gestured at Fallyn and the other werewolf. "Restrain him."

It was all just a little too much. "Is this really necessary? I mean, can't you just share some tips on how to control the beast, spot me a few hits of Valium, and maybe give me a couple of mantras and yoga poses to do for extra credit?"

One of the wolves behind me chuckled, and Samson sighed. "Look, Colin, there are other ways to go about this. But I've been around a long time, and for you I think the old ways are the best. I need to take you to the brink, so you can learn to hold your beast in check. Then, we're going to repeat the process, until you get better at restraining it. Gradually, you'll learn to control your ability to shift, and hopefully you'll gain full dominance over the beast by the time we're through."

"You mean tonight?"

Fallyn guffawed, and I blushed as her laugh echoed in the mine.

"No, son, not tonight. We'll be at this every weekend for weeks, possibly even months. It's up to you how long it takes, but no one learns to control their beast in a night. Now, let them shackle you so we can get started."

I walked up to the wall and snapped the first of the shackles on my wrist. Fallyn stalked up and clasped the other shackle to secure my free hand, while the other wolf secured my ankles. I tested the chains. They were incredibly heavy, and I had maybe six inches of play for each limb. Not enough to strike out, or even to avoid a blow.

Samson approached, and his eyes softened.

"This is going to hurt."

He pulled his clawed hand high behind him and raked it across my torso, eviscerating me in one clean swipe. My blood sprayed across the mine walls and ceiling, and I passed out just as my entrails hit the stone floor below.

AS IF IN A DREAM, I saw Samson ripping and tearing at my body, while Fallyn and the other wolf observed dispassionately. My consciousness was in that *other* place I went to when my Hyde-side came out to play. I felt myself begin to shift, then some force or presence exerted itself on my alter-ego's will, halting the change.

I sensed the Eye's presence coalesce in the emptiness around me.

-Intriguing. It seems the alpha is using his influence and magic to suppress your change. However, your Fomorian form is close enough to the surface to allow me to emerge. Shall I vaporize them?-

"No! I volunteered for this. It's the only way to learn how to control the change." Even though I didn't want the Eye to blast Samson into bits, I had to admit that I found its presence comforting under the circumstances. The Eye's personality was detached and neutral, but I'd always sensed a sort of ancient wisdom behind it. Once I had better control of my ability to shift and regular access to the Eye's powers, I'd delve deeper into the artifact's origins. But for now, I just needed to survive the night's activities without releasing my Hyde-side.

-Understood. I'm sure there are other methods that would allow you to gain control over your Fomorian form, but I can see how this method might be the most expedient. Incidentally, I won't be able to communicate with you for long. Not while he's suppressing your ability to change.-

"Got it. Do me a favor, Eye. Be ready to help me gain control if Samson can't hold the beast back."

-I require your intelligence and your Fomorian form's physical

abilities, in order to achieve my primary directive. I will do as you ask.-

"That's comforting. Just don't forget who's in charge here. This is my body you've taken up residence in, you know."

-I am temporally displaced, and therefore not residing within your body. However, I understand your meaning. Duly noted.-

"Smart ass."

-I have no reference by which I might interpret the intended meaning of that statement.-

"Whatever. Just don't let me kill the alpha. He's my only shot at getting this thing right."

-Again, noted.-

The Eye's voice and presence faded out, and my consciousness slid back into my physical body, just as Samson drew on the Pack's energy to heal me. As I came back into myself, I screamed and writhed in agony. Not only was the pain overwhelming, it was terrifying. Fallyn and the other wolf held my guts in while Samson healed me, using his will and the Pack's energy to knit the viscera, muscle, and skin back together. I felt my innards shifting back into the proper position inside my abdomen, and vomited all over Samson and the other two wolves.

"Oh, fucking hell," Fallyn muttered.

"Again," Samson declared.

Samson injured me and brought from the brink of death at least a half-dozen times. Each time, I found it easier to sense the change coming. And the last few times, I was able to predict the moment when the change was about to occur; that point when my consciousness stepped back, and my Hyde-side took over. In observing the process as it happened, I realized that if I could get in front of the change I could resist it, and even prevent it from happening.

By the night's end I was pretty sure I could learn to suppress the change, just as Samson had done. But could I also learn to stay in the driver's seat after turning into the beast? The last time I'd changed, I'd only been able to gain dominance over my Fomorian form with the Eye's help... and that was only for a few moments. I supposed that time would tell whether I'd have full control over my ability to shift. But I ever wanted to face down Fuamnach and the Dark Druid, only complete control would do.

When it was over, the alpha staggered back and sat hard against the wall. "That's enough for tonight. Unchain him."

I had to agree with him. Unlike the last time the Pack's magic had been used to heal me, this time I felt completely spent. After being ruthlessly injured and healed several times in a single night, I didn't think I could take any more. *The hell with getting a handle on my change.*

Fallyn and the other wolf released my bonds, and I collapsed to the floor. They unlatched the ankle cuffs, and the second wolf helped me to my feet. I stumbled to the wall across from Samson and sat, not even slightly concerned with my nakedness.

"Is it going to be like this every single time?"

Samson nodded. "Every single time."

"Shit."

Fallyn handed Samson a bottle of water. "Dad, if you don't mind, I'm going to clean up and go for a hunt. Need to recharge the batteries. Even a rabbit or opossum will do right now."

Opossum? Gross.

He nodded. "Take Sledge and Trina. Things are—unstable at the moment. You need someone to watch your back."

"I'll be fine. But I'll bring them along just the same."

The other wolf tapped my shoulder and I opened my eyes. I didn't remember closing them. The wolf held a bottle of water out to me, and I took it.

"Nice abs," she said. "Too bad you're not my type."

I recognized Trina's voice and chuckled. "Yeah, sorry to disappoint."

She laughed and followed Fallyn out of the chamber. I sat with Samson in silence, and heard the metal clang of the mine door slamming open a short time later.

I drank half the bottle, then crawled to my pile of clothes and slowly began pulling them on. "So, about Fallyn—"

Samson took a drink, pouring it down his throat. Werewolf lips weren't meant for plastic bottles. His long, pink tongue licked droplets of water from his snout and muzzle as he gazed down the tunnel after his daughter.

"Her mother died when she was just a child. Hunters, from the Circle's sister organization in Europe—folks with old scores to settle. I've raised Fallyn ever since. Well, me and the Pack."

I pulled my jeans halfway up my legs, then collapsed into the wall, exhausted. "And what happened to those hunters?"

"I ate their hearts. Fallyn watched as they died."

He said it as if to say, "I had eggs for breakfast," or "I like wool socks." Eating hunters' hearts in front of his offspring was apparently just another family outing for Samson.

"Must've been hard on her, losing her mom like that."

The alpha cocked his head. "She's always been—resilient. Daddy's little girl, I guess. Only, she's not so little anymore."

"She doesn't like me very much, does she?"

He took another drink and considered my question. "Well, she doesn't hate you. She simply resents your presence, because she thinks it jeopardizes my position as alpha. Fallyn is rather protective of me."

"Makes sense. But she does have a point, you know. I mean, it seems like you're going through an awful lot of trouble to help me. Why are you *really* doing this, Samson?"

"Like I said, I owe a debt. Besides..."

"Yeah? Besides what?"

"Never mind. Just do your best to get through this as quickly as possible. Tonight, you got a feeling for what it's like when your change starts to come over you, and now you have an idea of what it feels like to suppress it. Next time, I'll exert less of my power over your beast, and you'll need to exert your will to keep it at bay."

"So, the idea is to gain control over my beast, little by little, until I make it my bitch."

He shrugged. "More or less."

"You sure I can't just do yoga instead?"

He stood, ignoring my lame attempt at humor. "Take your time walking out of here. You'll want to show strength and confidence when you leave, because some of the Pack will be waiting around to see how you did. Any sign of weakness tonight will hurt your reputation and standing within the Pack."

"Good to know."

He turned to exit the chamber.

"Samson?" The old alpha paused at the entrance. "I know you hate doing this, so thanks."

He nodded once, then walked out.

8

Before leaving the torture chamber, I dug around inside my Craneskin Bag for a few energy bars, a Red Bull, and some ibuprofen. Once I'd downed those, I made for the front entrance. I exited the mine with my head held high, as instructed. A few wolves nodded at me as I walked past—whether in respect or solidarity, I couldn't tell. Others sneered or growled as I neared. I ignored them all, until one largish grey 'thrope stepped in my path.

I was in no mood to play games. I held eye contact with the 'thrope as I walked forward, stopping nose to snout with him.

"Samson might be fine with your kind joining the Pack, but I'm not," he growled. The werewolf spoke with a Midwestern accent, pronouncing "not" like "naught"—which grated on my nerves.

I readied a spell in my right hand as I spoke. "You have a disagreement with Samson, you take it up with him. But if you have a disagreement with me, *say when.*"

I watched and gauged his reaction. A slight narrowing of the eyes and tightening of the lips, as well as flexing his fingers—these all told me he was about to attack. I went first, triggering my flashbang cantrip and slamming my palm into his chest. On impact, there was a small explosion. The wolf was knocked back on his heels, his chest charred and set aflame.

He fell into a crouch and howled, beating his torso to put out the flames. Then he looked at me with murder in his eyes, baring his teeth in a growl.

That was, until he saw thirty inches of gleaming high-carbon steel, etched in silver, pointing at his left iris. Before coming out here I'd placed a few silver weapons close at hand inside the Bag, just in case I might need them. Looked like it was a good call. I suspected the werewolf would smell or sense the silver on the blade, and I was right. He visibly flinched away from the sword. I'd won this dominance game.

'Thropes murmured all around us.

"How could he dare to draw that here?"

"Silver—you just don't threaten another Pack member with silver."

"Serves Josh right. Hope he runs him clean through. That'll teach him."

And so on. I held Josh's gaze until he turned his eyes to the ground. Then, I spoke with a hell of a lot more authority than I felt.

"Let me make one thing perfectly clear," I said, with as much menace in my voice as I could muster. "If any wolf here is stupid enough to force me to release the beast inside me, it will slay them and half the Pack before it's subdued. That's not a threat; it's a fact. And if it means drawing steel on a Pack member—yes, even silvered steel—to keep that from happening, I will gladly gut any one of you to prevent a massacre."

Josh slunk away from me, eyes down. "This isn't over," he mumbled as he joined a group of 'thropes standing near the tree line. A few of them gave me hard looks, then they slipped into the night. I gripped the sword tightly as I looked around at every wolf present. Some held my gaze as it passed; others looked away; still others nodded their approval. After I'd made my point, I slowly walked out of the clearing and up the trail toward my car, sword in hand.

Adrenaline, nerves, and exhaustion kicked in about halfway there. My knees weakened, and I was about to stop and rest against a tree when a fully clothed Fallyn fell in step next to me.

"Uh-uh. Keep walking, even if it kills you," she whispered. "Trina and Sledge are in the trees to our left, but you're being watched from the north. They see you falter, and you're dead."

I kept moving, exerting every ounce of willpower to make it to the house and driveway. The sight of Sonny and two other wolves loading Sonny's bike into the bed of a pickup greeted me. That gave me a boost of energy, and I cracked a huge grin as Fallyn split off soundlessly, hopping on her own bike and cranking it up. I watched the trees on high alert, triggering my night-vision cantrip as an afterthought. As it kicked in, I saw a large and small shadow slinking through the cedars to my left, and four more shadows flitting through the woods to my right.

No one had messed with my car in my absence, so my tires were all intact. I traded the sword for my Glock, which I'd loaded with silver-tipped hollow points as a precaution. I slid into the front seat and placed the pistol on the passenger's side, saying a silent prayer as I inserted the key and turned the ignition. The rumble of the five-liter engine and dual exhaust roared in response, and I exhaled slowly. I kept my lights off as I made a three-point turn, releasing my cantrip and clicking the headlights on high as the car pointed toward the woods where Josh and his clique hid.

My headlights blinded four pairs of wolf eyes all at once, and I chuckled in satisfaction as they disappeared. I sped down the drive, putting the pedal to the floor as soon as my tires hit pavement. Forty-five minutes and two cups of bad gas station coffee later, I pulled into the junkyard parking lot. Despite being exhausted, I did a quick perimeter check to inspect my wards—just in case.

As I did, I reflected on recent events. There was certainly no turning back now. Samson had stuck his neck out for me, and I'd put his position as alpha in danger. If I quit, I'd make him look like a fool. And besides, the Pack would tear me to shreds. Self-preservation, and all that.

Nope, I'd have to see this thing through, one way or another. *Hashtag FML.*

I woke up feeling hung over and haggard, partially due to the previous evening's activities, along with a short night of restless sleep. All night long, I'd had nightmares about being eviscerated. The same dream had kept repeating over and over. In it, Samson opened me up with his claws and the rest of the wolves feasted on my innards as I watched, chained and helpless.

After I'd washed the sleep from my eyes and had a cup of Ed's horrible coffee, I spent an hour or so working in the yard, helping customers and troubleshooting the latest auction purchases. Then I cleaned up and checked my messages. I had texts from both Bells and Hemi. Bells had a lead on the missing kids case, and Hemi said he was working an angle based on a tip that Sal had gotten.

Speaking of Sal, I had voicemails from him as well—several, actually. He was frantic with worry, which surprised me. I guess I just didn't see him as being the loving, caring, fatherly type. Funny how people—and especially fae—could do horrible things, and yet still show affection to their loved ones. Then again, cold-blooded killers and sociopaths wore a mask of civility around their family and friends. I'd seen it dozens of times while working cases as a hunter. Even a bloodthirsty fae like Sal had to go home to someone —somewhere, sometime. I didn't know if seeing this side of him humanized him for me, or if it made me hate him more for the things he'd done. Red caps were brutal killers, and in the old days they'd loved staking out lonely waystations off the beaten path, catching lone travelers unawares. They delighted in savage acts of murder. It was their way—whether by custom or genetics —and they'd never change.

So, why was I helping Sal? I guess because I believed that even among the most vicious of fae, there had to be someone worth saving. And maybe that someone was Little Sal. If you stood by and watched the lone flower in a field of briars choke away and die, you may as well have plucked it out by the roots yourself.

I called Sal back, and he answered on the first ring.

"Druid, have you found anything?"

"I'm working a couple of leads. Humans took your son. I'm still not certain if they were working alone, or with fae. What have you heard since we last spoke?"

He exhaled, and his voice shook. "Nothing. No one amongst the fae knows nuthin'. No other fae kids have gone missing, and even though Rocko's had everyone asking all over for info, it's turned up squat." He sobbed a bit into the phone. "I just want my boy back, druid. That's all."

Shit. Before long, I was going to start feeling sorry for Sal. "I'm doing what I can. Look, if you hear anything, call me. And if I get a solid lead, I'll let you know, alright?" I considered hanging up, but guilt got the best of me. "Hang in there, Sal. We'll find him."

"Thanks, druid." He ended the call, leaving me with

conflicted emotions about the entire case. I decided to see what Bells had for me.

"Heya, loverboy. Found something juicy for you."

"Please tell me it's a solid lead on Sal's kid."

"You bet. Kids have been coming up missing from all over central Texas. Austin, Cedar Park, Round Rock, Marble Falls, Oak Hill, Bertram, Liberty Hill, Pflugerville—all foster kids, runaways, or undocumented immigrants, or they came from shitty, abusive homes. The kind that don't get a lot of news coverage when they disappear, you know? I put the eggheads in research on it, and they scienced the shit out of the data. Turns out all the missing kids come from within a fifty-mile radius, and guess what's dead center in the middle of the map?"

"Wild-ass guess? Something evil, and not altogether human," I replied.

"Exactly. The geeks found that the abductions center on the known location of a very nasty, European-style witch. One of those old-school fae witches—the kind that eat children. I have a location for her cabin, somewhere off FM 1431 between Lago Vista and Marble Falls."

"What the hell? I was just out there, last night."

"For?"

"Doing Pack shit. Trust me, you don't want to know."

She giggled. "Bestiality and frolicking in the nude under a full moon?"

"I should be so lucky. Look, you want to help me check this out?"

My request was met with momentary silence. "I go on shift in an hour. But, I could call in—if you really need me." She didn't sound at all like she wanted to come along, and it wasn't because she was afraid of witches.

"Naw, that's alright. I'll see if Hemi can ride out with me. He's always up for a good scrape."

"Um, okay then. Right." We shared several seconds of uncomfortable silence.

"I hate this, you know that?"

"So do I. We still haven't had that talk."

"And I take full responsibility for that." I blurted it out too quickly, desperate to fix things.

"Call me later?"

"I will, unless I'm baking in some witch's oven."

"I'm the only one who gets to take a bite of you, loverboy. And don't you forget it."

She hung up on me before I could respond, leaving me more confused about the state of our relationship than ever.

I DECIDED it would be best to speak with Maeve before investigating the witch. She knew more about fae creatures than perhaps anyone else, including Finnegas. How much she'd dish was up for speculation. But she was my best resource for info, now that Finn had up and vanished.

I hated the idea of going back to ask for more help. However willing Maeve seemed to be in providing me with information and resources, I always ended up holding the short end when dealing with her. I slid into the front seat of the Gremlin, and beat my hands on the steering wheel. Not hard enough to damage the car, but enough to vent my frustrations.

"Damn it, Finn. Why can't you ever be around when I really need you?"

I exhaled heavily, fogging up the windshield. I reached for a shop rag from the floor. But before I could wipe off the glass, writing began to appear on the windshield—as if someone was etching a note with their finger. I recognized Finn's handwriting immediately. Leave it to Finnegas to weave a supernatural texting spell into an automobile windshield.

Talk to Samson. Don't trust the fae.

"Um, Finn?"

Keep at it. News soon. —F

"Okay, then—I guess I need to speak with Samson." I wiped off the windshield, then drove to the Pack's clubhouse. When I walked in, Sledge and Trina were sitting in a corner, sipping brews and conversing in hushed tones. They looked up when I walked in, and called me over.

Sledge grinned from ear to ear. "Druid! Hell of a thing you did last night. The whole Pack is talking about it."

"Huh? I'm not following." I really wasn't, because I was too tired to think straight.

"Kid doesn't miss a beat," Trina quipped. "You don't remember your run in with Josh?"

"Oh, that." I shrugged. "It was no big deal."

Sledge laughed as he leaned back in his chair. "No big deal, he says. Hah! 'Course, some say you went too far, using magic on Josh and threatening him with silver. Others say you proved you're no pushover. That's enough for most wolves. We just want to know you have some spine."

Trina took a long swig of her beer and chuckled. "Sure as hell means no one is going to fuck with you from here on out, that's for sure. Especially not after the way you walked out of that mine. Most pups crawl out, or exit on a stretcher. Some don't come out at all, their first night. Then you put Josh in his place." She shook her head. "One thing's for sure, you know how to keep things lively."

"Thanks for having my back, by the way."

Sledge frowned. "Those assholes don't understand what it means to be Pack. They think it's all about being a wolf. Sure, that helps. But it's about having your brothers' and sisters' backs, and following your alpha into hell when they ask. These new school 'thropes, they don't get it. Family's about more than blood, as they say."

I let what he'd just said stew for a moment, then Sledge raised a finger off his bottle. "Doesn't need to be said, druid. Just know—me and Trina here, you earned our respect."

I swallowed hard. "Thanks."

Trina slammed her beer down and gave me a hard look. "I swear, if you fucking cry, I will reach down your throat and yank your ovaries out by the tubes. Fuck! Bad enough having to put up with Sledge. This asshole will cry at the drop of a hat."

He laughed and finished his beer. "Bitch."

"Pussy."

Sledge reached under the table and grabbed two more beers out of an open cooler. He popped one and gave it to Trina, then opened the other and held it up. "To the Pack. May it see the final days."

Trina tapped bottles with him. "May our enemies be mighty and the tales of our glory be told for generations."

They both chugged, then Sledge belched loudly. "Shit, prospect. Relax. Grab a brew and sit a while."

"Can't. Working a case. Is Samson around?"

He nodded toward the back room, and I headed that way. "Keep shaking things up, McCool," he yelled after me. "It was getting pretty gods-damned boring around here!"

Their laughter faded behind me as I approached Samson's office. The door was cracked open a hair.

The alpha's voice rang from inside the room. "Come in, Colin."

I pushed the door open, and found Samson sitting behind his desk, feet propped up as always. Fallyn sat on the desk's edge.

"Can't say much for your taste in clothes or vehicles, but

your timing is impeccable," Fallyn said, with a wry smile on her face.

Samson kept his eyes on me as he addressed his daughter. "Ask Sonny or Sledge to get this kid some cuts, will you?"

She frowned. "You're not going to patch him in yet, are you?"

If Samson was perturbed by her challenging tone, he didn't show it. "No, but he's the only one in the clubhouse wearing a trench coat. And, he needs to show some allegiance to the Pack. Damned kid already sticks out like a sore thumb. No need to make it worse."

I held my hands up in protest. "There's a reason why I wear this coat, you know. Lots of pockets, and it's good for hiding swords and guns."

Fallyn cocked her head. "I get that, but what's with the man purse?"

I snagged my Craneskin Bag, plucking it by the strap and holding it in front of me. "What, this? Never leaves my sight. Bad things happen when the Bag leaves my sight."

She smirked and shook her head. "Looks girly as shit."

I ignored her. "Samson, you got a minute?"

He held a hand up. "I know why you're here. Told you, you were expected. Finn and I go way back, and he knows how to get in touch when he needs something."

"Old bastard is always needing something." Fallyn pulled out a wicked-looking dagger and started cleaning her nails.

Samson gave her a long-suffering, fatherly look. "As I was saying, Finn reached out. He said you needed help looking into a witch—and not the modern, love potion-making type."

"How'd he—never mind, I don't even want to know. Anyway, this witch is more like the Hansel and Gretel kind. Fae, and possibly very old."

He scratched his chin. "Could be trouble, then. I've dealt with a few fae witches in my time. The real faery tales—the old ones—they don't come close to telling how dangerous those things can be."

Fallyn continued cleaning her nails, never looking up as she spoke. "Dad's from the old country. Still thinks everything back there is ten times worse than what we have here." She chuckled. "Whatever this witch is, it sure as hell can't come close to that wendigo we had to deal with a few years back. Finally had to trap it in a pit. Took a shitload of Semtex to put it down."

Samson rubbed his neck and stretched his shoulders, exhaling long and slow. I suspected a lot of his stress came from keeping his daughter in check, and not from handling political infighting in the Pack.

"Be that as it may, I don't want the prospect walking into this alone. Fallyn, you're going to back him up while he's checking out this lead. And I want you to stick with him while he investigates this case."

She looked up at me, then at her father, and stabbed the knife into his desk, leaving it to vibrate as she leapt to her feet. "Me? Why do I have to babysit the noob? Can't you send Sledge or Trina or someone else to look after him?"

He fixed her with a stare. His face was calm, but his eyes were hard. "I have my reasons." He looked to me, then to his daughter. "Keep each other safe."

With that, Samson turned his back to us and grabbed a bottle of whiskey, pouring a healthy two fingers into a bourbon glass. Then he kicked his feet up on his desk again, stared off into space, and sipped his bourbon. Obviously, he was done with the discussion.

Fallyn tongued her cheek and grabbed the knife, sheathing it at the small of her back under her leather jacket. "C'mon, druid. That means we're dismissed. Let's go see what the hell makes Dad think this witch is such a big deal. Who knows? It might be fun."

She walked out without another word. I looked at Samson, but he was busy staring into the depths of his whiskey. As I headed out the door, he spoke.

"She's the best part of me, druid. Trust her instincts. She won't steer you wrong."

I nodded and followed after his daughter.

9

We drove out to the witch's place in the Gremlin—or rather, I drove, and Fallyn napped in the back seat like a lazy dog on a hot summer day. She seemed content to let me drive while she caught up on all the rest she'd missed the previous evening. I was fine with letting her crash out while I drove. That meant I wouldn't have to converse with her, and I could spend the drive working through what I knew so far about the case.

My forebear a couple of thousand years removed was Fionn MacCumhaill, legendary Irish hero and one of Finnegas' first students. Shortly after they'd met, Finnegas had tasked Fionn with capturing the Salmon of Wisdom, which he'd done. Then the lazy old bastard had told Fionn to cook it for him, because supposedly whoever ate the Salmon would gain the wisdom it contained. Fionn had burned his thumb in some grease while preparing it, and by sucking on it, he'd transferred the Salmon's magic to himself. "Accidentally," of course. Finnegas was still miffed about it, two millennia later.

I'd inherited a portion of that magic, and although it had

weakened over the generations, it was still potent enough to help me solve cases. Its only drawback was that I had to suck my thumb to trigger the magic. Thus the constant teasing I'd received as a child, for sucking my thumb whenever I faced a difficult problem or situation. As I got older, I'd learned that chewing my thumbnail worked just as well, while attracting less negative attention. I nibbled on my thumbnail as I drove and let the magic take over, while I mentally reviewed the facts as I perceived them.

One. Somebody was taking kids, from all over the central Texas area.

Two. The kids they were taking were society's throwaways, the kind hardly anyone cared about who wouldn't be missed. The kind sex traffickers liked to abduct.

Three. To my knowledge, all the kids except Sal's boy were human.

Four. Little Sal's abduction was probably a mistake. I figured he'd been taken by humans who thought he was just another kid.

Five. The abductions centered on the witch's residence. However, correlation did not equal causation. Circle members were trained to look for supernatural anomalies. When all you have is a hammer, every problem looks like a nail. So, the witch might not be involved at all.

Six. We were acting on a hunch by heading out here. But it was a hunch worth checking out.

Seven. Despite the fact they were throwaways, everything combined added up to a lot of missing kids. More than enough to bring a hell of a lot more attention than the cases were currently getting. That led me to believe there was magic involved. It was likely that someone was either magically mind-wiping families and witnesses, or casting forgetfulness curses on law enforcement and anyone else who showed an interest in those missing children. And the creatures who were best at casting that sort of magic were the fae.

Human trafficking was a huge issue in central Texas. Typically, the pattern criminal organizations followed was to bring in sex slaves from Mexico, Central America, and beyond. Once they were stranded with no passports, no contacts, and no money, the women and kids they enslaved were easier to control. Jesse and I had stumbled across such an operation while hunting down a *brujo* involved in human trafficking. We'd rescued the women and killed the *brujo* and every last one of the sex traffickers, making it look like a rival gang had done it.

It was the first time I'd killed a human. And I felt no remorse over it.

But based on past experience, the pattern here didn't make sense. Sex traffickers might occasionally abduct Americans to ship them overseas, especially if they had a wealthy client with special requests. People had a hard time believing that sort of thing happened, but it did. Yet, the sort of criminal who ran sex slave operations knew how to avoid attracting notice. If they abducted someone locally, they were immediately shipped away. Girls who worked an area were kept isolated and in unfamiliar surroundings. It was all about control, and escaping notice.

Due to the sheer number of kids who had been abducted, and the fact that it wasn't drawing more attention, I was almost sure we were dealing with the fae. Possibly even a fae serial killer, which was not an uncommon thing to come across in my profession. I gripped the steering wheel tightly as I drove, seething with rage that a supernatural creature would have the audacity to operate this way, in my city, under my nose. Even after Jesse had died, and during the time I'd crumbled emotionally and stopped hunting, the supernatural community had still feared me. It wasn't just my curse that made the fae fear me; it was my reputation for killing the ones who stepped out of line.

Some fae had crossed a line they should've known not to cross. And it would be their last mistake. I just hoped I could figure out who it was in time to save... someone. I was a realist, and I accepted that the children might already be dead. But if there was even the slightest possibility they were still alive, I was going to find them. I'd save those I could, and send the responsible party or parties to hell or back across the Veil. And in the worst way possible.

WHEN THE MAP told me we'd hit the address Bells had provided, I nearly missed the driveway. Only a rusted, overgrown cattle guard and gate marked the entry to the property—a common sight in the Texas Hill Country. Whether the overgrowth had been intentionally allowed or if it was a product of neglect was unclear, but based on the old and fading look-away spell on the gate, I'd say someone didn't want to be found.

I overshot the drive by several yards, and backed up as I pulled off on the shoulder in front of the entrance. Fallyn was still napping in the back. Wary of getting stabbed for waking her, I slammed my door shut as I exited the car, yelling, "We're here!" as I walked to the gate. She sat up, bleary-eyed, and flipped me off as she stretched and yawned. The wards on the gate and property were old and weak, and failed to present much of a barrier. A thick chain and padlock locked the gate securely, but a quick bit of magic opened it in short order. I pushed on the gate, straining to free it of the weeds and undergrowth that held it in place. Finally, it swung open.

Fallyn was in the passenger seat by the time I hopped back

in the car. She popped a pill and took a swig of water from a bottle she'd found on the floorboards. "It's just caffeine," she explained.

"Hey, I'm not judging. But it is nice to know you won't be half-asleep while you're watching my back." I nudged the car through the gate, cringing as tree limbs scraped the roof, quarter panels, and doors.

"Seriously? You're worried about the paint on this old bucket of rust?" She thumped the dash with a fist, a little harder than necessary. "If you ask me, a few scratches might improve how it looks. And who says I'm going to be watching your back?"

I slapped her hand away from the dash. "Your dad, that's who. And take it easy on the dash. It's a classic."

"Classically ugly." She pushed her seat all the way to the rear, and kicked her booted feet up on the dashboard. "So, what's your plan here, mighty druid?"

I glanced at her feet in annoyance, but decided to let it go, keeping my eyes on the narrow dirt drive as I leaned over the steering wheel. I dropped my head almost to the dash to see past the overhanging limbs currently blocking the view ahead. "No idea. I figured we'd just find the house, and play it by ear from there."

She harrumphed. "Brilliant fucking plan. I thought you had to be smart to do magic."

"And I didn't know you had to be a pain in the ass to be an alpha's daughter." She started to protest, but I held a hand up to silence her. "Sssh. Look."

As we drove further, we began to see small, handmade fetishes dotting the trees. They were made from various pieces of trash and debris—everything from old soda cans, to corn husks, to plastic cutlery, to twigs and leaves. The fetishes were creepily reminiscent of tiny, tortured, and misshapen people, and gave off a definite Blair Witch vibe. They were just the kind of folk art bric-a-brac I'd seen my mother's clients and friends pay huge amounts of money for at art shows. I'd hate to think of what might happen if some enterprising gallery owner stumbled on this place and started selling them. No telling what curses might have been woven into each doll and figure.

Fallyn grinned ear to ear. "Shit, if that doesn't say 'wicked witch lives here,' then I don't know what does. Think it'd be a bad idea to grab one on the way out?"

"Very bad," I muttered, concentrating on the path ahead. "Unless you want to pick up a nasty curse. Could be anything from a bad luck hex to magical syphilis. Trust me when I say you don't want to take home a souvenir from this little outing."

She tsked, sucking in air through her teeth. "Right... guess I'll take your word for it, then."

I drove slowly, taking my time as I scanned the long dirt drive for signs of magical traps or alarms. It was strangely devoid of any such spell, although the remnants of long faded castings were apparent. About fifty yards past the first doll, the roof and second story of a dilapidated farmhouse appeared above the trees, so I slowed the car to a halt. Paint peeled from the white clapboard siding, shingles were missing, and at least one window was broken.

Fallyn eyed the house with interest and scanned the woods all around us. "Cut the engine off." I did as she asked. She rolled down her window and cocked an ear. "Nothing but birds and wind. Let's get this over with."

She exited the car with a bit too much pep in her step, making me wonder if she was taking this witch seriously. I kept an eye on her as I grabbed my Bag, slinging it over my shoulder. Fallyn bounced on her toes with anticipation, but she kept her head on a swivel, easing my concerns somewhat. She swept her eyes back and forth in a full radius around the car, pausing momentarily to sneer at my Craneskin Bag as she scanned my side of the road.

"Still with the man purse?"

I shrugged. "If something goes down, you'll be glad I brought it."

"If something goes down, you'll be glad you brought me," she said as she pointed a thumb at her chest. "I'm taking point."

She stalked silently into the tree line without waiting for a reply. "Wait, there could be traps—"

She was already gone. I reached into the Bag to make sure I had some surprises of my own ready, and followed after her.

I CAUGHT brief flashes of the "War Wolves" club patches on the back of Fallyn's jacket as I pursued her through the woods. She moved a hell of a lot faster than I could, probably in an effort to leave me behind so she could do... well, I really didn't know why she was so eager to get to the witch's house. Maybe just so she could make me look foolish. I had no idea what motivated her, and that meant I couldn't depend on her to watch my six. I cursed under my breath and moved as silently as possible through the trees until I spotted the 'thrope crouching in the shade of a juniper cedar ahead.

I slipped under the foliage beside her, following her line of sight through a gap in the needle-like leaves. Beyond the trees ahead sat the old farmhouse, sagging and worn, looking empty and long uninhabited. An aluminum screen door hung at an awkward angle, its rusted screen torn and draping down at the corner. Detritus, trash, and live oak leaves littered the porch. A pair of smallish work boots sat discarded on a pile of newspapers. Piles of animal scat sat on the tilted steps, which looked as though they might collapse if stepped on.

"Looks like a dead end," I whispered.

Fallyn held a finger to her lips and shook her head slowly, keeping her eyes plastered on the scene ahead. Somewhere in the distance, behind the house, a chain rattled.

She leaned in close and spoke at the lowest volume possible. "There it is again." Fallyn cocked her head, and I swear her ears swiveled a little as she panned left and right. "I need to shift," she said, and began undressing at an alarming speed.

I backed up a little to give her room, and busied myself with my Bag. I pulled a few useful spells out and placed them in my jacket pockets, then grabbed my Glock and slipped the holster onto my belt. It was still loaded with silver-tipped ammo, which would work well on certain types of witches, just like it did on 'thropes.

Witches fell into three major categories. First were hedge witches, humans who were typically herbalists and wise women who also practiced some minor healing magic. Most were harmless. Then you had those humans who dabbled in black magic, practicing spells to curse and hex their enemies, trading small parts of their souls to demonic entities and unseelie fae in exchange for raw power. They often charged for their services, which ranged from locating people who didn't wish to be found, to poisoning victims from afar, to forcing the unwilling to develop an infatuation with a spurned admirer. The Circle took down most who got out of hand—but those kind could always be found, and they were always trouble.

Then there were the fae kind—the baba yagas and striga, the soucouyant and skin walkers. They were the wicked witches of faery tales and folk legends the world over, the ones who lured unsuspecting children and travelers, gaining their trust so they could kill and eat them. Most of them were cannibalistic, and they preferred the taste of human flesh. I suppose since they weren't human, you couldn't call them cannibals—but they all ate long pig nonetheless. And, they used human bones and flesh for magic and rituals, perhaps to prolong their lives or harm their enemies. They were deadly and crafty, and the rule was to kill them whenever you came across one—with silver, beheading, or fire.

According to the intel I'd received from Bells, that's what we were dealing with here. However, it looked as though the witch who'd once lived here was long gone. Still, something was making noise out there. And, from the sound of it, the thing was getting closer. I checked to make sure I had a round in the Glock's chamber, and shifted my vision into the magical spectrum.

I looked in the direction I'd last heard the clanking sounds and saw the glow of a fae creature stalking toward us. It had been invisible to my normal human vision, but now it emitted a sickly green color, in the vaguest outline of a large dog or other four-legged mammal. However, it walked on its hind legs like a 'thrope.

I placed a hand on Fallyn's furry arm, and pointed as I sighted down the barrel of the pistol. She nodded with a low rumble in her throat. *Good, she sees it too.* Wishing to make certain it didn't disappear and flank us, I stepped from the trees and threw a handful of blessed salt at it, which would hopefully short-circuit its glamour. It did. As its form coalesced, a pony-sized dog took shape before my eyes, draped in thick black chains. It gripped the ends of those chains in long, clawed hands, much like those of a werewolf.

I recognized what it was immediately.

"Son of a bitch. It's a kludde."

I fired on it without hesitation, striking it twice center mass. The rounds didn't slow it down, but they sure pissed the thing off. As it shimmered into view in front of us, it roared and howled all at once. Fallyn answered with a roar of her own. She erupted from the trees, now fully in her werewolf form, growling as she made eye contact with the thing. I realized very quickly that I was standing dead center between the two beasts.

Then, they charged at each other.

10

I leapt out of the way, diving into a roll and coming up on my feet facing the direction of the 'thrope and kludde, who were now locked in mortal combat. It was a lot like watching two alley cats scuffle, but magnified times ten. They moved in a near blur, ripping and tearing and biting at each other with terrifying ferocity.

Kludde were considered by some to be a kind of tormenting spirit, but really they were a type of cu sith, albeit of the Germanic tradition. Ireland and Scotland had their own versions of kludde, including barguests, yeth hounds, black shucks, gwyllgi, and the like. Kludde were particularly nasty, however, due to their bipedalism and their use of the large chain draped around their bodies as a weapon to ensnare, entangle, and strangle their prey.

Like most fae, they were notoriously fickle. Sometimes, they'd merely play tricks on humans, and other times they'd chase and kill them. Legends said they were born from the ashes of a witch, but that wasn't precisely true. In fact, that was merely how they normally crossed the Veil into the human realm. Since the preferred method of dealing with witches was fire, many witches cast spells that would release a kludde from their ashes upon their death and cremation. Kind of a final "f-you" from the grave. Nasty, but I'm sure it gave many an overzealous villager second thoughts about burning the local witch alive.

The real pain in the ass about releasing a kludde was they were notoriously hard to kill. Born of fire, they were resistant to it. Being creatures of death, cold didn't harm them either—nor did drowning them under water. To my knowledge, no one had tried suffocation, but I assumed it would likewise have little effect. As one of the only kinds of fae that used iron as a weapon, iron and steel didn't harm them in the slightest. And being incredibly strong and quick, they were tough to capture as well. A single kludde could easily take out a three-person hunter team in short order, especially if it got the jump on them.

But against a werewolf? I hadn't a clue. The last time I'd dealt with a kludde, we'd killed it with a rowan spear. I suspected that any magically-enhanced wooden weapon would do, but I didn't have time to carve and enchant a spear at the moment. I hoped like hell that Fallyn could hold her own against the thing. If not, I would need a plan B.

Steel was out, bullets were out, and fire was out. I didn't have access to the Eye's magic, so that wasn't an option, either. Poison might work—but again, nothing on hand. I looked up from shuffling through my Bag to see how Fallyn was doing. She was definitely putting up a fight, matching the kludde bite for bite, blow for blow. However, she was already bleeding freely from a half-dozen wounds, while the kludde looked none the worse for wear.

I continued to watch as Fallyn ducked a vicious sweep of the kludde's razor sharp claws. She rolled past it and swiped her own claws across the monster's thigh muscles, shredding them to the bone and causing it to stumble. But as she rolled and pivoted for a killing blow, the kludde's muscles knitted back together. It spun quickly, swinging its chain in a huge arc. The chain wrapped around Fallyn's neck and locked in place, and the kludde began reeling it in, hand over hand.

Fallyn's eyes bulged in her wolf skull, and her muzzle opened in a silent snarl, gasping for air. She gripped the chain with both hands, digging her feet in and pulling in the opposite direction to try and create slack in the chain. However, as she created slack in the links between her hands and her neck, the chain curled itself more tightly around her neck, constricting like an anaconda.

Oh, hell, this isn't looking good, I thought as I kept rummaging in the Bag. *C'mon, Bag—give me something that'll help!*

Just then, I felt something shift inside the Bag—like the space around my hand and arm *moved*. It was much like the sensation of holding your arm straight out the window of a moving vehicle, just to feel the wind rush past. It only lasted a second, then my hand landed on something solid. I immediately *saw* what it was in my mind's eye... one of the toys I'd lifted from CIRCE before they'd shut down.

Perfect.

I pulled it out and checked it to make sure it was fully functioning. Yep, batteries at a full charge. I glanced over at the two combatants, and things were looking desperate. Fallyn had fallen to her knees. Her face was strained, and the skin around her mouth had taken on a purple, bruised color. The poor girl's eyes looked as though they'd pop out of their sockets, and the chain had squeezed her neck to half its diameter.

How she was still fighting was beyond me, because anyone else would've passed out by now from loss of oxygen. If I didn't act immediately, she'd be dead for sure.

I pulled the trigger on the huge red and black taser I held in my hands. It was an experimental model, designed for taking down large animals and livestock. Like the tasers that law enforcement used, it shot two darts out at supersonic speed. The darts were attached to the weapon by hyper-conductive wires, which delivered an electric shock in excess of 100,000 volts— twice that of the type used by law enforcement to subdue humans.

The darts shot from the muzzle of the gun, piercing the kludde's hide. It looked down at the darts with a puzzled expression, laughing in a feral, ghastly voice while keeping both hands on the chain that was choking the life out of Fallyn. I continued to depress the trigger, but nothing happened.

Misfire.

"Shit, shit, shit," I mumbled, slamming the side of the taser with my palm as I released and squeezed the trigger repeatedly. Suddenly, the thing jumped to life, emitting a high-pitched clicking noise accompanied by an electric hum. I turned my attention away from the taser in time to see the kludde seize up and stiffen, head to toe, and fall over in full-on KTFO fashion.

I DID A MENTAL VICTORY DANCE, then ran over to help Fallyn remove the chain from her neck, still depressing the trigger on the taser to keep the kludde down. Unfortunately, the chain appeared to be a fine conductor of electricity, and Fallyn was now both choking to death and being shocked into spasms along with the kludde. Realizing my mistake, and wondering if she was going to try to kill me when she came around, I released the taser's trigger and unwrapped the chain from around Fallyn's neck.

Fallyn's lupine features were a gnarly purplish color, her eyes were bloodshot and bulging from their sockets, and she didn't appear to be breathing. The kludde was beginning to stir, but I was more concerned with the fact that I might have just killed the Pack alpha's daughter.

"Ah, shit-shit-shit-shit-shit-shit-shit. Breathe, Fallyn— breathe, damn it!" I slammed my fist down on her chest, hoping that a good old-fashioned precordial thump might do the trick. *Nothing.* I thumped her chest again, and she took a quick, shuddering, wheezing breath through a severely constricted airway.

"Yes," I murmured under my breath. "Now to deal with tall, dark, and ugly over there." I glanced up, but the kludde was nowhere to be seen.

"Oh, you *have* to be kidding me." I looked around in the magical spectrum, but the thing was gone. There was the barest trace of an essence trail that led past the house. If I hurried, I might be able to track it down and finish it. I had one more set of darts left in the taser, and another jolt would put it down long enough to stab it with a stake from the vampire hunting kit I kept in my Craneskin Bag.

But one look at Fallyn told me I wasn't going anywhere. She had shifted back into her human form, and her neck was bruised, torn, and deformed. I was surprised she was even breathing, and could see her severely damaged windpipe collapsing with her every breath. I needed to do something about that windpipe, and fast.

One of my wilderness emergency medicine instructors had been a special forces medic who served in the war in the Middle East. He'd showed our class how to perform a field cricothyrotomy, where you cut an airway into the throat of a patient with a severe crushing injury to the trachea. The idea of cutting someone's throat to save their life had freaked me out at the time, but now it made sense. Fallyn's lycan healing capabilities wouldn't be able to save her from oxygen deprivation. She needed medical intervention, and fast.

I hesitated as I glanced down at her, unconscious and struggling for breath. If I screwed this up, it could kill her.

"C'mon, Colin. Shit or get off the throne."

Screw it. She'd die anyway if I did nothing. I reached into my pocket and pulled out one of the thick Sharpies I kept on hand for drawing runes, pulling it apart and using my hunting knife to cut off the end to turn it into a tube. Then I laid Fallyn on her back, gently tilting her head up with pressure under her chin, wary of any spinal injury she may have sustained. I felt her throat with my fingertips to find the thyroid and cricoid cartilage, above and below the area I was supposed to cut.

Considering how mangled her neck was, I did the best I could, making a vertical cut through her skin to expose the trachea, and a horizontal cut into her windpipe. Finally, I inserted the makeshift breathing tube and secured it with duct tape from my Bag. Soon, I heard the whistling of her breath through the Sharpie barrel, and noted that her color was returning and her breathing was much less labored.

I waited with her and monitored her as she recovered, a process that took some time. Within a few minutes she had regained consciousness, and I had to explain to her what I'd done and why. Unable to speak for the moment, she gave me a look that seemed to be a mixture of gratitude and frustration. I waited until her throat had healed, then helped her remove the tube and sealed the hole with duct tape until it closed on its own.

Another fifteen minutes or so later, Fallyn sat up. She placed a hand to her throat as she swallowed, then croaked out a few words in a soft, raspy voice.

"Did you kill it?"

I shook my head. "Sorry, but you weren't breathing and your heart had stopped. It was gone by the time I got you going again."

She pursed her lips and inhaled deeply through her nose, letting it out slowly before she replied. "Pissed you didn't kill it. Can't complain since you saved my life."

I smiled. "It was a difficult choice."

She grabbed a stick and tossed it at me, hitting me in the chest with enough force to hurt. I pulled off my coat and handed it to her, then offered her a hand. She took the coat but refused my help, standing up with nary a wobble as she draped the trench around her. She tried to speak again, but her voice gave out.

"Give it a minute," I said. "Werewolf healing is pretty amazing, but it has its limits, right? I'll go find your clothes."

She rolled her eyes as she pulled the coat closer around her, more for my comfort than her own. I fetched her clothing from the trees where she'd left them, and returned to find her searching the ground where the kludde had fallen. After getting dressed, she sniffed the ground closely, then nodded and walked to the house, entering with much more stealth than she'd used in our initial approach. Thankfully, the kludde was long gone, but Fallyn took her time as she searched the house for clues, following a scent trail that appeared to be much more interesting to her than that left by the kludde.

She led me into a bedroom upstairs, where someone had dragged several moldy mattresses along with moth-eaten bedspreads and blankets. The paint was faded and peeling inside the room, and the plaster was falling off the walls, but even I could smell what had drawn Fallyn to this room. It was the scent of human children.

AFTER FALLYN HAD RECOVERED her voice, she explained what her superhumanly sharp werewolf senses had revealed about the most recent occupants of the witch's house. She gestured at various spots around the room and cleared her throat, speaking softly as she described the scene.

"Five children, maybe six. They came through here at different times—except for two who came through together. Each one slept here overnight, then they were taken elsewhere."

She sniffed her way around the space, duckwalking and sometimes crawling on all fours. Occasionally, she'd pick up discarded trash and pieces of clothing or linens, taking a whiff of this or that as she narrated the story. One trail led us downstairs, to a dirt-floored basement that was one mass shallow grave, filled with the skeletons of dozens of children.

Fallyn knelt and sniffed the dirt. "Old. Decades, even. These aren't the kids we're looking for, Colin."

"But they're somebody's kids."

I knelt and touched a tiny skull poking up from the dirt. These were all missing children. Somewhere, someone was still wondering what had happened to them. I felt a bit of impotent rage, that this witch had been allowed to operate here for so long. I'd have to get Maeve's people or the Circle in here to remove all the cursed objects, before we tipped off local law enforcement about the graves.

Fallyn stood. "C'mon. We can't help these children, but we might be able to help the others. Let's backtrack and see where my nose leads us."

Reluctantly, I nodded and followed her back upstairs.

One of the other scent trails led us through a kitchen in the rear of the house and out to a crumbling back porch. I followed her as she pursued the trail, through the overgrown backyard and down a dirt path that led to a small clearing a few hundred yards distant.

She squatted and surveyed the scene. I got the impression she was using all five senses to work out what had happened there. She dropped to one knee and touched two fingers to a shallow impression in the dirt, where an adult-sized boot had left a waffled pattern in a wet patch of stony clay. Fallyn sniffed her fingers, rubbing soil between them.

Her nostrils flared and she bared her teeth. "I thought I caught the scent inside, but I wasn't sure. There was a 'thrope here."

"A 'thrope, as in a wolf? Are you sure?"

She looked at me with a frown, and nodded. "And a fae—something bound to nature. It smells—earthy. But no doubt about it. There was a wolf here, not two days ago. Back at the house, the smell of residual magic was confusing the scents. But out here, it's as plain as day."

"Probably some charm or spell the witch had on her house to confuse anyone who might come looking for missing kids."

Fallyn continued to search the clearing as she spoke. "Think she conjured the kludde?"

"Must've done it when she died, to guard her home or something. The question is, why didn't it attack the werewolf who brought those kids here?"

Her lips curled in a snarl. "That, druid, is a very good question. Only thing I can figure is the fae used magic to keep the kludde at bay."

"Or to control it. But it'd have to be hella powerful to do that."

"Hmph." She walked carefully in a small circle, examining the ground and squatting to touch the trampled grass. "This was where they handed off the kids." She stood and looked to the north. "Let's see where this trail leads."

I had no compunctions about letting her take the lead. For one, I could tell she was pissed. Back in the house when we'd first found those graves, her expression had indicated she was just as upset about it as I was. But now that she had proof there was a 'thrope involved, she was downright furious. Something told me she was going to see this case through to the end. After witnessing her tracking abilities, I had to admit that I was happy to have her assistance.

The trail ended roughly fifty yards beyond the clearing, at a single lane blacktop road that stretched off into the hilly distance. "Trail ends here. They got into a vehicle and left."

We searched the area for any other clues. Fallyn squatted on the shoulder opposite from us and motioned me over. She pointed at the ground.

"Tire treads. Probably a truck or van of some sort."

I compared it to the photo I'd taken at the trailer park. They were a perfect match.

I handed her my phone. "Take a look at this and tell me if my eyes are deceiving me."

She nodded and handed it back. "Same vehicle. Where'd you take the photo, if you don't mind me asking?"

"Where this red cap's kid was abducted. He's my client—and yes, I know it's weird. You think the fae you smelled might've been him?"

She cocked her head. "Could've been, but the scent was from something old. You know how their magic smells, the older fae. It's stronger than the young ones—and richer, with more layers to it. Whatever it is, it smells dangerous, and ancient."

Damn it. That was all I needed, to be mixed up with yet another ancient, powerful fae.

"Well, at least we have a lead. I'm going to have a friend look into these tire tracks. Think you could ask around, and find out if there are any wolves who might be mixed up in something like this?"

She looked at the ground as she considered my request. "I can, but don't tell Dad."

"What, you think I'm going to tell him that I nearly got you killed?"

She gave a toothy, nearly humorless grin. "Considering that it was right before you saved my life, I think we can call it a wash." The wolf girl looked up, and the smile left her face. "But listen to me, druid. Things are more than tense in the Pack right now—they're at a breaking point. You start stirring up more shit than you already have, and Samson could end up with a full-scale mutiny on his hands. You just sit back and let me sniff around, and I'll let you know what I find. Deal?"

"Deal. But if you do tell your dad about what happened here, do me a favor and make sure it's not before my next training session."

She shook her head. "Quit being a pansy, will ya? All Pack members go through the same thing, and nobody ever whines about it. It's considered to be poor form, for a 'thrope."

It was my turn to chuckle. "You forget, I'm no 'thrope."

She didn't reply, and instead made a show of examining the tire tracks. I ignored the implied meaning of her silence. Not that acceptance by the Pack was important to me, but I was rapidly gaining respect for this particular wolf. Her opinion mattered, more than I might have cared to admit.

"There is one good thing about nearly killing you with that taser."

She looked up at me with a frown. "And what might that be?"

"Bet you won't make fun of my man purse now."

"Pfft. You wish. Now grab your sissy bag and take me back to the clubhouse. I'm starving."

11

The following weekend, I had another grueling session of "training" scheduled at the Shaft. This one was supposed to be much less traumatic, as it merely involved slowly bleeding me to death. The idea was to gradually bring me closer to the point when the beast wanted to take over, so I could get a better feel for when it came on and how to control it.

Apparently, my first visit to the Shaft had been meant to be gruesome and shocking. Whether by tradition or design, Trina told me they did it to weed out those 'thropes who wouldn't be able to complete the training, as early as possible. Some would break and turn feral during that first, highly traumatic training session, and they'd be put down. Others would refuse to come back, and were seen as a liability to the Pack. They would also be put down, if they didn't run away first. It was a brutal methodology, and brutally efficient.

I never mentioned that I nearly hadn't come back for my second trip to the Shaft. I'd been up all night long debating the pros and cons of allowing Samson to rip my guts out again, versus saying "screw it" and taking on the whole Pack as they attempted to put an end to me for failing the trials. Either way, I figured it'd be bad. However, my chances for survival were much higher if I continued the training. Plus, I wanted revenge. For that, I needed to control my Hyde-side in order to harness the power of the Eye, so I could track down the Dark Druid and end his miserable existence.

And after that? Well, there was a certain fae sorceress who I desperately wanted to introduce to the concept of mortality. But, I had to learn to control the change first. So, off to the Shaft I went.

Samson paced back and forth in his wolf form as I got undressed.

"We're going to take it slow tonight, Colin. Just a few precise incisions. You'll barely feel it. Just tell me when you're ready."

The scent of blood was still strong in the chamber, and it triggered recent memories of being gutted. Between that and the cold, I began to shiver as I finished disrobing. I allowed them to chain me up again, and stalled for time by taking several deep breaths. I tried to achieve a state of calm, but the whole process was terrifying beyond belief. The raucous laughter of the were-wolves outside echoed down the tunnels, faintly disturbing the quiet in the torture chamber and increasing my anxiety. Finally, I decided to just get it over with.

"I'm ready."

Without hesitation, Samson extended a single, scalpel-sharp claw, and opened the veins in each arm with surgical precision. He was right. I barely felt it.

"It'll be a few minutes before you lose enough blood to trigger the change. Remember, this time, you have to exert your will in concert with mine, so you can start learning how to control your beast."

I nodded, and glanced over at Fallyn and Trina. I was still shy about being naked in front of them, and had chosen to wear a pair of boxers this time, much to the amusement of Trina and contempt of Fallyn. Trina eyed me with no small amount of concern, at least to the extent a werewolf's expressions could convey. I was becoming accustomed to seeing the Pack members in wolf form, and gaining more skill in reading their expressions and body language. Fallyn, however, just looked bored.

I decided to pass the time with some conversation. "Samson, why don't the other Pack members ever participate in these training sessions? Why is it just you, Trina, and Fallyn?"

Fallyn chuckled. "I'll answer that one for you. It's because he doesn't trust anyone else to do this. In other words, he's afraid you might have an 'accident' if another wolf was allowed in here."

"Oh, that's just peachy," I replied. I looked at Samson. "If your daughter is the closest thing to a friend that I have in this Pack, I'm screwed."

Samson bared his teeth in what I assumed was a grin—a rarity for the alpha in any form, human or beast. Trina snickered in her wolf voice, a hyena-like cackling that wasn't meant to sound sinister, but did. Fallyn merely hitched her shoulders and ignored my comment. As Trina's laughter died out, I realized that being the lone outcast among a Pack of werewolves was no laughing matter.

I noticed the growing puddle of blood on the floor of the chamber, and began feeling incredibly light-headed. Rather than come on all at once as it had in the past, I felt the change approach out of the recesses of my mind like a slow-moving train. I closed my eyes to help me focus, and Samson's voice echoed in the still quiet of the chamber.

"See the beast in your mind, Colin. Watch him as he approaches. Observe him as you would a worthy adversary, an opponent on the field of battle. Take note of his strengths, and his weaknesses. See the beast and know that you are his better, his master. Because he is you, and you are the master of your body, mind, and spirit."

That last bit threw me a little. *He is you?* What the hell was that supposed to mean? My ríastrad wasn't me. It was a curse that had been cast on me by that evil fae bitch, Fuamnach. But for all that mattered, I was entirely committed to defeating it on the battlefield of my mind. So, I did just as the alpha asked.

I WENT to that *non*-place in my head, that vacuum of nothingness where my consciousness retreated on every occasion that my ríastrad took over, and my Hyde-side came out. It felt a bit like standing under a spotlight on a completely darkened stage, except there were no echoes made by my footsteps, no gentle breeze coming from the ventilation system above, no scent of perfume and cigarettes and sweat from the players and audience. Instead, it was just me, standing in the middle of nothing. I could see my own body if I looked down at my arms, legs, and torso, but there was nothing solid or real to indicate my position in space or time. Strangely, it felt *safe*.

Then I saw it approach from a distance. Or rather, *him*. He loped toward me at a rapid, yet unhurried pace—in a strange humpbacked gait that required him to use one elongated, misshapen arm and closed fist as a sort of third leg, much in the manner of great apes. It might have taken hours or milliseconds for us to close the gap—and I do mean *us*, because in truth I felt as though I was being pulled toward him, as if by magnetism or gravity. In that place, I couldn't have avoided that other side of me if I tried.

As we drew closer, he fixed me with a wicked grin. The thing's mouth was malformed, and showed way too many teeth as it smiled. He came to a halt within striking distance, still propped up on that longer, thickened, club-like appendage. He leaned forward on it and rocked ever so slightly, back and forth. I got the impression he wasn't sure what to do. Each and every time I'd shifted forms in the past, the beast and I had traded conscious control in an instant. In fact, we'd never had the opportunity to meet in this manner.

I examined him more closely. The resemblance was subtle, but there. Although the bulging forehead, thickened jaw and lips, and massive cauliflower ears hid them well, I could still see my own features on this creature's face. What was creepier than that was seeing my own eyes, staring back at me. It was a lot like looking at myself in a funhouse mirror, except this funhouse was more like a house of horrors, and no one was laughing—not even the beast.

"You," he snarled. "My time. My turn."

"No," I replied. "I am in control."

He reared his head back and laughed, full-throated and hyena-like, ending in an angry roar. "You? You are weak. Even now, your human body is dying. Set me free, or we both die."

"No. Not again. Never again."

"Then I take what is mine."

The thing leapt at me, bowling me over in that non-place. We tumbled through an eternity of nothing and darkness, fighting like two alley cats over a discarded fish head. He was stronger, I was slower, and he was definitely more vicious. It wasn't long before I was losing the fight.

He pinned me under his massive weight, although I couldn't understand how there could be gravity in this place of nothingness. The beast flipped me over on my stomach, wrenching an arm behind me in a shoulder lock—one that I'd done myself hundreds of times in training and battle.

"Submit, weakling. I can break you as easily as stepping on a twig."

"No!"

He twisted my arm viciously, and I felt something give in my shoulder.

"I will rip it off. Submit."

At that moment, the Eye's voice cut through my pain.

-Haven't you wondered why he hasn't simply ripped your head off your shoulders and been done with it? Or how he has you pinned, in a place where the laws of physics do not hold sway?-

"Not now, Eye!" My head was twisted to the side, and I looked at the beast. He stared back at me, one crazy eye bulging from under that bony ledge of a brow, the other sunken and nearly closed. I considered the nature of the creature. Everything about him was disharmony and imbalance, as if he was made of pure chaos.

"Who do you speak with? The god's eye? It speaks to you?"

-Surely you've worked this out already. Consider that, if you and he are one, how can he hurt you without also injuring himself?-

"You might have mentioned that before he started ripping my arm off!" I growled.

-I'd hoped you'd figure it out on your own. While this whole scene is playing out as a physical struggle, this is merely your mind's way of interpreting what is actually a battle of wills. You against your darker side.-

That pissed me off. "We're not the same. He is *not* a part of me."

-So long as you insist on making that distinction, you will never gain complete control over your Fomorian form. So long as you insist on remaining separate, you will never subjugate the beast inside you.-

The beast glanced around furtively, then frantically. "Where is it? Why does it not speak to me?" It twisted my arm again. "Tell me!"

The beast leaned on my arm, yelling angry obscenities all the while. My arm snapped. I screamed, the beast roared, yet he sounded as if he was in just as much pain. Then I felt a sort of pressure settle on us both, and the beast faded from sight. I turned over on my back, cradling my arm and panting heavily—even though there was no air in that place.

No air.

Was this all just a product of my imagination?

-As you are so fond of saying, Colin... Bingo.-

The pressure intensified, and I blacked out.

⸻

WHEN I CAME BACK to reality, I was still inside the mine. I guessed that I had been out for a while, because Trina and Fallyn were both in human form and fully dressed. Trina was leaning against the wall, and Fallyn was seated opposite. They both looked pretty wiped out, and they weren't chatting or doing much of anything other than watching me. I was still chained up, covered in dried blood, but my wounds had been healed. Samson, however, was nowhere to be seen.

Trina pushed off the wall and walked closer, leaning over and propping her hands on her knees to get eye level with me.

"Holy shit, Colin—you alright?"

I sagged like a rag doll in my shackles, feeling drained. I blinked and hung from my chains for a few seconds, gathering my strength and getting my bearings. Then I struggled to get back to my feet. I noticed that Trina wasn't attempting to help me. She actually backed up a half step when I began to stir.

"How long was I out?"

Trina closed one eye and arched the other eyebrow, looking at the ceiling. "Hours? When you went under, Samson had quite the fight on his hands. I think he almost didn't keep your beast at bay. Took the piss right out of him. He stumbled out of here about an hour ago, told us to keep an eye on you until you woke up."

"If I was out, why am I still chained up?"

Fallyn stood up and spoke. "Because that was the creepiest shit any of us has ever seen. For one, Samson has never had to struggle to keep any 'thrope from changing. Ever. And second— well, none of us have ever seen a shifter do what you did."

I lifted my head to make eye contact with her, leaning against the wall and holding myself with the chains in an effort to remain upright.

"You'll have to elaborate, because I don't remember jack after I blacked out."

Fallyn and Trina looked at each other, then back at me. "You don't remember any of it?" Trina asked.

"Nope, not a thing. What happened? I feel like I just ran a marathon carrying Sledge on my back."

Fallyn crossed her arms and stared at me. "You sure you don't feel like you're about to change? That your beast isn't coming back?"

"Fallyn, I doubt I could walk out of here right now. I think everyone is safe."

"Alright, let's get you down and then we'll tell you what happened."

A few minutes later I was sitting outside the chamber, sipping water and waiting for one of them to speak. "So, are you going to tell me why you're so freaked out?"

Trina raised her hands in exasperation, or resignation. "I don't have words for what I just saw. Maybe Fallyn can take a stab at it."

The alpha's daughter tongued a molar and closed her eyes. Then she opened them and fixed me with a stare. She opened her mouth, closed it, then opened it again, and shut it again.

"Any time now, Fallyn. C'mon, it can't be that hard to explain."

She laughed, then took a deep breath and let it out through pursed lips. "Okay, let me see if I can describe this. Parts of you kept shifting, like the beast was bubbling just under the surface of your skin. Pieces of you would shift into your beast, and then shift back to human."

"But the weirdest thing was his eyes," Trina blurted. "Tell him about his eyes."

Fallyn pursed her lips. "I was just getting to that, Trina. Damn. At one point, you looked up at us and grinned, all evil-like. Then, one of your eyes got really bloodshot and changed color, 'til it was so brown it was almost black. Creepiest damned thing I've seen in a while."

"And freaky, too," Trina interjected.

Fallyn's brow wrinkled as she glanced at the other 'thrope. "I thought you were going to let me describe this to him?"

Trina shook her head. "Hey, I'm just saying, it was weird. Even to us werewolves. And we have seen some cuh-razy shit."

Fallyn turned back to me and blinked a few times. "Anyway, it was freaky—"

"Really freaky," Trina said.

Fallyn closed her eyes and took another deep breath, opening her eyes as she let it out. I figured she was counting to ten, although it could have been that she was struggling for the right words to describe what I'd done when I was out.

"It went on for a while. You were pulling on the chains so hard they started to stretch, and cracks appeared in the wall around the anchors. No 'thrope has done that before, ever."

"Nope, not ever," Trina echoed.

"Then your arm snapped, I guess from the strain. But it almost looked like someone grabbed it and twisted it."

Trina whistled. "Nasty spiral fracture, compound. Sticking

right out of the skin. Ugh." She shivered. "Haven't seen one that bad in a long while."

Fallyn tilted her head at the other wolf. "Trina works EMS. If she says it's bad, it's bad. Sounded like a gunshot when it broke. Then you seized up, and Dad too. Samson broke out in a sweat—"

"And werewolves don't sweat," Trina added.

"No, they don't—not normally. But Dad broke out in a sweat —straining to contain your change, I guess. Then, your skin finally stopped bubbling, or whatever it was doing, and you were you again. You collapsed, Dad healed you—"

"Took about everything the Pack had, mind you," Trina commented.

"Yes, it did. And then Dad told us to keep an eye on you, and he staggered out. That was maybe an hour ago." Fallyn grabbed my water bottle and took a swig, looking at it before handing it back. "Wish this was vodka. Shit, I need a strong drink about now."

I leaned my head back against the cold stone wall of the mine and closed my eyes. "Uh huh. So, I scared the shit out of you two."

Trina laughed. "You could say that, and I wouldn't deny it."

I cracked my neck, keeping my eyes on the ceiling. "So, now you know why I need to control this thing. Imagine if I lost it one day, and that thing got loose? If my Hyde-side can scare a couple of hardcore 'thropes who have seen it all, consider the consequences if I don't get a handle on my change. I don't even want to think about it."

Fallyn sniffed and scratched her nose. "I have to say, now I see why Dad is so eager to help you. Although, I wonder why he didn't kill you when you first moved into town." I looked at her, and she shrugged. "Hey, just sayin'. Normally, Dad kills anything that moves into our territory that shifts and is a threat to the Pack. Just the way it is."

"Well, maybe he should have. At least everyone would be safer."

Fallyn stood, wiping her hands on her pants. "Well, I'm not one to question Dad's judgement. He's the alpha, and it's not my place." She dropped her chin to her chest, and paused before she continued. "But I'm here to tell you, Colin—if he says we have to put you down, I'll be the first one to slit your throat. And that's a promise I intend to keep."

Trina looked away, purposely staying out of it.

I smiled ruefully. "It'd be a mercy if you did, Fallyn. And I wouldn't hold it against you."

12

T rina left while I was getting dressed, but Fallyn hung around, doing her best to look like she wasn't monitoring me for signs of the change. While I dressed, I grabbed a few protein bars, some Red Bull, and more water from my Bag. I tossed some spares to Fallyn, which she accepted without comment.

We sat there in silence, chewing on protein bars and sipping water. It took us a while; turned out, even werewolves had difficulty chewing protein bars. All that jaw power, and they still had to chew every bite like twenty times. Who knew?

I decided to break the uncomfortable silence. I spoke in a radio announcer's voice. *"This meal was brought to you by our sponsor, magic.* So, Fallyn, do you still think it's fair to hate on my Craneskin Bag?"

She tried to maintain her stoic expression, and failed. "I have to admit, it's growing on me. What's the deal with that damned thing?"

"Are you a gamer?"

"Never had the desire. Too busy turning a wrench or

learning how to survive as one of the lone female werewolves in the Pack."

"Well, I was going to say it works like a bag of holding. Ring any bells?"

"Only the 'I'm talking to a nerd' bell."

I clucked my tongue. "Never mind."

Fallyn wiped the smirk off her face. "No, seriously, I want to know. You carry that thing everywhere, and it's a damned bottomless bag of tricks. What's the deal?"

I pulled it in front of me and plopped the Bag in my lap. "Well, it's a fae artifact—one that's been in my family for generations. And, like most 'gifts' that come from the fae, it's both a blessing and a curse. The Bag has a mind of its own, and it's fond of letting things out when I'm not there to keep an eye on it."

Fallyn's eyebrows scrunched together. "You say 'things,' meaning—"

"Oh, mostly magical objects that cause mischief. Chameleonic backbiting blades, a potion of truthfulness disguised as a can of soda—or my personal favorite, rose-scented water that causes persons of either sex to throw themselves at the wearer's feet in desperate, humiliating adoration."

She shrugged. "That last one doesn't sound so bad."

I laughed bitterly. "The Bag replaced my cologne with it. I couldn't leave my room for a week, because every time I did I started a riot. Until you've had a soccer mom, a three hundred-pound defensive lineman in drag, and a pair of Mormon missionaries fighting a death match over who gets dibs on your snot rag, you can't fully appreciate how dangerous said situation can be."

She chewed her lip and crinkled her forehead. "Just curious, who won that fight?"

"The soccer mom. She was carrying pepper spray and knew krav maga. Although the lineman nearly had her; he was choking the life out of her until she sprayed him in the eyes. But those Mormons never stood a chance. One of them had half the hair on his head ripped out at the roots. The other lost an ear, chewed clean off by the soccer mom. Then she spat it back in his face." I paused and took a deep breath. "To this day, I still don't wear cologne."

Fallyn gave a sympathetic nod. "Sounds like the clubhouse on tequila night. I can relate."

I heard the echo of rapid footsteps coming down the tunnel. We both sprang to our feet, and I reached in my Bag for the first weapon at hand, which happened to be my war club. I stepped away from the entrance, off to one side with the club hidden behind me. Fallyn hid to the other side of the door, ready to ambush whoever came through.

Trina came bolting through the door, a concerned look on her slightly reddened face. "Folks, we got trouble."

Fallyn stepped into view. "What's the situation?"

Trina rubbed the back of her neck. "Josh managed to gather up a handful of his pencil-dicked buddies, and they're waiting outside for Colin."

"I take it they're not planning to jump out and yell 'Surprise!' with cake and party hats?" Both women looked at me with impatience, but I was too tired to care. "Hey, I just figured I'd ask, on the off chance that Josh decided to apologize by throwing me a surprise party. I could really go for some cake and punch about now."

Fallyn's jaw clenched. "Are you done making jokes? Because I don't think this is at all funny. Josh is more or less staging a small mutiny outside, and if they manage to take you out it'll undermine Dad's authority. Someone will challenge him for sure."

Trina guffawed. "Nobody's gonna take Samson out. Plenty

have tried, and in the end, they all ran off with their tails between their legs. Those that still could, mind you."

Fallyn glanced at Trina, then at me. "That may be true, but something about the current situation has my hackles up. I have a funny feeling somebody in the Pack is stirring up trouble so they can make a run at becoming the new alpha. And I don't think they're going to play fair when it happens."

"What makes you think that, Fal? Something you overheard?" Trina's brow crinkled, and she looked seriously pissed at the thought. "If so, let's just go take those fuckers out, and save Samson the trouble."

"It's nothing solid, Trina, and that's the whole problem. If I had something concrete to go on, I'd have already taken it to Dad. No, this is strictly based on intuition."

I held my hand up and cleared my throat. "What about the rest of the Pack?"

Trina shrugged. "Mostly neutral parties, waiting to see which way the wind blows. I wouldn't expect any help from them."

I wiped a hand across my face and sighed in frustration. "Then what are we going to do about Josh and his merry gang of bloodthirsty 'thropes?"

Fallyn crossed her arms and cradled her chin in one hand. "I could easily handle this for you, but it'll only make you look weak in front of the Pack."

A wicked grin broke across Trina's face. "You thinking what I'm thinking?"

Fallyn nodded slowly. "Yep." She turned and clapped a hand on my shoulder. "Druid, how would you feel about fighting a werewolf?"

I held up my war club. "Can I use this?"

"Nope. Not if you want to squash this for good. No magic, either."

"Well, in that case, I'd rather wear party hats and eat cake."

———

THE PLAN WAS SIMPLE. As soon as I exited the Shaft, I was to challenge Josh before him and his crew had a chance to jump me. That way, he'd be forced to fight me alone, fair and square. Well, sort of. He'd be able to shift into his werewolf form, and I'd be stuck in my current, puny human state.

Which meant I was royally screwed. But hey, when had that ever stopped me from picking a fight? Just to even the odds a little, I'd dug out my warded motorcycle leathers from inside my Craneskin Bag, as well as the matching boots, gloves, and helmet. All were spelled to protect against physical damage. They'd do nothing to even up the difference in strength and speed, but they'd at least keep me from being shredded out of the gate.

Hell if I was going to fight a 'thrope in jeans and a t-shirt. I might have been born at night, but not *last* night.

I paused just inside the door with the helmet under my arm, and looked at Fallyn. "You sure you can keep the rest of them from jumping in?"

"Sure as I can be. Believe it or not, I hold third position in the Pack—and I didn't get there by being Daddy's favorite. So, most of those wolves out there won't dare raise their backs to me."

I cocked an eyebrow. "Hang on a minute—what do you mean, 'most'?"

Trina chuckled. "What she means is that some of them are too stupid to know better. They're either new, or not the most gifted in the common-sense department. But don't worry. Fallyn'll teach 'em quick."

I shook my head and turned to exit the cave, imitating

Fallyn's voice under my breath and making bitchy faces while I spoke.

"Got this great plan, Colin. Go take on the werewolf who has every natural and supernatural advantage, without any weapons or magic. Oh, and just so you know, you might be outnumbered. Trust us, it'll work."

Fallyn called after me. "Don't get killed, or Samson will be pissed!"

I flipped her off over my shoulder, just before I threw open the door to the Shaft. It crashed against the rock wall with a loud, metallic boom.

I screamed at the top of my lungs. "Josh, you weak-ass, shit-for-brains excuse for a werewolf—where the hell are you?"

There was, in fact, a group of 'thropes waiting for me just outside the door. However, they hadn't expected me to come barreling out of the Shaft looking for a fight. I did my best to appear pissed off and crazy, looking at each and every wolf as I pretended not to see Josh in the middle. Finally, I allowed my eyes to land on his face, and held them there.

"There you are, you lying sack of shit. Heard you were telling everyone I was cheating the trials with magic."

Josh looked slightly confused, because this wasn't how he'd imagined things going down. Instead of coming out and begging for mercy, I'd insulted him right off the bat, and I was staring him down. That was as close as you could get in werewolf society to directly challenging another werewolf, without outright doing so. Which was what I was about to do.

Josh recovered some composure and narrowed his eyes. "Now hang on there, druid. I never said any of that. But I do say you're a coward, and unfit for joining the Pack."

A few other wolves around him muttered their agreement, but most were watching us both carefully, to see how this played out. Which was exactly what I wanted. *Time to light the fuse on this idiot plan and see who goes up in smoke.*

"You calling me a liar? Fuck that, let's settle this right now, shifter to shifter!"

Josh cocked his head and grinned nervously. "Are you seriously calling me out?"

"Did I stutter? I said let's settle this, right here and now. Do I have to come up and slap you in the face to make it official?"

He rubbed his jaw and smiled stupidly, looking around as he addressed his buddies. "This is just a trick. The last time he pulled silver on me and used that druid bullshit. I'm not falling for it a second time."

The other wolves muttered amongst themselves. Josh was losing face in front of his little clique.

I cackled like a madman as I looked skyward and howled. Then I stopped abruptly and stared Josh down, hoping I wasn't overdoing it. I wanted them to think I was DGAF-crazy—not stupid-crazy. The first would make them wary of me, but the second might get me killed. Wolves wouldn't tolerate a Pack member who was a liability... which, incidentally, was more or less why Josh had it in for me in the first place.

"I agree to fight you without any magic or weapons." I held out my arms and spun around, holding the helmet extended in one hand. "Just with what I have on me. And if you won't agree to that, then I say you're a coward."

That got his attention. He roared and began shifting. Josh growled a reply as his voice changed from human to that scratchy, full-throated lycan voice so many of the younger 'thropes had in their wolf forms.

"I—am—not—a—coward!" he bellowed.

I smiled and nodded. "Prove it."

I slapped the helmet on, just before he leapt a good ten feet across the clearing, tackling me to the ground.

THE SMART STRATEGY would have been to stay away from Josh's claws and teeth, but that would only work if I was using a weapon or offensive magic. Unfortunately, I'd stupidly agreed to forego such advantages. That meant my next best alternative was to get in close enough so he couldn't use his strongest weapons effectively, and hopefully grapple him into submission.

Grapple with a werewolf. *Great plan, Colin.*

On top of the obvious problems with my strategy, I'd recently witnessed how long it took a 'thrope to pass out from asphyxiation. Even with the kludde's chain wrapped tight enough around her neck to practically pop her head off, Fallyn had remained conscious for at least a minute or two. That was a long time in a fight—long enough for Josh to rip off my helmet and tear my throat out.

So, I needed a different plan. As he tackled me, I took the brunt of it and went with it, taking a shoulder to the chest as my helmeted head bounced off the rocky ground. Shaking off the impact, I immediately pulled guard on him by wrapping my legs around his waist and locking my ankles. At the same time, I used my arms to hug him tightly, one arm over his shoulder and the other under his armpit on the opposite side. I latched my hands behind his shoulders, and held on for all I was worth.

It was like riding a rabid bull. Josh went mad, clawing at me with reckless abandon. Fortunately, he couldn't use his full strength against me, because he didn't have the space to wind up and take a good swipe. And in this position, he couldn't effectively bite me, no matter how hard he tried. With his elongated werewolf muzzle and snout, he couldn't get enough space to get a decent mouthful of my head or shoulder. Even so, his claws and teeth scratched the hell out of my helmet and leathers, reminding me why I'd chosen to wear them.

The only problem was that eventually he'd get through the magically-strengthened Kevlar and leather covering my torso and shoulders. I already felt his claws gaining a bit more purchase with each swipe. The wards could only take so much damage. Once he got through them and ripped the protective panels out of the jacket, he'd shred me like last week's TPS reports.

So, I needed to improvise. And it was going to hurt. I hadn't had time to adjust the strap on the helmet before Josh had jumped on me, which was just as well. I had tucked the faceshield tight to his head and neck as soon as I'd locked onto him, to keep him from grabbing the helmet and twisting my head off like a beer bottle cap. And while the helmet was doing a great job of protecting me, it was also preventing me from using the only useful weapons I had in this position.

Namely, my teeth.

During our training with Finn, he'd encouraged Jesse and me to cross-train in as many other fighting styles and martial arts systems as possible. So, we'd picked up a little of everything, from aikido to vale tudo. I was always looking for instructors who taught down and dirty stuff, and that's how I'd found out about kinamotay.

It supposedly came from the Philippines, and the style was all about biting and eye gouging at close range. Not very useful against paranormal creatures, as you usually wanted to keep your distance. But in this case, it was my best shot at putting Josh down quick. If I could rip out a carotid artery and hang on, he might just bleed enough to pass out, which would give me the win. Being a werewolf, as long as we patched him up quick he'd recover—and then hopefully allow me to go on my merry way.

At least, that was the plan.

As Josh rolled around on the ground, frantically clawing at

my back and scrambling for a way to get me off him, I pulled my jaw in and back, working it around to get the strap over my chin. I waited for the right moment, when the pressure of Josh's teeth on the back of the helmet had relaxed. Then, I reached up quickly with one hand, slipping a thumb under the edge to pop it off.

In my kinamotay training, we'd practiced chewing through steaks wrapped in a t-shirt—no lie. I got good enough to chew through a nice sirloin in under twenty seconds. It was gross, but after class we'd barbecue, so at least the meat hadn't gone to waste. Remembering what that crazy-ass instructor had taught us, I drove my face into Josh's neck, using my mouth to feel for his blood pulsing under all that thick, hairy skin and muscle.

Josh must have sensed what I was doing, because he went nuts, rolling over and over and trying to use those huge canines of his to gnaw a hole in my skull. Unfortunately for Josh, I had the better position. With my face under his jaw, he couldn't bite my head if his life depended on it. That being said, his claws were another matter.

With his first swipe, he opened a gash on the back of my head that gushed blood down my neck and shoulders. The wolves cheered as they smelled first blood, but it barely registered as I searched for Josh's pulse. It probably looked like I was necking with him, but I didn't care; I had to find the right spot before he maimed or killed me.

There. Amidst a mouthful of fur and skin, I felt the *thoomp-thoomp-thoomp* of an arterial pulse. Without hesitation, I gnawed through skin, fur, and flesh, as if my life depended on it.

H is werewolf skin was tough, a lot tougher than raw steak, and it took me a while to chew my way through. By the time I hit the muscle beneath, the skin that once covered the back of my skull had been torn loose, and it flapped against my neck. I was feeling woozy—whether from psychogenic shock or actual blood loss, I wasn't certain. All I knew was if I passed out, I'd be dead. Or, my ríastrad would trigger, and Fallyn and Trina would be dead. I could care less about Josh and his goons, and I'd be glad to see them killed by my Hyde-side. But the girls didn't deserve that, so I held on and kept gnawing, like a lion on a gazelle's neck.

Then I felt it, just like my crazy-ass self-defense instructor had said—the hot spurt of an arterial bleed in my mouth. I thought I'd be grossed out by it, but instead it tasted *good*. The warm, metallic blood in my mouth excited me, and my pulse quickened as I kept chewing. I ripped larger chunks out of his neck, feeling energized as the scratching and scraping of the dying wolf's claws on my skull became weaker by the second. Then Josh went limp, but I couldn't stop. I didn't *want* to stop. The smell and taste of his blood spurred me on, and when he collapsed on me I rolled his massive body over and landed on top of him. Despite the fact that he was no longer conscious, I kept ripping and tearing at his throat with my teeth, rearing my head back and spitting out flesh, then diving back in for more.

Blood was everywhere. It was all over my face, neck, and chest. Whenever I reared back for another bite, it splattered across the wolves standing nearby. When the blood flow finally slowed to a trickle, I wasn't certain how long I'd been savaging Josh's neck. But underneath me, a human body had replaced the massive werewolf I'd been locked in combat with moments before.

Josh was dead, and killing him in that way had felt as natural as tying my shoes.

I glanced down at what was left of Josh's neck. Most of the flesh was gone from between his shoulder and ear on the left side, as well as his windpipe in front. A vertebrae was exposed in the back of his neck, the white bony protuberances standing in sharp contrast to the red gore surrounding it.

I should have been repulsed. I wasn't. That thought was what snapped me back to awareness.

I looked up. Fallyn stood directly in front of me, just inside the circle of wolves. She was crouched slightly with her arms loose at her sides, her blade in her hand. Her feet were splayed, and she had most of her weight on the balls of her feet. She watched me, wary, wondering if I hadn't fully lost control. As our eyes met her body relaxed, and the tautness around her eyes and mouth gave way to an expression of relief.

She stepped forward and raised my arm above my head.

"The druid has won his challenge. Are there any other takers?"

I glanced around at the rest of the wolves. Some looked angry, while others hid their reactions. All were strangely silent.

As I scanned the crowd, every last wolf looked down or away. No one else would challenge me; at least, not this night.

The wolf girl dropped my arm, and I let it fall loosely to my side.

"Then we're done here," I said softly, keeping my head high and my eyes level. No one spoke as the wolves began to disperse. Within minutes, all who remained were Fallyn, Trina, and me. And, of course, Josh's corpse. Trina's face was pale in the moonlight. She chose to avoid making eye contact with me, pretending to be occupied with watching the wolves as they departed.

Fallyn had no such issue, and she knelt in front of me as she looked me in the eyes. "For a moment there, I wasn't sure if you were coming back or not."

"Back from what?" I asked, but I was fairly certain I knew.

She exhaled heavily and bit her lower lip. "Your skin was doing that bubbling thing again, just like it did earlier tonight. Parts of you kept shifting at random. Thought I might have to put you down."

I looked at Josh again, and felt sick. "Next time, don't stick around. Run."

"Wolves don't run, druid. At least this one doesn't."

"You should learn," I said. "Help me up."

I stood, and the ground tilted beneath my feet. I stumbled, but Fallyn grabbed my arm and guided me to sit on a stump nearby. "Your scalp's a mess. Don't know if Samson can heal you 'til morning. He was pretty spent after that struggle you two had earlier." She looked at Trina. "Get me something to wrap this in, so we can take him to the hospital."

Trina nodded once and shuffled off, quickly returning with a bottle of water, an old t-shirt, and a towel. Fallyn took the bottle of water and poured it over my head. The water stung and I winced as I felt it wash hot, sticky blood down my neck. She reached behind my head and under the skin that had been torn from my scalp.

"This is going to hurt." She replaced the flap of skin and hair hanging off my skull.

She was right. It hurt, but not as much as I thought it would. Mostly, I was just dizzy and disoriented... and a bit sick to my stomach at what I'd done to Josh. But only a little. I wondered whether it had something to do with getting closer to my alterego, or if I was just becoming a hard bastard. In this line of work, life had a way of doing that if you weren't careful.

"How bad is it?"

"I've seen worse. Looks like some of the wounds closed on their own when you were on the verge of making the change. We'll get you stitched up, then tomorrow Samson can heal you properly."

I sat still as Trina tore strips of cloth from the t-shirt. Fallyn held the skin in place while Trina wrapped the towel around my head like a turban, using the bandages she'd torn from the shirt to hold it all in place.

Trina smiled nervously. "At least it wasn't your face. All that hair ought to cover that scar up. If he'd caught you on the other side, you'd have to grow a beard to hide it."

"Oh, hell no," I said. "I'm not exactly the hipster type."

Fallyn laughed. "Could've fooled me. You're definitely not the biker type, that's for sure."

"Geez, what gave that away?"

Trina looked at me, then at the ground. "Might be the vocabulary. You kind of have that 'Phil Dunphy' thing going on. But after tonight, I'm fairly certain no one's going to give you shit for it around the clubhouse anymore."

I cracked a smile, which she caught as she nervously bounced her gaze off the ground and back to my face. She held eye contact a moment longer this time. Guess I wasn't as scary-looking with my scalp back in place. Or maybe I just looked silly in a turban.

I looked over at Josh's corpse. "What about him?"

Fallyn didn't spare him a glance. "We'll give him a proper wolf burial. Now, let's go get you stitched up. That towel looks ridiculous."

FORTY-THREE STITCHES AND SEVERAL THOUSAND DOLLARS' worth of medical debt later, I was laying on a gurney at Brackenridge ER, my head wrapped in gauze and my brain fuzzy from the painkillers they'd given me. We'd made up some story about a stray dog attacking me, and I was pretty sure the ER doc had bought it. I closed my eyes and allowed myself to float in a place only trauma and strong opiates could take a person.

I must've slept, because when Detective Klein's harsh voice broke through the fog of my dream state, I had no recollection of her entering the room.

"McCool, what the hell happened to you? Doc is telling me you claim it was a dog attack, but she's not having it and neither am I. Who tore you up?"

So much for my cover story. I blinked and rubbed my eyes with my knuckles. Klein stood next to my bed, arms crossed. Her face was a mask, but I saw just a hint of a smirk tugging at the corners of her mouth.

"How'd you know I was here?"

"ER staff calls us whenever they suspect an assault, and guess who was on duty tonight? I happened to hear your name as dispatch was assigning a uni to come over here, and volunteered to handle it. Curiosity, and all that. Glad I came, too. The ER doc said it looked more like a bear attack. Which is strange, considering your girlfriend was killed by a bear."

I was still muzzy from the drugs, and not up to a verbal sparring match with the detective. "Just some stray dog. I didn't get much of a look at it."

She rocked back on her heels and nodded. "Huh. Far as I know, dogs don't attack with their claws. And the doctor said your wounds had definitely been made by something claw-like, not by teeth. She said it could have been a bear, but her best guess says you were attacked by someone wearing those ninja claw thingies. Said she had a hell of a time stitching you up, too."

"Just my scalp. Guess I'll have to give up my spokesmodel gig with L'Oréal. Bummer."

She rubbed her jaw and tsked. "I just can't figure you out, McCool. It's obvious that you're deep into some serious shit— the kind of stuff Erskine was mixed up with. But you know what? I don't think you killed him. You're too damned goofy to be a cold-blooded killer."

I closed my eyes and sighed. "Um, thanks?"

She frowned. "Don't get all gushy on me. Doesn't mean I like you. But although you're still not my favorite person, I'll give you this—I think the same people who killed him are after you."

I yawned, then opened my eyes. I spoke slowly as I looked her in the face. "It was a dog attack, Detective. And that's all I have to say about it. Now, if you'll excuse me, I really would like to go back to sleep."

She cradled her jaw in one hand. "Fine, have it your way. But sooner or later, you'll be in over your head. When that time comes, you're going to need my help." She pulled out a business card, and dropped it on the bedside table. "Be seeing you, McCool."

"Not if I see you first."

I closed my eyes as she left, only to open them again a few moments later when I heard someone enter. Fallyn.

"Where's Trina?"

"They said it'd take a while to stitch you up. While you were in surgery, we went to get my bike, then she headed home. Said Suze was going to give her hell for getting in so late."

"Why'd you come back?"

"Dad said I needed to bring you by as soon as they released you. Told me not to let you drive. Any word on when you're getting out of here?"

"Soon as the CT scan results come back. Wanted to make sure I didn't have a concussion."

"Mmm. What'd the cop want?"

Again, my eyes had drifted shut. I cracked one to look at her. "Not much. She thinks I'm mixed up with something suspicious. Probably good you weren't here when she came in."

"Just don't let on about your connection to the Pack. We mostly stay off local law enforcement's radar, and we like it that way."

"Noted. Any other questions?"

"Not a one."

"Good. Then I'm going to drift off for a while. Let me know when they say I can go."

"Fine. But if you have to pee, you're on your own."

"I've seen your claws, Fallyn. Trust me, the thought never crossed my mind."

When I woke up back at the junkyard the next morning, Bells was sitting on the foot of my bed. The smell of fresh coffee was in the air, mingled with the faint scent of brake fluid, engine oil, and iron drifting in from the warehouse. Bells handed me a paper cup of coffee, still warm.

"Morning, sunshine. Heard you had an interesting night. Care to dish?"

I sat up and took the lid off the cup, sniffing the contents. "Mmm, Luther's special blend." I took a sip. "Ah, black gold. I'd kiss you, but I need to brush my teeth."

"Like I've never smelled your morning breath. Although, from the stories I've been hearing, I half expected to find a female 'thrope in here this morning."

That got my attention. I cocked my head and looked at her over the coffee, sipping as I assessed the situation. I might have been terrible with relationships, and horrible at reading people, but it wasn't for lack of trying.

"You're referring to Fallyn? C'mon, Bells. She's not even in your league."

She narrowed her eyes at me, crinkling her nose. "Hmm, you're getting better at this. Go on."

"She's way rough around the edges. Definitely not my type. Too tall, as well."

A slight smile played across the corners of her mouth. "You saying I'm short?"

I leaned forward and grabbed her hand. "I'm saying you're the perfect woman for me. In every way."

She laughed, and her eyes danced. "Since when did you become such a charmer?" She placed a hand on my chest and gently pushed me away. "Go brush your teeth, so I can have that kiss."

I grabbed a shirt and headed to the restroom, getting razzed by a few of the warehouse employees along the way. They'd never seen Belladonna before, and I had forgotten what an impression she could make. I took no small amount of pride in telling them she was taken. After I brushed my teeth, I checked my scalp, using a hand mirror to see if I had any bald spots.

Thankfully, there were none. Besides a faint, almost imperceptible line of scar tissue under the skin, there was no sign I'd been injured. The night before, Samson had called in the Pack members who had been part of the whole "let's ambush the druid" thing, and he'd used their energy to heal me as a sort of punishment. Afterwards, Fallyn had pulled out the stitches. Her dad wasn't too happy about Josh, though. I wondered what the fallout from that fiasco would be.

When I got back to my room, Bells was holding my bloody shirt. "This smells of werewolf blood, and yours as well. What the hell happened last night, Colin?"

"You know why I'm doing this, right?" She nodded. "Well, a lot of the wolves don't like the idea of a shifter who's not a 'thrope being in the Pack. So, they've been giving me hell about it. Last night, I challenged their ringleader—and I sort of lost control during the fight."

She crumpled the shirt, holding it tightly in her hands. "Rumor has it you killed that wolf, with your bare hands. Is that true?"

I looked at the floor. "Actually, I ripped his throat out. With my teeth."

She whistled. "You sure know how to get a point across. Doubt anyone is going to be messing with the crazy druid from now on. But from the amount of blood on this shirt—it looks like it cost you. How is it you look none the worse for wear today?"

I sat her down and explained the whole training and healing thing, as well as what Fallyn and Trina had told me about how I'd partially shifted between my human and Fomorian forms during the fight.

"Which explains how some of my wounds healed during the fight. And why I lost control. I'm not exactly proud of what I did. Even if Josh was going to kill me, I had no intention of doing the same to him."

She grabbed my hands, holding them in hers. "Yeah—but don't you see? It means you're making progress. I mean, you didn't hulk out and slaughter any innocent villagers, so that's something, right?"

"I suppose. But I wasn't even aware that I was shifting during the fight. Once I tasted blood, I lost all sense of time and place. All I knew was that I wanted to tear Josh's throat out—which I did. I couldn't have stopped myself if I tried."

She patted my hand. "Still, it's a step in the right direction. And, no one was hurt who didn't deserve it. I call that a win."

I wasn't so certain. My greatest fear was losing control and hurting someone I loved. Now, it seemed the two sides of me were drawing closer somehow. What if I lost control during a fight, and injured Bells? What then?

Belladonna snapped her fingers in front of my face. "Hey, druid boy, you with me?"

I blinked and came back to reality. "Sorry, I was daydreaming."

"Obviously. I was just saying how we need to go see Sal. Yesterday, he called looking for you, and I mentioned you found a possible werewolf connection. Well, the little bastard got all worked up and hung up on me. A few hours later, he calls again saying he has vital information, something that might crack the case and help us find his kid. Said he'd only tell us in person, in case the fae involved are tapping our phones."

"You think they're on to us?"

Bells cocked an eyebrow. "Who knows? Magic wire taps are virtually untraceable, and Circle wizards do it all the time. They still haven't figured out how to intercept texts, though—which is why I'm a sexting only kind of girl. Last thing I need is for those eggheads in research to get a recording of me and you talking dirty to each other."

"You can always use me as a threat. Tell them your boyfriend will rip their throats out with his teeth if they even think about doing something like that."

She leaned in and kissed me. "Trust me, they're already scared shitless of you. They spend half their time looking up amateur video of supernatural events, and reading secret online forums about the world beneath, so they can shut them down. They've heard every story and rumor about the 'Junkyard Druid.' You're kind of like the boogeyman to those jokers."

"Yeah, well—I'm not so sure if it's a good thing that random people are scared of me."

Bells pushed me down on the bed and straddled me, pinning down my arms with her hands. "Oh, you're not that scary. At least, not once people get to know you." She tweaked my nose playfully, then nibbled on my ear. "Now, I hope you don't have anywhere to be, because I feel the need to mark my territory. Just in case that wolf girl gets any ideas."

I swallowed. "Nothing pressing. I am yours to mark, mistress."

Bells reached under my shirt, scraping her nails down my chest as she bit my left nipple a little too hard. A wicked smile played across her lips. "Mistress, huh? I like that."

14

We met Sal at the Bloody Fedora, where he led us to a booth tucked way in the back for privacy. I was certain there were a few fae at the bar who could overhear our conversation, but they all worked for Rocko, and Sal didn't seem to care about their presence. He looked worn down and haggard, worse than when I'd last seen him. Normally, the dwarf looked like he could chew lead and shit bullets, but today his eyes were sunken and bloodshot, his face was gaunt, and he'd lost a few pounds. The pale blue silk shirt he wore had pit stains, and he smelled like a distillery. Obviously, the strain of not knowing where his son was had taken a toll on the little monster.

"So, Bells says you have a lead for us to look into. What'd you dig up?"

His breath smelled like blood and whiskey as he leaned across the table. "When the girl here mentioned a wolf might be involved, it reminded me of something. That she-wolf you been hanging out with—she's too young to remember. But a while back, there was this 'thrope that was diddling kids. Clarence something-or-other.

"This wolf, he hurt a ton of human kids. He'd turn into the big bad wolf to scare 'em after, kept 'em quiet by threatening to hurt their families. That's how he hid it from the Pack for so long—for decades, even. But Samson found out eventually, and—oh man, was he hot. Anyways, that's the wolf you need to talk to. If any 'thrope would have anything to do with taking my boy, it'd be him."

"Wait a minute," I said. "Samson didn't have him killed?"

"Killed? You kidding me? To the wolves, death is too merciful for a piece of work like that. No, Samson didn't kill him. He castrated the freak, and banished him from the Pack. Trust me, to a male 'thrope, that's a fate worse than death. Can't have no offspring, can't have a mate, and no other Pack'll take him."

I coughed into my hand. "Um, don't they—grow back?"

"Naw, when the alpha castrates one of his own, they stay that way. Something to do with the alpha's authority, I guess."

Bells lit up at that little factoid. "Neat trick. Might come in handy, say if a girl had a cheating boyfriend." She squeezed my knee under the table, smiling sweetly. I couldn't tell if she was joking or not. "Tell me this, Sal—why didn't Clarence commit suicide? One silver bullet, and 'poof,' he's free."

Sal sneered. "Should've, but that's the really cruel thing about how they punished him. See, rumor is Samson got some badass sorceress to cast a geas on the pervy little bastard, to prevent him from hurting hisself. I tell you what: I wouldn't want to get on that alpha's bad side, that's for sure."

I thrummed my fingers on the table. "Do you have any idea where we can find this 'thrope?"

He shook his head. "Nope. But she does." He inclined his head toward Bells. "The Cold Iron Circle has the goods on all the supernatural bad guys in these parts. All you gotta do is look him up back at your office. They'll know where to find him."

Belladonna's eyes narrowed to slits. "Be glad to. Do you have a last name for this creep?"

Sal looked off to the side, jaw askew as he inhaled through his teeth. In that moment, he reminded me a lot of Bill Murray's character from *Caddyshack*. "What the hell was his name? Bugsy, Bilbo, Bumpkins? B-something. Hell, I dunno. How many pervy werewolves could there be?"

Bells touched my arm. "Might be easier to check with the wolves. Can you ask that wolf-bitch you've been cozying up to about it? Or, better yet, Samson himself?"

"Hmm... I could, but what if it tips someone off? I'm on shaky ground with the Pack as it is, and we don't know if it's someone in the Pack or not. Could be a lone wolf, but I kind of doubt it. It seems like Samson has the 'thrope thing pretty locked down 'round these parts. I think he'd know if a loner was operating in his territory. No—we have to play this cool. Get the nerd herd on it and see if they can dig something up."

Bells sighed and pulled out her phone, texting away at light speed as she complained under her breath. "I'm going to owe those goofballs six months' worth of pizza delivery once this case is through. Should've just played strip *Magic: The Gathering* with them like they asked. Horny little fuckers would've given me free server access for life."

Pretending I hadn't heard Belladonna's muttering, I looked at Sal, who was watching us both with his beady little eyes. He wasn't my favorite person, not by a long shot, but I felt kind of bad for the short, bloody bastard. Or rather, for his son. "You want to come with, when we find this guy?"

"No, I'll have to sit this one out. Rocko says he doesn't want to start anything with the wolves. But when you find out what the fae connection is, you let me know. We got no trouble going to war with our own kind. Hell, it's sort of a tradition. And when the fear dearg go to war, we don't stop until our knives, caps, and hands are good and bloody."

I slapped the table. "Fair enough. Bells, what did the nerd squad say?"

She kept her eyes on her phone as she answered. "I have an address. But they're asking for takeout from Home Slice. We can get it on the way—and you're buying."

THE SKIES WERE gray and overcast as we drove out to Manor, a small town east of Austin that was home to the best outdoor shooting range in central Texas, and not much else. Besides the gas stations, barbecue joints, and greasy spoons that lined the highway, there was little in the tiny burg to recommend it. Normally, I kind of liked the whole small town thing, having grown up in one myself. But this town looked like a place where washed up meth cooks went to die.

Or pedophile werewolves. Truthfully, I couldn't imagine a worse monster to inhabit a young child's nightmares, and wondered if I could restrain myself in his presence. Belladonna's admirers in the Circle's research department had pulled up a definite hit on the guy, stating with absolute certainty we'd find him here. I had no patience for people or creatures who hurt kids, and took several deep breaths as I parked the Gremlin in front of a dented, ramshackle single-wide trailer, circa 1970—complete with a rusted washing machine and several mismatched sets of car tires strewn all over the front lawn. If you could call it a lawn, what with all the weeds, trash, and neglect.

Bells squeezed my shoulder. "You know, I could go in by myself and interview this creep. I promise to show some restraint. Kind of part of the job, working for the Circle. We don't always get to kill the bad guys—only the ones command gives us the green light to terminate."

I let out a long, slow breath, because at the moment I was

even doubting the limits of my own restraint. And I wasn't nearly the hothead Belladonna was—not even close. If I let her go in there by herself, I'd end up with a dead werewolf, for sure. Not that it would be a bad thing, but the last thing I needed was more complications with the Pack.

"I know you can handle yourself, but I'm not letting you go in there alone." I chuckled under my breath. "What you just said —it kind of makes me wonder if you're working for the right team. Maybe you should quit and team up with me. You'd make a lot more money freelancing, you know."

She pursed her lips and gave me a sideways look, then leaned in and kissed me on the cheek. "You know just what to say to make a girl feel special." She leaned back and placed a hand on the door release. "You ready?"

"Ready as I'll ever be. Let's get this over with." We headed to the front door, watching our footing on the makeshift cinder block steps. I knocked hard, causing the door and the wall of the trailer home to vibrate. "Baxter! Clarence Baxter. We're from the Circle, and we need to talk."

I heard someone approach the door with slow, shuffling footsteps. "Go away. Got nothing to say to you Circle folk. You want to talk to a werewolf, talk to someone in the Pack."

Bells stepped in front of me. "Mr. Baxter, I'm here on official Circle business." She wasn't, but I'd already lied about my status with the Circle, so I figured one more lie couldn't hurt. "Now, either you open the door and let us in, or my wizard here blows a pick-up-sized hole in the side of your trailer, and you freeze your ass off 'til spring. What's it going to be?"

I heard a sigh from the other side of the door, accompanied by a hacking cough. The door latch clicked, and it swung open slightly. "Come in, then. See if I care."

As the door swung open, the smell of stale urine and unwashed flesh hit us, as well as the sickly-sweet odor of advanced cancer. I recognized it immediately, having had it seared into my olfactory memory as a teen, when my mom's aunt had been dying of lung cancer. Clarence was already shuffling down the hall, leaning on a cane with every step. I only saw his back as we followed him to his living room, but it was clear that he'd once been a large man. Now, sickness and age had eaten away at his body, leaving him hunched, frail, and bone thin.

He turned to face us as he lowered himself into a tattered recliner with obvious difficulty. With shaking hands, he pulled a threadbare patchwork quilt around him and grabbed an oxygen mask from nearby, placing it on his lap. The faint hiss of air escaping came from the mask and the soft thrum of an oxygen concentrator echoed from behind his chair and side table.

Wisps of hair adorned his mostly bald head, and round, weeping sores dotted his skin. His face was long and gaunt, with dark circles and jaundiced eyes and skin. I suspected he had lung cancer that had moved to his liver, or vice versa, and obviously skin cancer as well. He leaned his cane against the recliner, leaving it within reach between his leg and the armrest.

"What do you want?" he asked, lungs rattling slightly.

I stood with my hands clasped in front of me, using my second sight to make sense of the 'thrope's condition. He was a werewolf; that was unmistakable. However, his supernatural healing abilities had been either weakened or suspended. In the magical spectrum, it was clear that he'd been cursed or hexed. An amorphous blob of magic covered much of his torso, with tentacle-like limbs that wrapped around his body and inside his chest. He'd been cursed with some sort of symbiotic entity, one that fed off his lycan energies, sucking off just enough magic to keep his body from healing itself. But not enough to let him die.

Shit, Samson is a hard bastard. Yet, when I reminded myself why he'd done it, I couldn't blame the alpha.

I cleared my throat. "Mr. Baxter, we're investigating a series of disappearances—child abductions—and we've found evidence that a werewolf is involved."

He chuckled, then broke into a rattling cough that cut off his laugh, forcing him to take several deep breaths from the oxygen mask before he spoke. "And you thought I might be involved. Sorry to disappoint. I'm hardly able to chase children around these days, as you can see."

BELLS TOOK a step forward at that, and I laid a gentle hand on her arm to calm her. Beating this guy up wouldn't do us any good, and killing him would be a mercy he didn't deserve. I wanted information from him, but I wasn't about to end his misery.

No, I hoped he stayed like this for a long, long time.

Clarence's eyes narrowed, and he leaned forward slightly to get a better look at me. "I know who you are, and you're not from the Circle. I still linger on the outskirts of 'thrope society, anonymously. Whole damned supernatural community knows who you are, but it's the wolves that have been passing your picture around, wondering what to do about the fae-cursed shifter in their midst."

I glanced around the room, spotting an ancient, filthy laptop sitting on his side table. Chances were good that he didn't just use it to keep up with the latest gossip. *Once a low-life, always a low-life*, I thought. I needed to get him talking, so I decided to play along. "And what do they say about me, Clarence?"

"Some say you're a menace, a threat to the Pack and the community at large. Others want you on our side, say it'll tip the balance in our favor, should the Pack go to war." He brought the mask up to his face, breathing in and out rapidly, his voice muffled as he continued. "Most just want you gone. You've upset the Pack order, and if there's one thing wolves can't stand, it's uncertainty."

"But Samson leads the Pack," I said. "That's about as certain as it gets."

Clarence laughed. "Oh, he's a right scary bastard, I'll give him that. But things are changing within the Pack. These younger wolves don't respect the old ways. Maybe they'll decide to gang up on the old wolf, take him down and put their pick in his place. Or maybe they'll hire outside help to get rid of him. Either way, I won't shed a tear."

He wheezed into his mask. "But you didn't come here to listen to me drone on about Pack politics. You came because you're looking for missing children. Bah! Wouldn't be looking if that fae child hadn't been taken. No one cares about the little ones. Not like I did."

Bells bristled. "You didn't care for those children. You victimized them. Hurt them, and used them for your own pleasure."

He raised an eyebrow at her outburst. "Did I? I protected them, loved them when no one else cared. And they loved me back. They liked playing my games, and looked forward to my visits. Who are you to say it's abuse, when both parties enjoy the relationship?"

Belladonna lunged at him, and I had to forcibly restrain her. I pushed her toward the door, whispering in her ear. "Don't. It's what he wants, and we need him alive. Wait for me outside, please."

She kept her eyes on Clarence, and barely held her fury in check as she left. After the door slammed shut, I watched out the window to make sure she wasn't coming back inside. Then I walked back to the living room.

Clarence smiled from behind his oxygen mask. "Oh, she's a

lively one. Too old for me, but I bet she was something else when she was young."

"You disgust me."

"Then we have something in common, you and me. I'm repulsed by your self-righteousness, your attitude toward the natural love I feel for children. You're just like Samson, all puffed up with your own morals."

More out of frustration than anger, I pulled a silver spike from my coat and lunged forward. I tackled Clarence in his chair, bowling him over and pinning him with my knees. He was too sick to shift, and too weak to struggle. I leaned over him, bringing the needle point of the spike within millimeters of his left eye.

"Clarence, I'm not going to do you the mercy of killing you. But I will take away the only thing you seem to care about. How would you like to live out the rest of your days as a blind man, never able to appreciate the thing you enjoy most?"

What I was insinuating sickened me, but I knew this was the quickest way to get him to talk. Threatening to take away his sole source of pleasure was the only leverage I had over him.

He coughed, his breath a soft puff of putrid air. His eyes flicked nervously to the side table next to us. "You wouldn't. You can't. The pictures of my babies—they're all I have left."

I almost shoved the spike through his skull at that moment. "Then talk."

He blinked, his rheumy eyes fixed on the laptop. "Okay, I'll talk. If you really want to find out if the wolves have something to do with the abductions, talk to Sonny. He'll know what's going on."

"Wait, what about Sonny? You're saying he's involved?"

The old 'thrope leered at me. "Sonny has his claws in lots of things that Samson doesn't know about. He keeps his secrets well hidden from the alpha. Half the time, Samson has no idea what's going on in his own Pack. Pathetic."

"Anything else?"

"The alpha and the queen work together. They've been allies for some time now. Ask Maeve how you got accepted into the Pack. You might be surprised at what she tells you."

I laid the point of the silver spike on his skin, directly under his eye. The old 'thrope's flesh burned and sizzled. "How do you know all this?" I whispered.

He cackled, in spite of the pain I was inflicting on him. "I know, because I was once Samson's second. Who do you think trained Sonny?"

Stunned, I rolled off the diseased bastard as his cackling turned into a wracking cough. Instead of righting him, I left him there. As I stood, I grabbed his laptop from the side table and cast a cantrip to fry his Internet connection. His mirth turned to horror when he realized what I was about to do. The old 'thrope wailed and cried for me to return his "babies" to him as I exited the house. I left the laptop in a smoking heap of melted plastic and metal in his front yard.

Watching him crawl out of his trailer to weep over the smoldering heap was small comfort, knowing what I knew about the atrocities he'd committed. Bells' eyes met mine as I headed for the car, and her expression conveyed grim approval, and some regret. Whether her regret was because I hadn't let her hurt Clarence, or because there was nothing we could do for the children he'd abused and raped, I couldn't say.

I slid into the front seat of the car, gripping the steering wheel with my eyes locked straight ahead. Bells and I sat in shared silence for several minutes, listening to Clarence sobbing. Finally, I cranked the engine over, put the car in drive, and sped off.

15

Bells and I sat in the car outside Luther's coffee shop, listening to raindrops patter on the roof of the Gremlin. There were too many prying ears inside to discuss what we'd discovered, so here we sat. Even though I was seriously craving a double-shot mocha with extra chocolate syrup—and a shot of Bailey's. Or a bourbon, neat. Maybe both.

"So, are you going to Samson with this?"

"I can't, Bells. Not yet. Not until I have more proof that someone in the Pack is involved." And not until I understood Samson's connection to Maeve, if there even was one. For all I knew, Clarence might have been lying the whole time.

"Are you at least going to confront Sonny?" The accusation in her voice was evident, and it said, *"Stop being a pussy about this, Colin."* I couldn't blame her, because I felt like a bit of a wuss for not immediately going to the clubhouse to beat answers out of him. But I really didn't have all the puzzle pieces yet, and it wouldn't do me any good to waltz in and start making accusations. Especially since Sonny might not be at fault.

No, I needed more to go on than the ravings of a depraved, perpetually dying werewolf.

"I will, but I need another perspective on this first, from someone with good intel."

"Maeve." Her voice practically crackled with anger. Bells held a serious grudge against the old fae queen, blaming her for much of the misery that had befallen me of late.

"Hey, I don't like her any more than you do. But she's been my best source of info since I got back in the game."

Bells snorted derisively. "You're only back in the game *because* of Maeve. She's been pulling your strings this whole time, and I don't like it." Belladonna placed a hand on the door latch. "Tell you what. You go run off and speak to The Red Queen, and I'll swing by headquarters and see what I can dig up on the connection between Clarence and Sonny."

"You want me to drop you off at Circle HQ?"

She shook her head and crinkled her nose. "Naw, I'll have one of the research geeks swing by. I just need a few minutes with a latte and chocolate croissant before I deal with those guys."

She glanced at me from beneath hooded eyes, and smiled shyly. I found her vulnerability disarming, and it occurred to me that in the close confines of the car, her scent was intoxicating. Either by instinct or common sense, I realized I might be losing her.

"Bells, are we ever going to talk about—you know—your family, and that plane ticket?"

She tilted her head, and the corner of her mouth turned up slightly. "Soon. I don't want to think about it right now. I just want to enjoy whatever time we have, you know?"

I sighed heavily. "That worries me. All of a sudden you're talking about not coming back, and acting as if we're on borrowed time. Bells, I just got you. I certainly don't want to lose you already."

She reached across the console, brushing a strand of hair

from my forehead. Her eyes sparkled, but I saw sadness there. Was that the regret I'd seen earlier? She kissed me, softly. I leaned into her, and she lingered with her forehead next to mine.

"You can't lose me. Not really. But where I'm going, you can't follow."

I pulled away so I could lift her chin and look into her eyes. "I won't lose you, Belladonna Becerra. Not without a fight."

Her eyes welled up, and she kissed me again quickly. Before I could react, she exited the car. I opened my door and placed one foot on the ground, popping my head over the roof as I waited for her to say something else. My sharper than human hearing caught her softly-spoken words as she walked into the coffee shop.

"Don't make promises you can't keep, druid boy."

THIRTY MINUTES LATER, I stood in front of Maeve's door, debating whether to knock or beat feet. The gargoyles hadn't bothered to twitch a single claw or shift even a pebble since I'd arrived. I figured they'd had their fun, watching those fae work me over, but it still made me edgy. Just as I was about to leave, the door opened. Maeve herself appeared in the doorway.

"Hey, what happened to Jack?"

"After your last visit, he casually mentioned that he'd like to drown you in the garden pond and consume your deliquescing corpse over a matter of several days. Since I didn't care to have my koi feeding on decomposing human flesh—they'd keep asking for it ever after, you know—I gave him the night off."

"Hmmm. And just when I was starting to like the guy. But that begs the question—how'd you know I was coming over? You still keeping tabs on me?"

"Always. One must take care of one's investments. Come in."

I tongued my cheek and inhaled deeply, letting it out as I crossed the threshold into her home. Things felt strange —*stranger*—inside. More impermanent than usual, if that was possible. I glanced down a hallway adjacent to the parlor as I followed Maeve inside, and could have sworn I saw a room at the end shift and change. It was dark, and maybe my tired eyes were playing tricks on me, but it reminded me a lot of a scene from that *Dr. Strange* movie. I rubbed my eyes and looked again, only to find the corridor cloaked in impenetrable shadow.

Rather than leading me into the depths of her home, Maeve had tea waiting in the front parlor. I declined, and the tray remained untouched. She sat in a high-backed chair, legs crossed and fingers steepled, watching me with predatory attention as she waited for me to speak. I returned her stare and waited as well. The silence stretched for what seemed to be an eternity, but it couldn't have been more than a minute or so before she spoke.

"Colin, you will grow old before I grow bored. Ask what you came to ask."

I tried to keep a smile off my face. Even small victories were worth savoring when it came to dealing with the fae. "Earlier today, I visited Clarence Baxter at his home."

"Yes, Samson's former second. I was the one who cast the curse on him. I hear he suffers a great deal these days."

I counted to ten before responding. "So, you and Samson really are allies. I didn't know if I could believe the stuff Clarence was telling me, but I guess it makes sense. Why else would they have let me in the Pack? I mean, I'm not really a shifter—at least, not in the classical sense. I'd just like to know why the connection was hidden from me."

A slight tilt of her head was the only physical reaction I got from her. "I've hidden little from you thus far, Colin, and that only to keep you safe. In truth, your ignorance stems from failing to ask the right questions. If you spent less time charging around like a bull in a china closet, and more time using the gifts you've been given, you'd save yourself a great deal of suffering."

"Are you saying I'm reckless?"

She smiled. "Fionn was ever the same as you. Brash, and a man of action. But he was too soft-hearted, and existed under the false assumption that his allies were as loyal as he. It cost him dearly, in the end. You should learn from his mistakes, and take his fate as a cautionary tale of sorts."

I folded my hands in my lap, to keep myself from fidgeting. "The lesson being to never trust the fae?"

"Perhaps. But I'd say the bigger lesson is to not be blinded by love. Love can cause you to let your guard down at the most inopportune times. And it has destroyed many a valiant warrior."

"That's rich, Maeve, but I call bullshit. I know who I can trust, and I don't count you among them. You know why? Because your people are only interested in amusing themselves at the expense of humans, and any 'help' the fae provide always comes at a price."

"Some, but not all, Colin. There are those of us who, for our own reasons, choose to see things from more of a human perspective. Especially when our interests align."

I crossed my arms over my chest. "See what I mean? It's always self-interest with the fae. You never offer any assistance to humans, except when it meets your own ends."

Maeve sat completely still, watching me over those long, delicate hands. After several seconds had passed, her eyes crinkled slightly at the corners. "As you say," she replied.

I sighed heavily, closing my eyes as I counted to ten, again. When I opened them, she was still staring at me. Maeve was obviously in the mood to play games, unlike my last visit. I didn't have the patience for it, so I decided to get down to brass tacks.

"Alright, tell me what I need to know so I can find the missing children. And while we're at it, if you have any insight on how I can learn to control my ability to shift, then I'm all ears."

The corners of her mouth curled in satisfaction. "Where should I start? With the children or your ríastrad?"

"Honestly, I don't care at this point."

"Well then, let's begin with the more selfless of your requests, shall we? Tell me, Colin, what do you know about changelings?"

CHANGELINGS WERE a staple in faery tales and legends all across Western Europe. As the legends went, the fae would steal human babies shortly after birth, replacing them with fae children glamoured to look like their human counterparts. The fae would take the human children to the Underrealms, raising them with no knowledge of their human origins, keeping them as slaves and abusing them for their own cruel amusement. The fae children, on the other hand, attempted to remain incognito among their human hosts for as long as possible.

These "changelings," as they came to be called, were known to raise all kinds of hell, which included everything from exhibiting disruptive and unruly behavior, to cursing crops and livestock, to murdering members of their host families. Changelings were experts at playing the innocent party, and usually set up a patsy to take the fall for whatever mischief or harm they caused.

What you got with a changeling was pretty much a crapshoot, and usually humans only ever figured it out after it was too late. But fae being fae, they would gradually reveal their capricious and sociopathic inner nature as time went on. Once their cover was blown, the changeling would drop their glamour and shock the hell out of everyone present, then vanish from sight. And often, the human child they'd replaced would never be seen or heard from again.

I cleared my throat. "I know what everybody knows about changelings. The fae swap human babies with their own offspring, glamoured to look like the human child, so the fae whelps can make life miserable for their human hosts. It's just one more sick joke your kind devised to fight the boredom that comes with being nearly immortal."

"That's more or less accurate. Give or take a few important details."

I gave Maeve a hard look. "Wait a minute. Are you saying that's what's going on here? That makes no sense, Maeve. These kids are gone, poof—without a trace."

She favored me with a grin worthy of any dragon or tax collector, one that was all teeth and all business. "As I said, your account is correct, save a few important details. Namely, the reasons why certain fae choose to steal human children. Sometimes it is done purely for amusement, with the fae parents watching as their offspring creates all manner of trouble for their human hosts. In these cases, the fae see their actions as an enormous prank, and eventually the human child is returned unharmed.

"But there are certain of my kind who steal human children for other, more nefarious reasons. Some fae have developed a... *taste* for human flesh over the years. The younger the better. Others crave human flesh, but their interests are more carnal and less gustatory in nature. And then there are those who find human children uniquely malleable where magic is concerned, which makes them highly valuable to fae magic users who practice the dark arts.

"As you can imagine, modern laws and technology have made it difficult for certain kinds of fae to abduct human offspring. Thus, the various tastes and desires of the unseelie fae have created a market for human children among the seedy underbelly of fae society. Sadly, now there exist those who specialize in providing human children, even infants, to fae in the Underrealms whose tastes and interests demand such distractions. For a price, of course."

I absorbed what she was saying, considering her words carefully before I responded. Over the years, Jesse and I had solved a few cases where children had been abducted by the fae. But we'd always assumed they were isolated cases. What Maeve was describing amounted to the fae engaging in human trafficking. I wondered, how many missing children and teens had been taken to the Underrealms, never to be seen from again?

"If what you're saying is true, then why haven't you done something about it? Understand, I'm giving you the benefit of the doubt here by assuming you don't approve of these crimes being committed against human children."

Maeve's eyes tightened around the edges, and her voice hardened. "I would never approve of such a thing, nor would I allow it in my demesne." She paused, and I wasn't sure whether it was to gather her thoughts, or her composure. "However, certain of the seedier of our kind continue to do so, despite my wishes. They normally reside in areas beyond my reach, sneaking into my demesne without my knowledge, and taking children in an express violation of my decree."

"And I take it you want it to stop."

She inclined her head just a hair. "As I said, our interests align."

I took a deep breath, blowing it out my nostrils as I chewed on my thumbnail. I let my magic wash over me as I considered her words. Even with my magical insight turned up to eleven, I could see no deception in her words, and no reason why I shouldn't cooperate.

"Fine. I want these dogs put down just as much as you do. More, I would think. So, got any leads or intel on where we can find them, along with the kids they've taken?"

"Only that you're headed in the right direction. Stay on the alpha's second, and watch him carefully. According to my sources, he's central to all of this. Also, the red caps know more than they realize. Ask them about the Rye Mother and her agents."

"The 'Rye Mother.' Got it. Now, about this whole process of taming my darker side—what advice can you give me?"

"You won't like what I have to say," she replied.

I chuckled. "That's never stopped you before. C'mon, Maeve, just tell me what I need to know. I'm tired of being chained up and bled half to death."

She closed her eyes, as if to consider what she would say. When she opened them, her gaze had softened a bit.

"I'll admit, Samson's methods are brutal, and perhaps necessarily so—at least where therianthropes are concerned. However, in your case, I believe you may benefit from a softer touch. You might consider a visit to the doctor you met at the Pack's clubhouse. He may be of more assistance to you than Samson at this juncture."

"You mean Dr. Ganesh? The weretiger?" I shook my head. "You might have told me that before I let Samson rip my guts out. At least that was a one-time deal. Now he just opens a vein and watches me bleed all over the floor."

"I regret that you're having to go through that, Colin. But it has been necessary that you work with the Pack to this point.

And now that you've come this far, Dr. Ganesh will likely be the better tutor for you."

The subtext here was that she'd needed me inside the Pack to do her dirty work. Yet, for the first time since I'd gotten back in the game, I didn't mind being manipulated by Maeve. Not much, at least.

"Okay—I'll take your word for it." I stared at her expectantly. "Yes?"

"I'm just waiting for the other shoe to drop, Maeve. You said I wouldn't like what you had to say. What am I not supposed to like?"

"Ah, finally you're beginning to ask the right questions. You're a quick study, if a little dense at times. I could tell you, but it's better that you hear it from Dr. Ganesh than from my lips. You're less likely to reject his wisdom than mine."

"That's the truth." I stood to go, but Maeve remained seated. I tipped an imaginary hat at her. "Cryptic as always, Maeve. Yet, your time is appreciated."

"It is the one thing I have in abundance, Colin."

"You mean, besides wealth and magic?"

She looked at me under hooded eyes. "Sarcasm really does not suit you."

"Yeah, but considering the company I've been keeping lately, on most days it's my only defense. See you around, Maeve. I can show myself out."

16

The next day, I caught up with Sonny at the clubhouse. After the show I'd put on out at the Shaft when I'd taken Josh out, no one took the opportunity to give me busy work when I entered the place. On the other hand, no one seemed to want to talk to me, either. I honestly didn't know which was worse, but at least I wouldn't have to wash glasses, clean puke and piss off the bathroom floor, and haul beer from the basement today.

Sonny was in the back, hanging out in Samson's office playing pool. I had no idea where Samson was, but Sonny sure seemed to be making himself at home in his absence. I knocked before entering, a sign of respect from a no-rank prospect to the alpha's second.

Sonny finished his turn, neatly sinking two stripes with a bank shot before scratching in the corner pocket. He stepped back from the table, leaning on his cue like a Viking holding his longsword in prayer.

"Well, look who it is. Our very own wolf-slayer. So, 'slayer'— you come to kill more wolves today?"

"That was self-defense, Sonny. Fallyn and Trina will vouch for me."

"Not the way I heard it. According to Josh's boys, you came out of the Shaft enraged and raring for a fight, and Josh just happened to be the poor soul you took it out on." He tsked. "Poor kid never had a chance."

He's trying to push my buttons. Interesting. Up until this point, Sonny had kept his feelings under wraps, at least around me. It made me wonder whether Sonny had been pitting Josh and his cronies against me all along.

I cased the room about thirty seconds too late, and realized there were no friendly faces present. Sonny was playing pool with three other wolves—all of them huge, thuggish types—and not a one of them was smiling. One concentrated on making his shot, but the others glared at me from their stools along the wall.

I realized that I might have made a tactical error, coming here alone to confront Sonny. But I wanted answers, and he was the one who had them. I decided to play it cool.

"I'll admit, once the fight started it got... out of hand. But he'd shifted and I can't even control my change. Whatever happened, it sure wasn't a fair fight."

He chuckled. "No, I'd definitely say it wasn't that. There was fae magic involved. But enough of that—what brings you here, druid? You looking for Samson? Maybe to beg his forgiveness for killing one of his Pack members without permission?"

Fallyn had told me not to worry about it—and besides, it had kind of been her idea in the first place. She'd already informed Samson about how it had gone down, and from what I understood I was more or less in the clear, at least where he was concerned. I decided to trust her and avoid taking the bait.

"Actually, I came looking for you. Can we can talk in private?"

He looked around and spread his hands, showboating for his

audience. "What, your fellow Pack mates aren't good enough to hear what you have to say to me? Or are you trying to get me alone, so you can do to me what you did to Josh?" His brow furrowed and he glared at me. "I welcome you to try, but I guarantee—it won't turn out like you expect."

I held my hands up. "No, nothing like that. I just have something to speak to you about that's best discussed in private."

"Again, whatever you have to say, you can say in front of your Pack mates. Klaus, Jaeger, and Claw here are like brothers to me. So, they stay."

Well, shit, you asked for it. I decided I'd test his reaction to Clarence's name, to see what he'd reveal. "Alright, if you say so. Do you remember a wolf by the name of Clarence Baxter?"

Sonny was sighting down the length of his cue, lining up a shot. "Hmm... nope, doesn't ring a bell."

"That's interesting. He says he's the one who trained you for your position. You know, to replace him when he got kicked out of the Pack."

Sonny sunk his shot and stood upright, looking like he didn't have a care in the world. "Oh, that old coot? Didn't he molest some kids or something? I don't know, that was a long time ago. Why do you ask?"

"I'm working a case. Investigating some missing kids. Clarence seemed to think you might have info that could be useful in my investigation."

The 'thrope raised an eyebrow. "My, my, but aren't we important. You make it sound all official, like you're working under some sort of authority. But everybody knows you're just a kid, nosing around in other people's business. Pfft. Pathetic."

His cronies chuckled, like crows cawing from the top of a fence. "You didn't answer my question."

He glanced at me, then sank another ball. "Kid, what would I know about a bunch of missing children? Probably got taken by some perv like—what was that old 'thrope's name again?"

"Clarence. Clarence Baxter. He used to be Samson's second." I watched Sonny carefully, looking for any crack in his facade, any indication that might tell me I'd struck a nerve. There was none. Damn, but he was good.

"Clarence. I should write that down, just in case anyone else asks." He began to clear the table, first sinking his own balls one by one, then the rest in rapid succession. "You know what, kid?" *Thunk.* "Maybe that old man just likes sending dumb fucks like you"—*thunk*—"on wild goose chases." *Thunk.* "Ever consider that?"

"The thought did cross my mind."

He walked around to my side of the table, setting himself up to sink the last few balls. He had an awkward shot to make, and sat side saddle on the edge of the table to get the right angle. As he did, I got a good look at the soles of his boots. They had a distinctive waffled pattern on the sole, with a series of chevrons down the middle. Just like the boot print Fallyn had found at the witch's house.

He sank the last few balls from his perch, then turned to face me as he stood. "Well, I guess that settles it, prospect. The old man was playing you. Now, go find something useful to do around here. My bike needs to be cleaned, so you can start with that."

He motioned to one of his crew. "Rack 'em up, Claw." I stood there for a moment after being dismissed, watching him until he noticed me again. "You need something else, prospect?"

"You didn't tell me if you wanted it gassed up or not. I have a natural way with fossil fuels. Druid magic, and all that."

He smiled, but only from the nose down. "I bet you do, kid— I bet you do. On second thought, I'll get someone else to clean it. Now get lost, before I find something else for you to do."

"You're the beta around here, Sonny. Whatever you say."

He didn't spare me a glance as I walked out. Couldn't say the same for his crew, though. I could feel every last one of them boring holes in my back with their hateful stares. Something told me that Sonny and I would be at odds, very, very soon.

Now, I was faced with a conundrum. I was ninety-nine percent sure Sonny was involved with the abductions, but I had no motive and no real, solid evidence to connect him with the crimes. If I took my suspicions to Samson now, he'd likely dismiss it and tell me to come back when I had something concrete to go on. And even if Samson did listen to me, it'd only put the Pack in even greater disarray if he acted on the info. As if my presence hadn't already done enough damage.

I needed to build a stronger case against Sonny and his crew, and I needed to find those kids. I only hoped I could get to them in time. From what I understood about traveling to the Underrealms, it was no small feat—especially if you didn't have access to a portal. And, those were generally guarded by the fae rulers in each demesne. No one got in or out of Underhill without the express permission of the fae king or queen who guarded each passageway.

Considering that Maeve wasn't about to let someone move a bunch of missing kids through her basement, I figured they'd have to take them elsewhere to move them. Also, they'd have to line up buyers, or set up some sort of auction to dispose of the kids once they were moved. For all I knew, they might already have that stuff in place, but if I was lucky they'd be keeping those kids somewhere that bordered Maeve's territory.

If so, there was a chance I could get them back. I drove by The Bloody Fedora to see if Sal's car was there. His Olds was right where he usually parked, so I headed inside to chat him up in person. I wasn't about to trust this conversation to the airwaves. If the fae were listening in and we tipped them off, they'd move the kids... or worse.

Walking in alone got me a few hateful stares, because it hadn't been that long ago that I'd trashed the place in a drunken rage. Thankfully, Sal spotted me immediately and waved me to a back booth, where he looked to be about seven shots deep in a bottle of something clear and liquid that lacked a label. The dwarf only slurred his words slightly as he greeted me.

"Back already? Hopefully it's good news. Lemme pour you a drink."

I slid into the booth and picked up the glass he pushed over to me. A quick sniff of the contents told me it was proofed somewhere between moonshine and paint thinner. I set the glass back down with a shudder.

"I'll pass, Sal. That stuff looks like it could eat a hole through a troll's stomach."

"Suit yerself. More for me. Now, tell me what you've found out."

"Some of it I can't discuss in the open, but I think I tracked down the connection we've been looking for. Only problem is, I need more evidence before I can take it up the chain of command."

"Uh-huh, I see. And your plan is?"

I leaned in close and lowered my voice. "What do you know about the Rye Mother?"

He swished his drink around in his glass, then set it down gently on the table. "Ah, the Roggenmuhme. She's bad news, druid, and not one to be messed with. German fae, a type of korndämonen. She's known to be a big baddie, old and vicious, with lots of magic to boot. I guess it would make sense, if she's involved."

Korndämonen were harvest spirits in Germanic myths and legends, nature spirits worshipped as deities in times past. Sometimes farmers would sacrifice to them to ensure a bountiful harvest. It was foolish to do, because once you fed a spirit or fae with blood, they developed a taste for it that would only grow over time.

Sure, you might get good crops for a year after sacrificing a cat or a goat to a harvest deity, but what about the next year when they demanded twice the sacrifice? Or ten years down the road, when they started demanding human blood? Before long, villagers would be having babies just to leave them in the fields. Nothing that came from the fae was to be trusted. They were always going to screw you in the end. *Always.*

Which brought me back to Sal's quip about the Rye Mother's involvement. "What makes you say that?" I asked.

The red cap downed his glass. "She eats kids, is why. Steals 'em, fattens 'em up by making them drink from her tit, and then eats them."

"Um, that's fucked up, Sal."

"Yeah, but she has other fae working for her now, doing the dirty work. You know how it is. The fae that survive here in the human realm eventually have to get with the times. As I hear it, she has an entire outfit dedicated to trafficking human children and selling them to fae in the Underrealms. Well, those she doesn't keep for herself. Heard she's mainly based in the upper Midwest and Northeast. Had no idea she was operating in this area. Maeve doesn't put up with that shit, ya know."

"So I've been told. You think you can put out some feelers, see if anyone knows whether they've run into her people working the outskirts of Maeve's demesne, maybe in Houston or New Orleans?"

Officially, Maeve was the queen of Austin, but unofficially, no fae took a piss within a hundred and fifty miles of the city without her knowledge. Houston was a sort of no man's land between her city and the Big Easy, where anything could be bought or sold for a price. New Orleans was run by vamps, and not the semi-friendly kind we had here in Austin. The New Orleans vamps were mean, nasty, on the take, and they could care less what went on underneath their noses—so long as it didn't bring any heat on them. Even the Circle stayed out of New Orleans, and that was saying something.

Luther somehow kept that element from influencing his people. How he did it, I had no idea. But the evidence indicated Luther was not a vamp that any of his kind wanted to jack with.

Sal motioned the huge half-ogre barkeep over and whispered in his ear. The guy nodded and left, and Sal turned to me and cracked his knuckles. "I told Shorty to put the word out. I should have something for you within a few hours. Keep your phone handy."

"I will. And you should stay sober, because once we get a location, I plan to move fast. The eggheads that work for the Circle say these child abductions have come to a halt of late. That probably means they'll be moving the kids soon, so be ready."

"I was born ready, druid. Drunk or no, I'll be there to take care of business when the time comes."

I stood. "Sal, you think that the Rye Mother's people would hurt your boy?"

The dwarf held up a hand and growled. "Are you asking if they'll eat him? Nah. Fae are predators, not cannibals. But if they thought he was a liability..." He sighed. "No matter what you think of my kind, we red caps look out for our own. Just get yourself ready and wait for my call, alright?"

"Sure, Sal. Whatever you say."

I left him to his drink, and headed back to the junkyard to

prepare. Because when this thing went down, I was going to make someone pay hell in dimes.

I GOT a text from Sal later that night.

-Meet me behind the Fedora in an hour. Come ready for action, and a long drive.-

I forwarded the text to Bells and Hemi. Both of them had been involved in the case from the start, and both wanted in on the action when shit hit the fan. I was about to put my phone away, but decided to forward it to Fallyn on a whim.

-Got a solid lead. Meet us in an hour if you still want to help.-

I gathered everything I needed within a few minutes. Most of what I required was within easy access in my Craneskin Bag. I'd been ready for this moment for days, since this whole messed-up case had started. Making sure I wasn't forgetting anything, I rifled through the top-level contents of the Bag, just in case. Silver-inlaid sword, check. War club, check. Glock with two extended mags, one filled with silver tips and the other with cold iron pellets jammed into the hollow end of each round, check. Possibles bag with a few nasty surprises, like magically-enhanced Molotovs and caltrops coated in wolfsbane, check. Burner phone, check. Snacks and drinks for the road, check.

And, the last item. I hefted it in my hand, inside the Bag. It was a rolled-up leather case—thick, bloodstained, and worn. It was something I didn't like to bring out, except in times like these. But ruthless enemies called for ruthless measures, and ruthless people to carry them out. I set the bundle back where it belonged, grabbed a new black army trench I'd enchanted with protection runes for just such an occasion, and headed out the door.

Bells and Hemi were already waiting for me at the Fedora,

along with Sal, Rocko, and the entire Red Cap Syndicate—a motley assortment of dwarves in eighties-style leather jackets, wool pea coats, fur trench coats, and every other tacky cliché accoutrement of Mafioso style imaginable. They stood in a half circle, slightly apart from Hemi and Bells, smoking and joking amongst themselves. The tension was thick as I approached. Sal greeted me as I entered the circle of dim halogen light.

"Druid, glad you could make it."

I nodded. "Sal. Rocko."

The clan chief of the fear dearg nodded in kind. "Druid. You know I don't care for you, especially not since you tore my place up. But, the queen said let bygones be bygones, and dis is Sal's show. So, I call truce. But you still owe me for the business it cost me."

Owing the fae anything was a mistake. "Consider this payment in kind, then. Besides, I can't take money for doing what's right. After this job is over, my debt to your clan will be paid. Deal?"

Rocko nodded. "Deal." He turned to Sal. "We ready, Salvatore?"

"Everyone is prepped. I'll explain everything, once we're on the road." Sal addressed Bells, Hemi, and me. "I arranged transportation for everyone. It ain't gonna be comfortable, but it was the only thing I could come up with on short notice to get us inside without drawing too much attention."

"Just where are we headed?" I asked.

He held up a hand. "In due time." The dwarf motioned for me to lean in close. As I did, his eyes darted left to right. "Spies. I'll explain on the road."

"But your intel is legit?"

He sniffed once, and dropped a hand to rest on the cleaver handle at his waist. "Oh, it's legit. And we're going to get our hands good and bloody tonight." The rest of his clan muttered their agreement. "Alright then," he said, loud enough for all present to hear. "Let's load up."

Hemi and Bells looked at each other, and then to me. I shrugged, and followed the red caps as they walked around the corner of the club to a waiting freight truck—not quite large enough to be a semi, but still plenty big. The sides were void of any markings or other identifying info. One of the dwarves knocked on the sliding door, and someone inside pulled it up, revealing cargo area that was empty except for a few couches and crates, arranged all willy-nilly inside.

Sal turned to me. "I know it ain't exactly riding in style, but it'll get us past their security. Trust me on this."

"I've ridden in worse. Let's just load up and get this thing over with."

Hemi smiled at Bells and hopped up on the tailgate, bypassing the loading ramp that had been set up for our diminutive traveling companions to use. Bells took one look inside and shook her head.

"Oh, hell no. I'm riding up front, where it's warm and I can roll down a window if someone farts."

"Suit yourself." I stood outside for a moment as the rest loaded up, looking around and trying to avoid being obvious about it.

"Expecting someone, mate?" Hemi asked.

"Naw, I guess not. Let's get going." I hopped in the back and shut the door, trying to recall a cantrip for dispelling foul odors as I latched the gate.

17

We spent the next three hours bouncing around in the back of that truck. As it turned out, the cantrip I'd prepared came in handy, because about a half hour into the trip one of the dwarves started ripping bombs. It was enough to make me lift the door to let in fresh air, which caused the temperature in the back of the truck to drop about twenty degrees.

Our driver pulled the truck into a gas station when we got close to our destination, and not a moment too soon. Although my cantrip had dispersed most of the foul odors the red cap had released, everyone jumped out immediately when the truck stopped moving. Hemi and I were first through the door, and we met Bells as she stepped out of the cab.

"So how was the trip, boys?" she asked with a wry grin on her face.

Hemi chuckled. "Things were pretty rough until Colin used his druid powers to clear the air. But even with the magical assist, we still had to leave the door cracked for most of the trip."

I watched over Belladonna's shoulder as the dwarves waddled into the convenience store. Tony G, the dwarf responsible for the foul odors, was getting bitched out by the rest of his group. Something told me that if he kept it up, he might be hitchhiking home from Houston.

"Never mind how our trip was—how was it riding with Sal?"

"I'll have you know that Sal was a complete gentleman. He even let me set the radio station and temperature in the cab. I have no complaints."

"It's because they're afraid of you," Hemi said as he kneaded his back with closed fists and stretched. "You Circle people have a rep for taking out unseelie fae like yesterday's trash."

I chewed my lip and grimaced. "Remember, though—for now, we're all one big, happy family. We're here to get these kids back, and that's all that matters. Then we can part ways with these Red Cap Syndicate boys."

I tilted my chin to let them know someone was approaching. "Sal, nice of you to join us. We were discussing the finer points of traveling Red Cap Bus Lines. I have to say the seating wasn't bad, but we could've used more ventilation in the back."

Sal didn't look like he was in the mood for joking. In fact, he looked more like he was in the mood for doing some killing. I felt the same way, but it was a ritual for me to joke before a big fight or mission. I wasn't about to change my traditions now—especially not for a bunch of unseelie fae.

The dwarf gesticulated angrily as he spoke. "Guess I better fill you in, since we're almost to the location. Here's the deal... we're heading to a warehouse on the southwest side of Houston. According to a tip we got from a púca a couple of hours ago, it's where the Rye Mother's people hide the children they traffic."

Púca were water fae that were known to have a taste for human flesh. I'd have to pay a visit to Sal's informant later, to find out how it knew where the kids were being kept. But that could wait until after we rescued the children. I nodded to acknowledge that I was listening, and let Sal continue.

"From what we was told, it takes them months to kidnap enough kids to make the trip to Underhill worth it. Crossing over in secret takes a lot of planning, and they have to grease a lot of hands to do it. In the meantime, they hide the kids out here to avoid being found out."

The more Sal talked, the angrier Hemi's expression became. He slammed one meaty fist into the palm of his other hand. "I got something for these pricks. Just wait 'til I get my hands on whoever we find in that warehouse."

"We all feel the same way, big guy," I said as I clapped my hand on his shoulder. "But we have to make sure we do this according to plan." I looked at Sal and raised an eyebrow. "We do have a plan, right?"

Sal cleared snot from the back of his throat and spat, hitting a rock near the road. "Yeah, yeah, we got a plan. You might've noticed that Rocko didn't ride with us in the truck. He drove on ahead in his Caddie and is posing as a buyer at the warehouse. He's going to get the grand tour, then sneak away to let us in through the back. We're gonna pull around to another warehouse close by, and wait for his signal."

Bells cracked her knuckles. "And that's when shit is going to hit the fan, right?"

Sal winked at her with his jaw set. I couldn't recall a time when the dwarf looked more determined. "You got that right, doll face," he said as he snorted and spat again. "And it's going to be bloody, the way us red caps like it."

Sal walked off to join his buddies inside the convenience store. I figured they were all buying alcohol and nicotine, tanking up for the big fight. I looked at my shivering companions and chewed my thumbnail in nervous excitement.

"This is it. The moment we've been waiting for. Just remember, our primary concern is getting the children back—it's not to deliver justice on these creeps. Even though that's what I intend to do. But getting the kids to safety comes first."

Hemi leaned in as he tongued a molar. "And once we get the kids out? What happens then, Colin?"

"Then? Then there'll be hell to pay. And I intend to collect with interest."

AFTER A SHORT AND much less odiferous ride to the warehouse, we parked the truck, then our entire group disembarked and hid behind a building close to our target. As I surveyed the area, I noticed several white vans and work trucks in the parking lot, with the lightning bolt symbol Click had described to us emblazoned on the side. The lettering beneath the logo said "Müller Site Services," a suitably vague and forgettable name that was likely to draw little attention from witnesses and onlookers. A plain white placard on the back door of the warehouse matched the name on the vehicles.

Bells and I busied ourselves with checking weapons and equipment, while Hemi just stood to the side like a big Maori statue. The red caps had gathered in another group nearby. Due to their peculiar affectations and preferences for Mafioso clothing, most of them were not dressed suitably for the weather. Except for Sal, they remained huddled together for warmth—rubbing their arms, stamping their feet, and passing around a couple of bottles of hard alcohol.

Sal remained separate from the rest of his crew, in order to keep an eye on the warehouse. He insisted on maintaining eye contact with the target building, just in case Rocko had to stick his head out the back door to motion us over. Likewise, I kept an eye on Sal, just to make sure he didn't go cowboy on us. After a few minutes, Sal noticed me watching him and waved me over.

"Okay, druid, here's the deal. Rocko's supposed to send me a text when he has a way for us to get in. When he does, we have to move fast. Once we're inside, me and the boys are going to go through that place like a reckoning, and we intend to kill everything that ain't a child."

"I can't argue with that plan," I replied, pulling my trench coat tighter around me. "But I want you to keep a couple of the fae alive. I need intel to get to the bottom of this whole mess, which means I gotta have someone to question—so I can find out exactly how the Pack is connected to this operation."

Sal continued to keep his eyes on the warehouse where the kids were supposedly being held. One thing I had to say about the bloodthirsty little shit: he was focused. I just hoped his desire for revenge wouldn't put our mission at risk.

"I can't promise anything, druid, but we'll do our best. Just keep the kids safe, get them out of the building, and leave the killing to us. Alright?"

"Try to keep the bosses alive, Sal. That's all I ask." Sal's only response was slight bob of his head, barely perceptible in the dim light behind the warehouse. At that moment, Sal's phone vibrated in his hand. I glanced over his shoulder to read the text on the screen.

-Rear entrance southwest side, two minutes-

"That's our cue." I gave the signal to Hemi and Bells to get ready to move.

Hemi produced a short, flat war club from under his shirt, and began smacking it in his open palm. Normally he'd already be chanting to activate the wards that protected him in battle. But we'd agreed there would be no magic—at least not until we were inside. We didn't want to take any chances that they might sense our presence. Never one to be outdone, Bells produced a shortened automatic 12-gauge shotgun from under her long leather coat. I was positive the heavy firepower would be put to good use.

We waited for Sal to move his crew into position, then followed them across the parking lot, staying close to the wall as we crept to the entrance Rocko had found for us. The red caps all had blades drawn, and they crept like cats as we moved to the doorway. Within seconds, the door cracked open and Rocko popped his head out.

"You waiting for an invitation?" Rocko whispered. "Get in here before they figure out what's going on."

The red caps filed in the door, one by one, and we followed close after. Once inside, it didn't take long for my eyes to adjust to the gloom. It was nearly as dark in the building as it was outside. We were in a high-ceilinged warehouse, in a corridor that led ahead about twenty feet before taking a sharp right. The walls in the hall ran straight to the ceiling, ending where they met metal beams and joists approximately twenty-five feet above our heads.

That told me there was probably a second floor, which could complicate our search for the children considerably. From somewhere ahead, electronic music with a heavy bassline pumped incessantly, and flashing lights reflected off the shiny white paint that covered the walls. The only other light came from LED strips that ran along the baseboards, a dim blue-white glow that barely lit the hallway and added to the creep factor inside the building.

I cast a cantrip to enhance my hearing, to determine what we might find ahead. As the spell kicked in my ears popped, and sounds came to me from distant corners of the building, filling my heart with both hope and dread.

First, I caught the faint sounds of children sobbing. Then I heard laughter, mingled with conversation. After that, I registered the guttural grunts and moans of a man and woman in the midst of a sexual act, mingled with the terrified cries of a young boy.

"My God," I said, my voice trembling with rage. "This isn't just a place where they hide the kids they abduct—it's a fucking brothel."

My whole world went red in an instant, and righteous indignation drove me into action. I flew past the red caps like a bullet, using my hearing to home in on the horrible tableau my spell had revealed.

I BOUNDED down the hall with a short sword in my right hand and my Glock in my left. It was times like these when I wished I had a silencer for my pistol. Fortunately, the farther I got down the hallway, the louder the music became. I hoped the noise would mask any sounds of combat—at least until I could get to the child being tortured on the other side of the building.

I paid no heed to who might have followed me. There was no need to look, anyway. Two sets of footsteps matched my own; one set soft and light, the other set ponderous and plodding. Bells and Hemi required no explanations from me; they had my back.

Running at full speed, I turned a corner just in time to see a tall, thin man with curly, close-cropped hair and a ruddy complexion leading a young girl of about eleven years old on a leash. *On a fucking leash.* I shifted my sight into the magical spectrum without slowing; he was fae. His true form revealed him to be just as tall and thin, but with smooth, alabaster skin and platinum blonde hair that fell in an unruly manner around his preternaturally delicate facial features.

I shot him in the head without missing a beat. The girl dropped to the floor in a crouch, covering her head with both arms and cringing away from me. Without slowing, I spoke over my shoulder just loud enough for Bells and Hemi to hear.

"Get her to safety and start checking these rooms for more children. Kill any adults you find, fae or human."

A quick glance over my shoulder verified that Hemi was tending to the child. I tuned my hearing into their conversation as I ran farther down the hall, unsurprised to discover that the Maori warrior had a gentle touch with children. I caught just enough of their interchange to determine the child was taking Hemi to a room where the rest of the children were being held.

I ran on.

The child's screams grew louder, the closer we came to our destination. The grunting and moaning of the adults rose to a crescendo, then they faded off into momentary silence. The child's cries trailed off as well, transitioning into quiet sobs that tore at me in a way I hadn't felt since Jesse's death.

I skidded around another corner, nearly slipping on the smooth concrete floor. As I slid into sight, I revealed my presence to a pair of fae headed toward us. One was hulking and muscular, while the other was short and stocky. They were twenty feet down the hall and momentarily surprised at my sudden appearance. I took the opportunity to pierce their glamour with magic, so I would know what I faced.

The larger of the two was a buggane—a dark-skinned ogre-like creature covered in black fur, with large tusks and sharp teeth set in a vulgar red gash of a mouth. The smaller of the pair was your standard variety goblin—nasty little gray-green humanoids with a penchant for violence and cruelty. It only took a split second for the two of them to determine we weren't there to deliver pizza, and they shifted stance while spreading out to block our passage.

The buggane was on my side of the corridor, so I headed straight for it, knowing I could count on Belladonna to take out the goblin. I sped up as I ran toward the creature, firing bullets into its chest and drawing my sword arm back as if to take a huge swing at its neck. As I closed the gap with the buggane, the goblin's head exploded in a shower of bone fragments, blood, and gray matter. My opponent shrugged off the bullet wounds in its chest and lunged at me, just as I figured it would. Bugganes were tough bastards. I slipped under its grasp and slid feet-first as I stabbed upward at the monster's groin.

The sword met little resistance until it lodged in the buggane's pelvis, so I let it go as I slid past, skidding to my feet and firing at close range into the back of its head. And while the 9mm hollow-points didn't cause its head to explode, they did create a satisfyingly large hole in its eye socket as they exited. I grabbed my sword and kicked the thing in the back, wrenching the weapon free. I didn't spare it another glance as I sprinted on down the hallway.

We were almost there.

The hall ended at a doorway, currently secured by a rather sturdy-looking metal door and deadbolt. The child's sobs emanated from the other side of that door, punctuated by taunting jeers. I detected two distinct voices: a nasally female voice, and a deeper male voice. I holstered my gun and reached into my Bag as we approached the door, pulling out a hailstone and palming it in my right hand.

The Bag had kept the hailstone in stasis, and it was as cold as the day I'd collected it. I could've used an ice cube for the spell, but it wouldn't have been as powerful. Finnegas had taught me that druid magic worked best when it conformed to and amplified natural events. A raging summer storm had formed the hailstone; combining my magic with that power would make for a potent spell. It would do.

The sobbing on the other side of the door stopped, just as I whispered power into the irregular icy sphere. I threw it overhand, striking the door between the handle and the lock. As it shattered, a thin coating of frost appeared on the door near the jam, spreading to cover the door handle and lock.

"Bells, blast it," I commanded, my voice emotionless despite the anger I felt.

She complied, aiming her gun at a downward, oblique angle to avoid inadvertently hitting the child inside. As the double-ought buckshot hit the super-frozen metal of the door, the area around the locks shattered like ice. I kicked the door open and entered with both gun and sword at the ready. The two fae inside must have sensed our approach via magical means, because the male was already swinging a sword at my head as I stepped through the doorway.

I leaned back lazily, letting the blade pass within millimeters of my eyes, countering with a horizontal slash of my own. I angled the blade up to catch his wrist just past the pommel of his sword. I severed his hand neatly from his forearm with that cut, then stepped to deliver two more cuts, one just above the front of his knee as I passed, and another slicing behind both knees as I pivoted, hamstringing him completely.

Grabbing the fae by his hair, I held my blade at his neck. His body shielded me from his female companion, who was standing in the corner muttering a spell. Her hands weaved patterns in the air as she muttered, but that stopped abruptly when each of her hands disappeared in a fine mist of bone, skin, and blood—courtesy of Belladonna's precision shooting with the shotgun.

18

The female fae fell to her knees, eyes expanding in shock as she stared at the bloodied, ragged stumps where her hands had been. "Bells, keep her covered—and quiet."

I pulled the male fae's head back by the hair, my blade close to his neck. I took some small satisfaction in the sizzling sound his skin made as the cold iron seared it. I leaned close to his ear and whispered with as much menace as possible. It didn't take much effort.

"Who's in charge here?" I asked.

"You have no idea who you're dealing with, human," he replied. "I'm fae royalty. You've just signed your death warrant. When my father hears of this, he'll send a death squad to torture you. But first, I'll have them take you to Underhill, where they'll keep you alive for centuries while you suffer."

"Colin," Belladonna's voice quivered. "Look."

I glanced up at her ashen face and pained expression, then followed her gaze to the unconscious, broken form that lay on the bed across the room. The child had been bound and gagged, mutilated and tortured, raped, broken, and then discarded like some plastic dime store plaything.

I snapped, like a guitar string wound too tight that had been played too hard for too long. I thought back to the time before the Dark Druid had killed my dad, and how my life had been shattered by his death. I thought about all the hurt and heartache I'd suffered at the hands of the fae. I thought about my curse, and losing Jesse. And I considered how these children's lives would be forever changed by what the fae had done to them.

I'd had enough.

I drew my blade slowly across the male fae's throat, listening to him gurgle and drown in his own blood as he collapsed to the floor. Then I threw my sword overhand and watched it spin— once, twice—until it pierced the female fae's breast. Already on her knees and suffering from shock, she sank to the floor and expired in a pool of her own blood.

It was a death too swift and too good for them, but I was more concerned for the child. I rushed to the bed, quickly untying him and wrapping him in a sheet, careful not to cause further pain or injury. I hugged him to my chest, then laid him back down on the bed so I could do a proper rapid trauma assessment. While his physical wounds weren't life-threatening, what the fae had done to him was so horrifying, I had neither the presence of mind nor the emotional capacity to categorize it.

Sal and Tony G entered the room. "Druid, we found my boy, and the lowlifes that are in charge of this dump." He paused and took in the scene before him. By the look on his face, I realized there were things that could give even the fear dearg pause. "Oh, sweet mercy. Even in the old days, none of my kind would sink so low."

"Are we secure, Sal?" I asked, moving so Bells could sit at the child's side. She hovered over him protectively, like a mother bear guarding a wounded cub. Tears flowed freely down her face, and her eyes shone with a fierce rage that said death was too kind for the fae who'd committed this atrocity.

"Yeah, druid, we're secure. The place is locked down, and my boys ran through this place like the plague. I kept two alive like you asked—the fuckers that were in charge." He glanced at the kid on the bed and shook his head. "Shit, druid. My guys are fathers, brothers, and uncles, and most have families of their own. If they see this, those fae won't stay alive for long."

"That's a surprising revelation," Belladonna hissed, her voice dripping with venom. "Coming from such a bloodthirsty race."

Sal looked at the wall and bit his lip. He exhaled heavily. "Even the fear dearg have their limits, hunter."

I pulled my burner phone from my Bag and pointed at the two red caps. "Sal, you and Tony G keep this under wraps." Then I dialed one of two numbers I had programmed into the phone earlier that evening.

Someone picked up on the other end. "Colin?"

"Yeah."

He sighed with relief. "Thank goodness. Did you find them?" Earlier, I'd let Luther know we had a solid lead on the kids. He'd been waiting to hear from me, just in case we needed support or back-up.

"No time to explain, Luther. Contact Maeve, and tell her I need her at this address immediately." I rattled off our location. "And ask her to bring her best healer."

"Consider it done. Is everything okay?"

"Not in the slightest, Luther. Not in the slightest."

AFTER I MADE sure the child was stable, I followed Sal and Tony G to a set of offices situated above the lower level. Apparently, this area was used for admin purposes only, and the rooms up here looked like the same barebones offices in any nondescript office building or corporate warehouse. The contrast between the gaudy offensiveness of the rooms below and the eerie normalcy of the offices above raised my hackles. I seethed as I followed Sal to the office, where they were keeping the sole surviving fae.

The room we entered looked like something out of a 1970s cop drama. The walls were covered in cheap wood paneling, a large metal desk sat opposite the door, and the place smelled like cigarettes, cheap cigars, and spilled liquor. Inside, two fae had been tied up with extension cords and telephone line. Their mouths were taped shut, and both had been beaten bloody.

Currently, Johnny Dibs was straddling one of them, carving shallow bloody lines into the fae's chest as he squirmed and shrieked impotently. Rocko sat behind the desk with his feet kicked up, drinking a glass of whiskey and lighting a cigar. I assumed he'd found both in the office, but knowing Rocko, it was just as likely that he'd brought his own stash. He puffed on the thing until the end was cherry red.

"That'll be enough, Johnny," Rocko coughed, waving his cigar and flicking gray ash on the desk. He looked at the cigar like it'd bitten him, then tossed it in the trash can. "Like I said, the druid needs these two alive. You'll have to wait until after he's done with them before you get to have your fun."

Johnny Dibs gave his boss an "Aw, shucks," look, and slowly climbed off the fae he'd been carving, cleaning his knife on his victim's shirt. I spent a moment taking in the scene, trying to decide where I should start, and mustering enough self-control to resist killing my witnesses. I waited for Johnny Dibs to back away before I spoke.

"Who do we have here?" I said, to no one in particular.

"You're looking at the top dog and his assistant," Rocko replied. "They haven't told us much, but based on what we gathered from Sal's kid, they work directly for the Rye Mother. Turns out Little Sal got snagged on accident by a couple of humans who worked for them. Since he's fae, they didn't know what to do with him. They decided to make him their gopher, the dumbasses. The kid figured out the whole operation the first day."

"Why didn't he call his dad and tell him where he was?" I asked.

Rocko shrugged. "The phone lines are just for show. The warehouse doesn't have phone service, Internet—nothing. The only people who have cell phones are the bosses, and all the doors lock with keys from both sides. The place is set up like a jailhouse, and little Sal didn't have the juice to get himself out."

"Where is he now?"

"I got him downstairs with the rest of the kids," Sal said. "I didn't want him seeing whatever happens up here."

I rubbed my chin and took a few deep breaths. "I'm going to need to talk to him. Bring him upstairs—but keep him down the hall, alright?"

Rocko pointed at one of the nameless red caps standing around, and they sulked out of the office to comply—apparently miffed they were taking orders from me. I knelt next to the fae that Johnny Dibs had been cutting on, grabbing him by the chin and looking him in the eyes. "Which one of these guys was in charge?"

"Rupert, the guy I sliced up," Johnny Dibs said with a sneer. "That's why I was carving on him."

I flipped the other guy over on his side, so he had a clear view of what I was about to do. I'd already pierced their glamour with my magic, and knew that these were both high fae, with all the supernatural beauty and vanity their kind possessed. The boss wore a tailored Italian suit, silk shirt, and expensive pair of Italian-made wingtips. His underling wore creased white slacks, loafers with no socks, a designer polo shirt, and a cardigan tied loosely around his neck. I pulled the tape from the boss's mouth, and he spat in my face. I wiped my face clean with my sleeve, and gave him a solid, backhanded slap that drew a trickle of blood from his mouth.

He sneered at me. "I told you to stay out of our business, druid. Regardless of what you do to me, you will pay the price for your meddling. And believe me, I fear my mistress much more than I fear the likes of you."

I recognized his voice instantly; he was one of the fae that had tuned me up in front of Maeve's place. This didn't change things much, but it did make sense in light of what had happened. I'd thought the fae who'd attacked me were Maeve's people, but it had to have been these clowns, trying to warn me off from investigating Little Sal's disappearance.

I weighed my options for making them talk. Death wouldn't scare these two. Chances were good the boss was telling the truth when he said they were much more afraid of the Rye Mother than they were of dying by my hand. But I knew what they *were* afraid of, more than anything else. I would use that to my advantage.

I looked the peon in the eyes as I taped his boss' mouth shut again. Then I pulled my skinning knife from behind the small of my back, and grabbed his boss's nose at the tip before slicing it cleanly from his face. I held the skin and cartilage up, examining it with feigned disinterest before tossing it over my shoulder with a shrug. The one who had lost his nose had a fit, struggling against his bonds as he flopped around like a fish. The tape covering his mouth muffled his screams.

I made eye contact with his second-in-command again, as I pinned his boss to the floor with my knee. Then I grabbed his left ear and sliced that off too, tossing it away before slicing off the other one. The boss was frantic now, his breathing labored through his now unimpeded nasal passageways, which caused him to spray blood and snot all over my shirt. I didn't much care. It only added to the effect I was trying to achieve.

But I wasn't there yet. I reached into my Craneskin Bag, and pulled out the leather bundle that I'd placed there earlier. I untied the straps and rolled the leather case out on the floor, in full view of the second-in-command and his boss. Inside were pockets that contained all manner of hand tools—surgical instruments, knives, and razors. Some were silver, some forged of cold iron, and some were surgical steel.

I smelled urine; the underling had pissed himself. Now we were getting somewhere.

THE CASE WAS a holdover from the latter part of my training with Finnegas; and yes, it was a torturer's kit. Learning to torture monsters had been one of the final steps in my training. Not one that I'd relished, nor enjoyed—but something that Finnegas had insisted I learn, despite my moral misgivings. But honestly, I'd never thought I'd be grateful that Finnegas had made me learn how to interrogate monsters.

But now? Now I *wanted* to use it, to inflict pain on the creatures who'd hurt that child. Inside, I felt nothing but bright, burning rage that threatened to overwhelm me. It took all I had to remain in control, so I could finish what I was about to do. I'd felt remorse and pity for the vamp that Finn and I had tortured as practice. But now, in this moment, I felt nothing for the fae I was cutting on but hate.

I did have a brief moment of doubt, wondering for a second if I was trading my humanity for revenge. Had the "training" I'd been receiving from Samson damaged me somehow? Was I becoming inured to violence and killing? Was all this contact with my Hyde-side taking its toll? I couldn't remember ever feeling this callous and hollow before. But now wasn't the time to plumb the depths of my emotions and sanity. I had work to do.

Someone had to get justice for those kids. No matter what.

I looked at two of the red caps standing along the wall, noting the nervous, wide-eyed stares they were giving me. "Hold him down," I ordered.

They glanced at Rocko to get his approval before complying. He slowly nodded, grinning in grim approval. It wasn't so much that my actions had shocked the moral sensibilities of the red caps; it was that they had underestimated how ruthless I could be when pushed. As I moved out of the way, one of them straddled the fae's chest, and the other, his knees. Despite their small statures, like most dwarven fae their bodies were incredibly dense and muscled, and they managed the job with ease.

I took my time moving down to the boss' feet, and then removed each of his shoes with slow, precise movements while he struggled to free himself. I pulled off each sock in turn, balling them up and placing them inside their respective shoes. He was whimpering and crying now, but I ignored him. I leaned over my case of tools, moving my hand back and forth slowly, as if trying to decide which tool would be the best for this particular job. Finally, I removed a large pair of steel wire snips, clicking them in my hand as I moved back to the fae's feet.

I snipped off each of his toes at the first knuckle, one by one. After that, I went to work on his fingers, leaving him with nothing but bloody nubs. The entire time, I never asked a single question, nor did I remove the tape from his mouth. Finally, as a coup de grace, I scalped the fae, tossing the skin and hair in a wastebasket nearby. Then I gouged his eyes out. Only after I was through with that particularly gruesome task did I remove the tape from his mouth.

By now, his voice was hoarse and he could no longer scream

at full volume. Which was just as well. I grabbed his tongue with a pair of pliers while he was in mid-scream, using them to wedge his jaws open as I severed his tongue at the base with a scalpel. This too I tossed aside, just before I cleaned my tools on his now bloody silk shirt and suit jacket.

I looked at his second-in-command. "At this point," I stated as I cracked my neck, "you might think that I'm going to kill him. But you'd be wrong. Killing him would be a mercy, and a waste of all the hard work I've put into him so far."

I stood up and stretched, then rolled out my shoulders. Once I was good and loose, I knelt next to the underling and tore the tape off his face in one quick motion.

"Please, don't do that to me," he stammered. "I'll tell you whatever you want—anything you want to know. Anything. Just promise that you'll kill me before the Rye Mother gets to me."

"Fair enough," I replied. "So long as I get the information I want, I promise you a quick, clean death." His boss was gagging behind my back, drowning in his own blood. I glanced over my shoulder. "Turn him on his stomach, so he doesn't choke to death. I'm not finished with him yet."

The underling gulped loudly and stared at the bloody mess I'd made of his former boss. It had been grim work, and not something I'd ever be particularly proud of. But at least now, I'd have no problems getting the information I needed.

And, I was one small step closer to avenging the as-yet unnamed boy downstairs.

But damned if I was finished yet. In fact, I was just getting started.

19

The red caps flipped over the mutilated form of the brothel's supervisor. His breathing eased as he blubbered and bled all over the floor. I grabbed his former underling by the armpits and set him roughly in a nearby office chair.

"What's your name—and I mean your real name, not the name you took when you came topside."

"August. August Bockelmann," he stuttered, "but everybody just calls me Augie."

I grabbed my skinning knife from the floor where I'd left it, wiping it clean on the pale pink cardigan Augie wore around his neck. I tapped the tip on his chest, looking him in the eye as I smiled.

"Augie. That's an innocuous name for a feldgeister who steals children."

"I was never involved in fieldwork," he squeaked. "I never even went downstairs most days." He paused to swallow. "It's not like I enjoy this work."

I placed the tip of my blade just below his eye. "Careful what you say now, Augie," I whispered. "I promised you a quick death, but right now you're not convincing me that I made the right choice."

Augie's mouth opened and closed rapidly, like a fish out of water. Then he snapped it shut, evidence that he wasn't as dumb as he looked.

"Like I said, I'll tell you everything, everything I know. Just do me a favor and—" Augie looked at his former boss, writhing and moaning incoherently on the ground. "Just put him out of his misery, please. I can't think while he's moaning and bleeding all over the place like that."

"Sorry, Augie. Can't do that right now. I need him alive, to send a message to the Rye Mother. And that message is coming straight from the queen of the Austin fae." I paused and looked over my shoulder. "And speak of the devil herself..."

I recognized the crackle and pulse of Maeve's magic, just before she stepped into the room through a magic portal. Her effortless use of such high-level magic revealed her to be a power unto herself. She usually made an effort to appear innocuous around me, serving tea and chatting amiably in the pleasant confines of her home. But it was times like these that reminded me just how dangerous the queen could be.

Rocko, Sal, and the other red caps all dropped to one knee, bowing their heads in reverence to their queen as she stepped into the room. I merely looked at her nodded. "Maeve, thank you for coming on such short notice."

She glanced around the room and took in the scene blank-faced, even at the sight of Rupert bleeding all over the carpet. Another tall, slender, aged fae stepped through the portal behind her before it closed. The fae she brought with her wore a voluminous gray robe, with the hood pulled over her head. I knew she was female by her lithe shape, and saw she was aged by the pale translucence of what little skin her robe revealed. She reached up to pull back the hood covering her head, revealing that she didn't bother to conceal her appearance with glamour or magic of any kind.

"Druid," Queen Maeve addressed me. "Where are the children?"

"De-de-downstairs, my queen," Rocko stammered. "Sal, show the healer where the children are being kept."

Sal rose to comply. He bowed as he approached the tall elder fae in the robe, showing her deference in an uncharacteristic manner. It told me that not only was she ancient, but powerful and royalty as well.

Maeve glided toward the chair where Augie sat. I noted that the feldgeister's complexion had paled considerably since Maeve had arrived, and he quivered as he struggled to lower his head as much as possible in her presence.

"Q-Queen Maeve, it is an honor," Augie stuttered as she approached him. Her eyes narrowed as she appraised our captive, a rare display of anger from the normally composed regent.

"I can take over from here." She looked me up and down, her expression inscrutable. "Perhaps you should go clean up before the children see you."

I looked down at my shirt, pants, and shoes, like a child who had been caught playing in the mud wearing his Sunday best. I wiped my hands on my shirt self-consciously, then dropped them to my sides before Augie could notice my discomfort.

"Well—I'm sure you can get more information from Augie here than I could. And with much less mess, of course." I turned and knelt in front of Augie, so I could look him in the eye as I delivered my final threat to him. "Remember, Augie," I whispered, "you invaded *my* territory too. And you should know— the human children you hurt? They're under *my* protection. They were always under *my* protection. And I *will* have retribution."

I nodded to Maeve and left the room, closing the door behind me. I walked several feet down the hallway, then stopped and leaned my back against the wall. I suddenly felt weak, and my hands shook uncontrollably. My stomach roiled with nausea, and I ran into a nearby restroom, vomiting into the toilet. I hurled and hurled until nothing came up but bile and air. Then I removed every scrap of clothing I wore, tossing it in a metal wastebasket and immolating it with a spell.

I washed Rupert's blood from my skin with shaking hands, using paper towels, soap, and water. The fae's blood made little pink rivulets as it ran down the rusted drain, and I thought back to when I'd rescued Finnegas from Rocko and his crew, not so long ago. *How things change.* I splashed water on my face several times to shock me back to the present. Finally, I dried myself with a wad of paper towels, then retrieved a spare change of clothing from my Craneskin Bag.

After I'd dressed, I leaned against the sink and stared at myself in the mirror, looking for traces of that monstrous other side of me. Seeing none, I realized that the monster I had just let out had been all me. I closed my eyes, took several deep breaths to compose myself, and went to find Little Sal.

As I EXITED THE BATHROOM, I nearly bumped into Click, the fae from the trailer park. He was leaning up against the wall, smoking a cigarette. "You look like shit, druid," he said after exhaling cigarette smoke from the corner of his mouth.

"This day is just full of surprises. How in the hell did you know to come here? Did one of Rocko's boys tip you off, or have you been following me around this whole time?"

He dropped his glowing cigarette butt to the floor and

stamped it out on the tile with his boot. "Told you I was gonna help you, and I meant it. You gonna talk to Little Sal?"

"Yeah. I need to find out what he saw while he was here."

"Probably best if I go with you," Click said as he lit up another cigarette. "The kid was always a bit skittish, so things'll go better if I'm there to set him at ease. C'mon, I'll take you to him."

Little Sal was with his dad in another, smaller office two doors down from the space where I'd tortured Augie's boss. It occurred to me that I didn't even know his name, but I didn't care at this point. All I cared about was justice—justice for those kids downstairs, and justice for all the people in my life who'd been hurt by the fae. I felt thin and worn out, but I wasn't about to let that show. The kids needed to know someone was willing to stand up for them. Even if Maeve was going to mind-wipe them later, it didn't matter. They needed to know right now that somebody was going to make the bad guys pay.

Sal was sitting in a chair with Little Sal curled up in his lap. The boy was sucking his thumb and hanging onto his dad's shirt for dear life, while his father held him close. Sal's display of fatherly love reminded me that all fae weren't bloodthirsty creatures of instinct like nosferatu or kludde. Sure, they were capricious, aloof, and prone to treating humans like cattle, but they were also thinking and feeling beings, as the scene before me clearly showed. I flashed back to what I'd done earlier, and felt ashamed. I put the thought out of my mind and instead focused on the white-hot ball of anger in the center of my chest, and the image of that little boy tied up on the bed.

Sal nodded at us as we walked in the door. "Click. Druid. I think the kid's fallen asleep."

"Well, I hate to wake him, especially after all he's been through. But I do need to ask him some questions before I head back to Austin."

"I'm awake," a small voice replied. "I was just resting my eyes." Little Sal wiped his thumb on his dirty, stained shirt. Although his proportions were diminutive like his father's, he looked to be about eight or nine years old in human years. But, like Click, he could be eight, eighteen, or eighty for all I knew. The kid pushed off his dad's chest and sat up straight so he could look me in the eye. He bore quite a resemblance to Sal, yet his cherubic appearance stood in stark contrast to his father's weathered face, thick, calloused hands, and rough, unruly beard.

"I only have a couple of questions for you, Little Sal. It won't take much time."

He looked at me, and then at Click. "Hiya, Click. I talked to strangers. You told me not to do that."

"S'alright, ya little bugger."

"I'm sorry, Click. I won't do it again."

"No need to say you're sorry, kiddo. It wasn't your fault. I should've been there, looking out for you."

"It's okay, Click. They didn't hurt me. Not like the other kids." Little Sal looked down at his feet. He looked sad and forlorn—survivor's guilt, more than likely. Obviously, Little Sal wasn't struck from the same mold as the rest of his kind.

I dropped to one knee to get eye to eye with him. "Sal, I just need to know one thing. Did you ever see any 'thropes while you were here?"

His eyes wavered back and forth from my face to Click's. "I dunno what that is."

Click flashed a smile. "He means the blaidd, Sallie. Werewolves."

Sal's head bobbed up and down. "Oh yeah, they were here—a couple of times at least. They brought kids in, and met with Augie and Rupert every few days."

"So Rupert really was in charge—not Augie?" He nodded,

and I forced a smile. "Sal, do you remember the werewolves' names?"

"One of 'em. Rupert and Augie always talked about them after they left and called them names. Augie said they were 'rotten wolves,' or something. Him and Rupert talked about the one named Sonny a lot—I think they liked him the least."

I smiled again, and hoped it came across as sincere. "Thanks, Sal. That's all I needed to know."

He blinked and leaned back against his father's chest, pulling his knees up tight to his stomach and sticking his thumb back in his mouth.

Click walked over to him and gently ruffled the hair on his head. "I'll see you later, lad—back at the trailer park, and we'll play video games and read comics. How's that sound?"

Sal failed to reply, and his breathing became steady and slow as he nestled back into his father's arms. Big Sal waved us away out of the boy's line of sight. Then he addressed me directly in a quiet voice. "Druid, look me up back in Austin. I owe you, and that debt will be paid."

I said nothing, because nothing needed to be said. Click tilted his head toward the door and exited the room, so I followed him. But as I was leaving, Little Sal's sleepy voice spoke up behind me.

"I'm glad you hurt Rupert, mister. He deserved it. He hurt the kids worse than anyone."

I paused in the doorway and hung my head. "I... Thanks, kid. I needed to hear that."

"I know," Little Sal mumbled, as he nestled into his father's chest and drifted off to sleep.

WE SPENT the remainder of the evening sorting out the kids,

with Maeve's mysterious healer checking each child for injuries and treating them accordingly. For some of the children—those who'd been specifically set aside for powerful customers in Underhill—their injuries amounted to nothing more than being slightly malnourished, along with the odd scratch or bruise. But for other children—those who'd suffered the misfortune of being selected for abuse in the Rye Mother's sex trafficking operation—their injuries were unspeakable.

Many of the children cringed when anyone approached them, while others stared off into space with blank expressions. Those children refused to interact with us, no matter how much we attempted to coax them with food and drink. After about thirty minutes of witnessing the effects of the abuse they'd suffered at the hands of the fae, I couldn't take anymore. I needed to feel like I was doing something, anything to help them, but since Maeve was interrogating Augie, guard duty was all I could come up with.

I waited outside the rooms where the children were being cared for, standing guard against all threats real and imagined. While I doubted the wolves would show up before we left, pacing back and forth and running perimeter checks kept my mind off the children—and what I wanted to do to Rupert and Augie. Hemi and Bells followed my lead, each of us spurning conversation and company, choosing instead to process the events of the evening in silence as we made our rounds.

That was just as well, because I didn't much feel like talking. My mind was a whirlwind of thoughts and emotions, and I kept berating myself over would-have, could-have, and should-have scenarios. If I only *would have* been paying more attention to the news, I might've noticed all of the missing kids and gotten involved sooner. If I only *could have* cultivated better connections within the fae community, I might have been tipped off to what was going on and put a stop to it before any kids were hurt.

What it all boiled down to was simple: I *should have* been paying closer attention to whether there were any supernatural threats to the children in my city. These thoughts occupied my mind as I paced the halls and swept the perimeter outside the warehouse.

Another question nagged at me as well: how could The Cold Iron Circle be unaware of a supernatural child trafficking ring, one that had operated right under their noses? I saw the same question written on Belladonna's face, each time we passed each other in the halls. I had a feeling that after tonight, she was going to do some serious soul-searching with regard to her current employer. I wouldn't have been surprised if she started digging around to see if they were simply incompetent, or purposely oblivious to the Rye Mother's operations.

And as for Hemi? Tears ran down the Maori warrior's face, and he allowed them to flow freely without wiping them away. He made no attempt to hide how deeply affected he was by the whole situation. He appeared so heartbroken that I almost felt guilty for bringing him along. None of us had expected to see this level of depredation and evil at the end of our journey to find these children. As our eyes met in passing, we made a silent pact by determined stares and haunted looks; we'd see this thing through to the end and punish the perpetrators, no matter the cost.

About an hour later, Maeve exited the room where she and her healer had been treating the children. I made a beeline for her as she entered the hall.

"How are the children doing?" I croaked, struggling to speak without choking up.

While she appeared to be emotionless and distant, the lines around her eyes said it all. Even by the measure of all she'd seen during her incredibly long life span, she was still affected by what she'd witnessed this evening. Rather than responding to my question, she locked eyes with me and tilted her head toward the rear of the building.

"Let's take a walk, shall we?"

I complied and pretended to lead as we strolled down the hallway and out the rear entrance of the warehouse. Dawn would be breaking soon, and I worried that workers would be showing up at neighboring buildings and businesses. We needed to determine some reasonable arrangement for the children, and soon.

The crisp cold air outside failed to chill me, despite or perhaps because of the emotional exhaustion I felt. We strolled away from the building in silence. After we'd distanced ourselves from that cruel place, she spoke.

"We healed them physically, and I want you to know they will suffer no physical scars or reminders of the horrors visited on them."

I let my breath out slowly, and watched it form a small cloud that dissipated in the breeze. "That's certainly a relief, but I sense there's a catch."

"There is. I need to know how you want to handle this, Colin. As far as I'm concerned, you're the human representative for these children. Your voice holds the most weight, since you volunteered yourself as their protector and champion, and proved to be the only person who cared enough to track them down."

I bit my lip and gave a halfhearted shrug. "Not the only one. I was just the only person with enough information to connect the dots. Still, I was a dollar short and a day late, Maeve. The story of my life."

She released my arm and turned to face me, placing her hand gently on my chest and her finger against my lips. "Shush, sweet boy. You did more for those children than anyone else was willing to do, and now you will bear a greater burden than most would accept. Now, you have a choice to make."

"What choice?" I knew what she was getting at, but I didn't care to accept responsibility for that decision.

"Their minds and memories, Colin. You and I both know we can't allow the story of what happened here to reach the human authorities. It will only raise questions and spark curiosity in the minds of those who investigate such crimes. It will put those people in danger, as well as keep the children in a state of continued peril for as long as they possess knowledge of the fae.

"And there's more to consider. Many of these children are broken, emotionally and psychologically. For some, their minds have shut down almost completely. Removing their memories of what happened here would be a mercy."

I wrestled with the decision, and wondered if tampering with the minds of these children was morally and ethically superior to leaving them with the nightmare memories they currently possessed. I felt very strongly about fae meddling in human affairs, and even more strongly about them meddling with human minds. Wiping a person's memory with magic was such an intrusive act, some might consider it as heinous a crime as rape.

"Will they remember any of it?"

"I'll make certain they remember nothing. It will be as though they suffered a bout of amnesia, from the time they were taken until the time they are returned to their parents."

"A case of group amnesia is bound to raise a lot of questions."

"Yet, fewer than if their memories remained intact."

I swallowed hard and sighed. "Then do it. As long as it doesn't harm them, wipe every bit of it from their minds."

"Consider it done," she replied, locking arms with me again and leading us back to the warehouse.

Maeve squeezed my arm. "We'll still need to get them back to their families. We must do it in a way that involves the authorities, while giving them a story that satisfies the natural questions that will arise."

I had already decided how I would handle things, if I ever located any of the children. "I know someone who can help. But once we clue her in, I need your assurance that she'll be declared off limits to the fae."

Maeve was three steps ahead of me, as always. "I assure you, no harm will come to Detective Klein, should you secure her cooperation in returning the children and covering up the involvement of the fae in their abductions."

"Fair enough. I'll make the call, but I'll need your help convincing Klein once she arrives."

20

D espite the fact that Klein hated my guts, she was a good cop. Klein was clean as a whistle—the polar opposite of her former partner, the late Sgt. Erskine. Sure, she'd harassed me a bit while investigating her partner's death, but like I said, it was to be expected considering the circumstances surrounding his passing.

I waited for her outside the back door, enjoying a few moments of sunshine after a long, dark night. Detective Klein pulled up in an unmarked car. She stepped out with her shooting hand in easy reach of her sidearm, remaining behind the open driver side door of her vehicle as she scanned the area.

"McCool, you'd better have a good reason for dragging my ass all the way to the outskirts of Houston."

Earlier on the phone, I'd told her I had a reliable lead on the missing children. I'd insisted that she come alone, claiming that my source was skittish and would flee at the first sign of a bust. She'd treated my story with some skepticism, but in the end, she'd agreed to meet me at the designated time and place.

I kept my hands in clear view as I pushed off the wall. "Relax,

Detective Klein. I promise this isn't a trick, and that the trip will prove to be more than worth your time."

"So, where is this mysterious informant of yours?" she asked, as she shut the door to her cruiser.

"She's inside, waiting for us. But fair warning—I'm about to introduce you to a world few people know about. And, the knowledge I'm about to share with you will undoubtedly place you in grave danger."

She rolled her eyes and smirked condescendingly. "Kid, I've been a cop since you were in grade school. And let me tell you, I've seen it all. Dark web child porn rings, grisly hits done by cartel sicarios, and murder-suicide scenes that'd curl the hair on your head. Trust me, nothing you show me is gonna shock me or put me off from finding these kids."

For her sake, I momentarily considered calling it off. I could always find another way to get the kids back to their parents, one that wouldn't require her involvement. Once she became aware of the world beneath our own, her life would never be the same again. But, Maeve and I had gone over this before I'd made the call, and we had mutually agreed that we needed Detective Klein's help. One of Maeve's plants in the department just wouldn't do; we needed an investigator who had a reason for being the person to "find" these children.

"Don't say I didn't warn you," I said as I opened the door. "Now, follow me."

I led her down the hall a short distance and stopped directly in front of the room where Maeve waited. "Last chance to back out, Detective."

Her face reddened, and she exhaled sharply. "Just open the fucking door already."

I did as she asked and entered the room with Klein on my heels. Maeve was standing in front of a desk, looking for all the world like a high-class soccer mom who'd gotten lost on her way to a Rodan and Fields convention.

"Detective Klein, I'd like to introduce you to Maeve, queen of the Austin Fae."

"Fae? Come again?"

I wiped a speck of sleep from my eye. "Fae, as in fairies."

Skepticism and impatience played across Klein's face. "Is this a fucking joke?" the detective growled. "Somebody better tell me what the hell Betty Crocker has to do with the missing kids, or I'm gone."

I held my hands up in a placating gesture. "It's been a long night, Detective, so I apologize for not easing you into this gently." I looked at Maeve. "Maeve, if you would be so kind?"

Maeve dipped her chin in acknowledgment of my request, then she raised her arms to her sides, levitating until she floated several inches above the carpet below. As her magical disguise disappeared, her soccer mom outfit morphed into a gauzy white dress—a toga-like off the shoulder number that billowed and whipped around her, although there was nary a breeze inside the office. Her skin paled from her usual sunglow tones to become a flawless, unbroken expanse of alabaster, without a single blemish or scar to mark her as mortal.

Soft white light emanated from Maeve's chest, expanding until she shone with a frosty luminescence. Her face transformed from the refined, feminine visage she typically portrayed to the world, and was replaced by alien, supernaturally beautiful features. Her eyes changed colors, from silvery gray to icy blue, to blackest night and then back again. Sparks of magic danced all around her, like fireflies on a warm summer evening. I doubted any human artist could have ever accurately depicted her in her full queenly radiance.

Detective Klein's mouth fell agape. "What. The. Hell."

The corner of my mouth curled into a grin, despite the gravity of the previous night's events.

"So, Detective Klein, I guess it's time someone told you: magic is real."

A FEW MINUTES LATER, the real Maeve was hidden beneath her glamour again, and we sat in the office explaining things to Klein over rancid cups of convenience store coffee. Klein jabbered on as her mind reconciled details and events that she had previously written off, with what she now knew to be true.

"Shit, I knew it! There was no other explanation for how the evidence disappeared from Erskine's house. Not to mention all the other weird shit I saw during the time we were partners. I mean, Erskine was the ugliest man I'd ever seen—the guy was just repulsive. But some of the tail he managed to attract... come on, there was no way he could get women like that without supernatural intervention. Seriously, do you know how hard it is to get a date when you're a cop? Never mind getting laid on a regular basis. Still pisses me off, just thinking about it."

As Klein nattered on, Maeve's normally composed veneer wore thin. "Detective Klein, if we could get back on task? As you'll recall, Colin brought you here on the pretense of revealing critical information regarding the missing children cases."

Klein looked at her and shook her head. "Shit, Galadriel, give me a minute to process, would you? Do you realize how fucking weird it is talking to you like this, after finding out you're basically the chick on the Starbucks logo?"

"Um, that's a siren—entirely different type of fae," I interjected. "But getting back to the reason why I brought you here in the first place..."

Detective Klein nodded, her eyes still slightly unfocused and wide with the shock of learning that magic was real. "The kids—yeah, of course. Just listen to me yammer on. Son of a bitch, Stacy, get it together already. You got a job to do."

Maeve stood and needlessly straightened her flawless and unwrinkled clothing. "Perhaps we should just show you what we've found. Detective Klein, please follow me." Maeve led the way out of the room and down the hallway a short distance, stopping before a closed door. "Colin, I think you should do the honors, such as they are under these trying circumstances."

I took a deep breath, letting it out slowly. "Detective Klein, we—well, I'll just let you see for yourself." I opened the door and stepped aside so the detective could walk through. We followed her inside, where the children were sleeping on pallets, or sitting quietly while they colored or played with stuffed animals and toys that Maeve had conjured earlier.

If the detective had been shocked before, now she was completely beside herself. "These are the kids—all the missing kids."

"Not quite all of them," I said with a shrug. "But most of them, anyway. We suspect that some children, the ones not here, were actual runaways. Or, at least, that's what we hope."

Detective Klein pulled her phone from her pocket. "I have to call this in, immediately." She began dialing frantically. Maeve snapped her fingers, and the phone screen went dead.

"Please, Detective—before you contact your superiors, we must first discuss how this very delicate situation is to be handled and contained." I detected just a hint of magic in her voice, a slight authority behind Maeve's words. It was just enough to get the detective's attention.

Klein shook her head, staring at the now blank phone screen before putting it away. "Okay, but how? I mean, how'd you find them?"

I glanced at Bells, who was sitting on the floor coloring

puppies with a young boy and girl who couldn't have been much older than eight or nine years old. Hemi was crashed out not far from her, sitting with his back against the wall with one small child curled fast asleep under each of his massive arms.

It was somewhat comforting to see the children resting, relaxed and safe under the care and supervision of two people I trusted most. But my heart still felt heavy knowing what they'd been through, and I knew it would remain so for quite some time.

"Honestly, Detective Klein, that's a long story—and one we should discuss out of earshot of the children."

The message I wished to convey registered plainly on my face, a dark and pained subtext that gave Detective Klein pause. "Considering everything you've told me and all I've seen, I suppose I'm obligated to give you the benefit of the doubt. But I'll have one hell of a time explaining this to my lieutenant. Never mind the field day the press is going to have with this story."

"I understand that," I said. "But once you hear the story I'm about to share, you'll know why this needs to be handled so delicately."

AFTER LOTS of discussion and deliberation, we managed to convince Detective Klein that a measure of subterfuge and misdirection would be necessary in returning the children to their families. At first, she wasn't on board with faking evidence and lying to her superiors, not to mention filing false police reports. But after we pointed out how difficult it would be to explain the involvement of myself, Maeve, Hemi, Bells, and the fae, she then agreed to follow our plan.

Bells called in a team of fixers from The Cold Iron Circle—

specialists they employed who were skilled both in magic and in forensics. They quickly removed all the bodies that wouldn't jibe with Detective Klein's report, and made the gunshot wounds look like they were made with the detective's sidearm. Finally, with Maeve's assistance, they removed all trace of any forensic evidence that might have pointed to the involvement of persons other than Klein.

The story we were going with was simple: Detective Klein had received an anonymous tip that some of the abducted children were being held in a warehouse on the outskirts of Houston. Admittedly foregoing protocol regarding jurisdiction and cooperation with local law enforcement authorities, the detective had followed up on the lead solo, thinking that it was probably a dead end. She would report that she'd had every intention of involving local authorities if the lead panned out.

Upon arrival at the warehouse, she'd heard screams from inside the building. Being in a cell phone dead zone—a technical detail Maeve was able to arrange with some minor spell work—she was unable to call for back-up and decided to enter the building alone. Inside, she was attacked by unknown persons, returned gunfire, and killed two assailants. Upon a quick search of the building, she'd located the children, who had apparently been drugged to keep them compliant during their abduction and subsequent unlawful detainment.

Of course, the detail about drugging the children would hopefully quell any doubts or questions regarding their case of mass amnesia. The fixers from the Circle planted evidence to support that detail when the forensics teams swooped in to investigate the case. I was nervous, because I knew federal law enforcement would soon be involved; however, Maeve assured me that she had contacts and people working for her at the highest levels in all federal agencies in the area. Her assurances were enough to calm my nerves and convince me that we weren't putting Detective Klein's career at risk.

After it was done, Maeve opened a portal back to Austin. Leaving the premises in that manner would ensure that we left no trace of our presence, and no one would see us leaving the building before Klein called in the incident. We left the moving truck that we'd arrived in where it was, and the Circle fixers planted forensic evidence taken from the children inside the vehicle. It would look as though the truck had been used to transport the children during their abductions.

"Meh, it was stolen anyway," Sal informed me. "One of the boys nabbed it from a nearby neighborhood a few weeks back. We'd been keeping it hidden in case you found Little Sal. Figured we'd need to mobilize the whole crew on short notice."

"I appreciate the faith you placed in me," I replied.

He scowled, but I could tell his heart wasn't in it. "Druid, I know we had our differences in the past. But I won't forget what you did for me and Little Sal." He reached out and clasped forearms with me. Then he nodded, picked up Little Sal, and followed the rest of Rocko's crew through the portal.

Maeve cast a spell over the children to gently put them to sleep, and then she stood next to the portal, waiting for me to pass through. "Colin, you haven't much time. I might be a faery queen, but I do have my limits."

I stood shoulder to shoulder with Detective Klein, getting one last glance at the sleeping children. "Klein, do you think they'll be okay?"

"Colin, I know you're beating yourself up for about a dozen reasons right now. But I gotta tell you—you're nothing less than a flippin' hero. And I'm glad I was wrong about you."

I shook her hand. "I sincerely hope you don't get in trouble for this, Detective."

"Not gonna happen, kid. I'm one of the few female detectives the department has, and City Hall is all about the diversity. I might even get a promotion out of this—even if my lieutenant is going to chew my ass royal. Now, get outta here so I can call this in and get these kids back to their families."

With that final reassurance from Detective Klein, I headed for the portal. She was already on the phone as I stepped through, and I turned to watch as Maeve followed and closed the portal behind her. We were standing in the garden behind her home. None of the others were present, which surprised me, since they had gone through just seconds before.

"Your friends are all safe and sound. I sent them elsewhere and directed us here so I can have a moment to speak with you alone."

I cocked an eyebrow and tilted my head. "Is this when the other shoe drops?"

The stern look she gave me put me in my place. Maeve had gone out of her way to assist our efforts and the children. After all the help she'd given, it was rude of me to question her motives.

"I take that back. You're the last person I should be rude to at the moment."

Her expression softened. "There is no other shoe to drop. I merely brought you here to tell you how proud I am of you. And also, to advise you to take caution in how you share the information we've obtained with the Pack."

Just then, my cell phone started going crazy. Since Maeve had fried the cell phone towers near the warehouse, I hadn't had service for several hours. A quick glance told me I had about a half-dozen missed calls, all from Samson.

"Hold that thought, Maeve. I have a feeling that my relationship with the Pack is about to get very complicated."

21

The fae queen's expression was grave. "It's Samson, isn't it?"

"How'd you know?"

"Call it intuition gleaned from many centuries of dealing with intrigue and subterfuge. I suspect Sonny knows we found the warehouse and the children, and he has decided to make his move."

I looked at the first text from Samson.

-Mutiny. Fallyn missing. Stay away from clubhouse.-

"Shit."

Maeve's eyes narrowed. "Then it's as bad as I suspected. I take it Samson has instructed you to stay far away from the Pack for the moment?"

"Got it in one. But how did Sonny know we found the warehouse?"

Maeve shook her head. "Such details are inconsequential. The priority at present is to contact Samson to determine his status, as well as yours with the Pack."

I scrolled through the texts Samson had sent me, which detailed all that had transpired in my absence. "No need. Samson says he'll be out of contact for the next several hours, and that I should stay off the grid. Something about a conclave, and my being excommunicated from the Pack."

Maeve crossed her arms and rested her chin on one hand. "It appears that Sonny has played his trump card. I would assume that he called a gathering of the Pack, either to challenge Samson's authority, or to get you removed from the ranks of prospective members. Or both."

I listened to the voicemails Samson had left. "Huh. These messages are pretty much a play-by-play of Sonny's every move over the last twelve hours. Dammit! How am I supposed to learn how to control my change now that I've been kicked out of the Pack?"

Maeve cleared her throat. "You're overlooking an important detail about how the Pack deals with shifters who fail to control their change."

"You mean the whole thing where they kill them? But I haven't even completed my training—surely that has to count for something, right?"

Maeve tapped a finger on her chin. "It all depends on how much power Samson has retained within the Pack. If he remains in control, even nominally, then they should still allow you to attempt the trials. Operating on that assumption, that means you need to disappear while you receive further training in controlling your change."

I yawned and rubbed my eyes. "You know what, Maeve? Going to the Pack and Samson for help was a really shitty idea."

"I said precisely the same thing to both Samson and Finnegas, and asked them to discourage you from going that route."

I knuckled my forehead. "Since when did you guys get so chummy? Never mind, it's not important right now. Just tell me what you think I should do."

"Now that Sonny is certain you know of his involvement in

the child abductions? And that you have witnesses and means to prove it? Well, I assume he'll try to sway as many Pack members as possible to his cause. He likely sees you as the greatest threat to his plan to challenge Samson for the leadership of the Pack, and he'll attempt to kill you without leaving any trace of evidence leading back to him.

"Thus, he'll send his underlings to do his dirty work. Rest assured, werewolves are searching the city for you right now. However, Pack law says you get a chance to prove you can control your change. Stay alive until your trial, and you have nothing to worry about."

I rolled my eyes and threw my hands in the air. "Great... so all I have to do is dodge a few dozen badass werewolf bikers, who all know where I live, where I like to hang out, and whose houses to stake out to find me." I glanced at an imaginary watch on my wrist. "I give myself—oh, about four hours on the streets of Austin before I end up in a very public and bloody brawl with members of the Pack."

"My dear boy," she sighed. "I have the situation in hand..."

The distinctive howls of two werewolves on the hunt cut Maeve off, followed by a huge crash that caused the ground to shake beneath our feet.

Maeve cocked an ear toward the ruckus occurring in front of her home. "Well, it seems as though the wolves have found you already—along with my gargoyles. My, but Sonny is getting bold. He must want very badly to see you dead."

The crashing noises were getting closer. "So, Maeve, are we gonna fight, or flee?"

"You will flee, while Adelard and Lothair deal with our intruders. They might think little of you, but they'll give their lives to protect my home." She winked at me. "Although, I don't think that will be necessary in this case. While werewolves heal quickly, they tend to be very squishy."

She waved a hand, and a portal opened in the garden a few feet from us. "I'm sending you to someplace safe. Run along and enjoy a few days of peace. My staff will see to your every need. I'll be sending someone to assist you shortly."

"But—"

"There's no time. I can assure you, Ms. Becerra and Mr. Waara will come to no harm in your absence." She snatched my phone from my hands, then shooed me toward the portal. "They'll be able to track you if you have this—and besides, you won't need it where you're going. Now please, leave, before I'm forced to physically intercede on your behalf. As it stands, I will have to spend a considerable amount of time convincing my council that we are not at war with the Pack."

"All right, I'm going. But one of these days I want you to show me how to do this portal thing."

"Certainly—just as soon as you have a few decades to spare." She shoved me through the portal with a great deal more strength than I would've ever suspected she possessed.

───────

WHEN MAEVE HAD SAID "SOMEPLACE SAFE," I had assumed that she meant a cabin tucked in the woods, far outside of Austin where no one would find me. I got it half right. In fact, Maeve transported me directly into the presidential suite at a full-blown retreat and lodge located on the northwest side of Lyndon B. Johnson Lake. Apparently, she owned the place outright. True to her word, several staff members bustled into the suite within moments of my arrival.

Thirty minutes later, I was freshly showered, fed, and resting on the enormous king-sized bed, watching Jack Hanna play with a pair of leopard cubs on TV. Earlier, the hotel staff had brought me room service consisting of Belgian waffles, thick cut bacon, fluffy scrambled eggs, and plenty of toast, jam, butter, and real maple syrup. Even though I was exhausted, I felt guilty for sitting on my hands while Sonny and his goons were still at large.

But, running off after them would likely result in a full-on ríastrad incident. I'd attack them, they'd nearly kill me, and then I'd transform and my Hyde-side would cause widespread chaos and destruction. Not cool. So, I decided to get some rest. Eventually, the huge meal and lack of sleep took their toll, and I was dozing off when a knock on the door roused me.

"Go away," I yelled. "I'm about to go into a food coma."

Dr. Ganesh's British-accented voice replied from the other side of the door. "Mr. McCool, I was told you were expecting me. However, I can come back later if you like."

I groaned and rolled out of bed, pulling a thick white terrycloth robe around my body. I stumbled to the door and looked through the peephole, just to make sure it was the doctor and not an impostor. Assured that it was indeed Dr. Ganesh waiting outside the door, I opened it and rubbed my eyes.

"Sorry for being rude, but I had a rough night. Come in." I stepped aside as he entered. He wore dark gray slacks, polished black dress shoes, a black leather belt, and a golf polo. He looked as though he had gotten a lot more sleep than I had, and appeared to be quite chipper despite the early hour.

"My apologies, Mr. McCool. While I understand that you've experienced quite a lot over the last twenty-four hours, we have work to do. Maeve filled me in on the details. In fact, it's all the talk among the shifter community in Austin. The Pack is cleanly split in two, with Sonny taking a slight lead in the number of Pack members who have chosen to take his side.

"Samson retains enough power to ensure that you'll still be allowed to attempt your trial. However, my sources inside the Pack inform me Sonny is pushing to hold your trial in less than a week's time. With Samson's daughter missing, he'll likely be too preoccupied searching for her to exert much of his dwindling influence to move the date back."

I sucked on my teeth as I considered the implications. "Hmmm... So what you're saying is, I have to accomplish in a few days what was supposed to take me months. Think it's possible?"

"Possible? Yes. Probable? No. However, I know something that you don't. And that is what the trial consists of. Would you like to hear it?"

I shut the door and locked it, then flopped into an easy chair. "Aw, what the hell. Thrill me, Doc."

"Robert Downey, Jr. said it better," the doctor quipped with a grin. "But points for making an *Iron Man* reference during such a trying time. Now, here's why you don't need time on your side. Traditionally, the exact nature of the trial that the shifter goes through to prove they can control their change is kept hidden from them. The reason for this is so they take their training seriously."

"I'd say getting my guts ripped out and then being bled half to death every Saturday night for the last few weeks was pretty serious. I mean, it's kinda hard to show up for that sort of thing and consider it slacking."

Dr. Ganesh sat across from me on a couch. "I don't disagree. And honestly, I believe the Pack's methods to be brutal and excessive. Especially when you consider that all you have to do to prove that you can control your change is to do just that— keep from changing."

"Dr. Ganesh, I don't understand. I thought I had to fight a bunch of werewolves and survive, or something equally insane."

Ganesh laughed. "Oh no, nothing that dramatic. In fact, most of the drama happens long before you ever make it to your trial. All you have to do to demonstrate to the Pack that you are in control of your ability to shift—in other words, in control of your beast—is to resist changing in the face of temptation."

"Could you be more specific? Because I'm going on about thirty hours without sleep, and it's starting to catch up with me."

"Certainly. The test is simple: they lock you up in the Shaft with a baby goat for three days and nights. You get no food or water. If you don't kill the goat, you pass. Lose control, shift, and slaughter the poor creature, and you fail. In which case..."

"In which case, the Pack kills you."

Ganesh inclined his head. "Just so. However, I believe that the nature of your beast will work in your favor during your trial. You see, Colin, your beast isn't driven by the same sort of prey drive that most shifters possess. In fact, from what I understand, you only shift when you are on the brink of death. Is that correct?"

"Pretty much," I responded.

"Which means that you're home free. The trial is going to be a breeze for you. Even so, I think it's prudent for us to spend the next few days productively. During our short time together, I intend to do my best to teach you how to control your change, and resist it or call upon it at will."

"I don't know, Doc. Samson did his damnedest to get me to that point over the last several weeks. Best I could manage was to hold it off with a hell of an assist on his part. But if you think you can help me, I'm willing to try anything. Because I need to have control over my Hyde-side, if I'll ever..." I let my voice trail off, not sure if I wanted to let Dr. Ganesh in on my personal shit.

He raised a hand and stood. "Say no more; your motivations are your own. I am merely here to help you learn to control your beast, in whatever way I can. Now, get some sleep. Tonight, we begin."

Without another word, he exited the room. I sat in silence for a few moments, trying hard not to brood. But it was a wasted effort; within minutes of Dr. Ganesh's departure, I fell fast asleep in the chair.

I SLEPT AWAY most of the day, and woke up hungry, with the phone next to my bed flashing. I picked it up and retrieved my messages. One was from some random fae, telling me that Maeve had everything under control back in Austin; Hemi and Bells were safe, and they had been informed that I was in hiding. The second message was from Ganesh, saying he'd meet me at my room after nightfall.

After another shower and more room service, I did some stretches, working out a few kinks that had cropped up since the previous night's events. I'd had nightmares while I slept, all about the children, and they had left me tense and irritable. The last thing I wanted to do right now was hide; I'd have much rather been hunting down Sonny and his crew, and taking them out for their involvement with the abductions and trafficking operation.

But, ríastrad problems. I plopped down in an easy chair, flipped on the TV, and tried to take my mind off it while I waited for Dr. Ganesh.

True to his word, he showed up just after dark. "Well, it seems you are well-fed, and hopefully well-rested. Let us begin, shall we? Sit, please."

"You mean we're not going somewhere isolated? Far away from other people?"

He smiled. "This is not necessary. Most of what we will do involves little in the way of violence. You will present no harm to others while we work."

I sat cater-cornered to him on the couch, while he took the easy chair I had been occupying earlier. "No offense, Dr.

Ganesh, but you haven't seen that side of me. When it gets out, I can't control it."

"Can't, or won't?"

I bristled at what he was insinuating. "Trust me, if I could control it, I would. Once I change, it's like I'm a passenger in my own body. I have almost no control."

He leaned forward with his elbows on his knees. "Colin, what if I were to tell you that your ability to control your beast is mostly a psychological process, rather than a magical one?"

I sniffed and cleared my throat. "Well, I'd say you were flipping crazy. See, I wasn't born like this. My change was brought on by a curse, by fae magic. There's nothing psychological about it, except in the aftermath when I lose control."

"But you are still aware of what's going on after you change, correct?"

"Absolutely. It's horrifying. I can see what's happening, but I have no way to stop it."

He stabbed a finger at me. "That's where you're mistaken. The reason you have no control when you transform is because you're allowing the beast to take control."

I began to protest, but Dr. Ganesh leaned forward and held up his hands to silence me. "Now, it's certainly not your fault, and I'm not blaming you. No one ever told you what to expect or how to control the change. But, to gain the control you seek, there is an important truth you must accept. This truth is the crux, the key to developing control as a shifter. And this is something that weretigers, my kind, are taught from the time we are very young."

"What, that I am 'one with the universe'?" I replied with acid in my voice.

He held up a finger, like a teacher recognizing a particularly brilliant answer from a pupil. "Close! It is that you are one with your beast."

My hands curled into fists in my lap. "No. No way. That thing and I are nothing alike."

"On the contrary, that thing and you are one and the same. You see, when a human becomes a shifter, it's different from being born as such. Whether you are infected by another shifter, or you develop therianthropy from a curse, the result is the same. Magic alters your gene structure, in such a way that your body, mind, and spirit are conjoined with bestial magic. I was born this way, and you were made as you are by magic. Yet, all that magic did was awaken some latent genetic code that allows you to tap into shifter magic."

"But I don't turn into an animal, or an animal-human hybrid. I become—"

"You become a hybrid of a human and a Fomorian. That is your curse, but it is also a part of you, now. And by denying it, you remain separate from that other side. Thus, the beast-nature remains in control after you shift."

He waited patiently as I mulled over what he was saying. "If that's the case—and I'm not saying it is—but if that's so, then how do I learn to stay in control after I transform?"

The doctor's smile faded, and his voice became more serious. "The solution is simple. You must reconcile your two sides, so they become as one—without giving up control to the beast."

22

It took Dr. Ganesh quite a while to convince me that my Hyde-side was as much a part of me as the body I was born with. Well, perhaps I should qualify that statement—I couldn't completely accept that my evil alter-ego was just another aspect of my personality and being. However, I could at least accept that I needed to reconcile with it to learn to control it.

What he was saying made sense to me; it was no different than learning to control my natural magical talent. Finnegas had once informed me that the reason why I was able to use magic was because I had just the slightest bit of fae blood running through my veins. Apparently, this was the way it was for all human magic users; every single one of us had some genetic connection to the fae. That genetic link was what allowed us to see, harness, and control magic.

So, it wasn't much of a leap to believe that when Fuamnach tampered with my genetic code, she'd created a means by which I could manipulate a different form of magic: shifter magic. And, as Dr. Ganesh explained, whether that magic caused me to shift into an animal or some Fomorian nightmare, it was still *my* magic to control.

Now it was time to get down to business. I lay on the couch in the suite, eyes closed and my hands clasped over my stomach. I listened to Dr. Ganesh's instructions as he guided me through the process of learning to control my beast. He spoke to me in a calm, soothing voice, explaining the philosophy behind his approach.

"Colin, the first step will be finding that place within yourself where you and the beast coexist. To this point, you and your beast have been in a battle for control of your body whenever you have found yourself on the brink of death. Due to your weakened state, you were unable to exert any control over that other side of yourself. So naturally, it took control, shifted into the form it needed to protect you both, and then acted by instinct to do so."

I open one eye to glance at him. "So, what you're saying is that all this time my Hyde-side has been trying to protect me?"

"In a manner of speaking, yes. But you have to understand that your beast—any 'thrope's beast, actually—operates on the level of a wild animal, or in your case, a violent fae creature. The beast knows only self-preservation and survival. It doesn't act based on morals or any social contract. It only knows how to kill, eat, and live. Left to its own devices, the beast is always an incredibly destructive and dangerous force."

"But once I confront it, won't it fight me for control?"

"Well... perhaps." He settled into his chair and crossed his legs, clasping both hands over his knee. "But let me ask you a question. Can you be at war with yourself?"

I knew why he asked that question. If my beast was indeed part of me, of who I was as a person, then the only reason the beast and I struggled for control was because I chose to be at war with that part of my nature.

"In many ways, Colin, what we're doing is somewhat similar to personality reintegration therapy. At present, you and the beast are split, and when one side takes over, the other side takes a back seat. We need to create some kind of harmony between you and that other, bestial side of you, so you can gain control after you shift. But based on my experiences growing up among therianthropes, I believe that the hardest part of this process will not be harmonizing with your beast. Rather, it will be forgiving yourself for all the things you've done when you let that other side of you take control."

I'd already considered that I was ultimately responsible for every horrible thing that happened when I let my Hyde-side take control. What Dr. Ganesh was suggesting to me was nothing new, as I'd been blaming myself for Jesse's death since the day it happened. Whether I'd be able to forgive myself— today or at some time in the distant future—well, that remained to be seen.

Right now, mission number one was vengeance: for Jesse, for the children we rescued, and for everyone else in my life that had been hurt by the fae. That required achieving some level of harmony with my beast, so I could control my ríastrad and access the power of Balor's Eye.

"Dr. Ganesh, I accepted responsibility for my actions long ago. I know I can't change the past, but I can act in the present to change the future. You just tell me what I need to do to kiss and make up with my Hyde-side, and I'll do it."

Ganesh remained quiet for several heartbeats. "Very well then—let us begin."

———

THE DOCTOR TOOK me through a guided meditation that was a sort of self-hypnosis. I soon realized that the exercise was quite similar to those Finnegas had taught me when I'd first started using magic.

When I'd begun studying spellcraft, I'd had to learn to recognize my magic and isolate it, before I could channel it into spells and cantrips. The process was painstakingly slow at first, but now it was as natural as breathing. Knowing there was some crossover between what I'd learned previously and what Dr. Ganesh was teaching me gave me confidence that I desperately needed.

Dr. Ganesh had already explained what I had to do, so I tuned out his voice and began controlling my breathing, slowing my heart rate and triggering the mental state that was most conducive to complex spellcasting. Being in that place allowed a spellcaster to bridge the gap between the physical and the ethereal; this was essential for tapping into any significant magical power source or reservoir.

But as I went deeper into my trance, I was unable to access the void where my consciousness resided when my ríastrad took over. I shook my head in frustration.

"It's not working, Dr. Ganesh. I'm not there yet."

"Then you'll have to go deeper. Don't fight it. Relax, and focus on slowing your breathing even further, then allow yourself to fall into the void where your other self resides."

I did as he asked. I quieted my mind and surrendered to the journey inside myself. At first I counted my breaths, then I allowed my focus to drift. As my breathing and heart rate slowed even further, I slipped deeper inside myself until I was floating in the Void.

Being in that non-place again was frightening at first, but it was also peaceful there. As long as I avoided focusing on the vast emptiness of it, I averted panic and was able to relax. I floated in that state, oblivious to the passage of time and the presence of my physical body until something *else* arrived. My alter ego appeared in that vast nothingness, and we stood—or floated, I suppose—face-to-face.

The creature eyed me, and we maintained a quiet detente for an inestimable length of time. Then, he spoke, with a voice that rasped like a whetstone drawn across a rusted blade.

"You have no place here. Leave, while you are still able."

Despite the verbal warning, it made no move to follow through on the threat. For that reason I said nothing, wondering if this other side of me really saw us as two separate entities. I myself questioned whether we really were two facets of the same being. Yet, the longer I observed the creature in front of me, the more that theory proved itself to be possible.

Upon seeing that I wasn't going to respond, the creature became silent, fuming as he paced in the emptiness between us. All the while he kept his eyes on me, glowering from beneath his protruding brow, and bared sharp, crooked teeth. He clearly hated me, and I wondered why he didn't attack. Then, Dr. Ganesh's recent words echoed back to me.

Can you be at war with yourself?

Suddenly, I realized this was the first time I had faced this other side of myself without seeing it as an adversary or enemy. In the past, it had always appeared as an invader, a trespasser within. But after my earlier conversation with Ganesh, I had at least partially accepted the possibility that this beast was a part of me.

And, that meant that I was in control. It also meant that I was safe. I looked at the creature with new eyes, no longer repulsed by his presence. I took in every scar, lump, deformity, and callus, every warped and twisted angle of his mutated physique. I gazed at his humped back, his limping gait, and the almost simian way he moved. I looked at his face and saw the usual hatred there. But beneath it, there was more.

What I saw there was fear.

Fear was an emotion that I knew well, one that had been a constant companion of mine for years. In truth, fear was what drove me. Fear of losing the people I cared for most. Fear of not being there to save them from danger. Fear of pain, fear of loss, fear of heartache, fear of loneliness.

When I looked in the creature's eyes and saw that he was afraid, that's when I knew. He was me.

AS I CAME to that realization, the creature stopped pacing and began to back away from me, with limited success. Despite the vast emptiness in which we floated, it was as if he hit an invisible wall. My Hyde-side scrambled frantically to escape, but his efforts were futile. I took a step forward in the emptiness and closed the gap between us.

As I did, the creature flinched and growled as he shied away.

"It's okay," I whispered. "I think I finally understand."

"Stay away from me," he muttered.

I took another step.

"No, no, no, no... you can't! I won't allow it. You're too weak to protect us!"

I continue to approach as my beast did all he could to avoid me. First, he squatted, turning partially away while hunching his shoulders and covering his head. Then he continued to make himself as small as possible, curling into a ball on his side. With my every step, the creature appeared even more frightened and pathetic.

Finally, he began to change. At first, the changes were subtle; a shift of the bone structure here, a smoothing of the skin there. But the closer I got to the creature, the more rapidly the changes occurred, until soon I towered over him as he cowered and mewled at my feet. But at this point, it was no longer a creature at all, but instead a person I knew very well; in fact, it was someone I'd lived with all my life. The small quivering heap before me was now no Fomorian nightmare, and it certainly was no cold-blooded killer. I stood looking down at myself, only a younger version of me. This was the pudgy, uncoordinated, insecure Colin McCool, who had emerged soon after my father had died.

I realized that for years, I'd hated this kid. I'd hated his weakness, his vulnerability, and his inability to protect himself. I hated that he'd cried himself to sleep every night in the weeks and months after Dad passed away. I hated that he'd let the other children pick on him, that he was picked last for teams at school, and that the only girl who would talk to him was a skinny little tomboy who was just as much of an outcast as he was.

The sight of that small, frightened boy broke my heart. I looked at my former self, the scared little guy I used to be, and felt nothing but compassion for him... and for myself. My emotional epiphany brought the nature of Fuamnach's curse into crystalline focus. She had taken all my fear, all my self-loathing, all my loneliness, and used it to fuel her curse.

That's why when the ríastrad had taken over, I'd been powerless against it. I'd already been at odds with that side of myself, with that scared little boy I kept deep down inside who was still afraid of his own shadow. And instead of having empathy and compassion for a lonely child who had tragically lost his father at an early age, I'd had nothing but contempt. Somehow, she'd seen right into the deepest part of me and used my innermost fears to destroy me... and Jesse.

But no more. I knelt before the child and extended my hand.

"Shhh, don't cry. I'm not going to hurt you."

My younger self looked up at me over a tear-soaked arm. "B-b-but you h-hate me."

I shook my head. "I don't hate you," I whispered. "How can I hate myself?"

I reached out to the little boy and touched his shoulder. Initially, he cringed away, but I remained still until he relaxed and relented. As he did, I gathered him in an embrace and felt a warmth and comfort that I had not allowed myself to feel for many, many years. Then a bright light suffused us both, increasing in intensity until the Void faded away, and I returned to reality.

* * *

MOMENTS LATER, I opened my eyes to find I was still lying on the couch in the suite. The first rays of dawn were creeping through the windows, and Dr. Ganesh was sitting in the same spot he'd been in the night previous, observing me beneath hooded eyes.

"Geez, Doc, have you been up all night?"

He smiled and rubbed his eyes. "Mostly," he yawned. "Although I must confess that I did take a catnap here and there. You had me concerned, you know—most shifters don't stay under that long when they first confront their beast. I take it you had quite the inner battle."

I sat up and swung my legs off the couch, leaning forward and taking a moment to rub the sleep from my own eyes. "I guess you could say that, although I don't know if you could rightly classify it as a battle. And, in retrospect, I would hardly call that other side of myself a beast."

The doctor's brows lifted slightly in surprise or puzzlement. "You don't say? Well, I suppose it would be different in your case, considering that the nature of the creature you shift into is fae— or, well, Fomorian—and not a natural predator."

I closed my eyes and took a deep breath, letting it out slowly as I attempted to put a name to what I was feeling inside. Then I realized what I felt was a foreign, once familiar state of being. I chuckled and leaned back against the couch, sighing with relief.

"What is it? What happened to you while you were under? Obviously, you've experienced something profound."

"Peace," I stated simply. "For the first time in years, I'm at peace."

Dr. Ganesh was grinning from ear to ear, his eyes bright and friendly. "That makes me very happy, Colin—very happy indeed."

"Me too, Doc. Me too."

23

After breakfast, Dr. Ganesh and I agreed that we should both get some rest and then reconvene later in the day. The sense of peace I'd felt earlier didn't last, because as soon as I thought about Sonny and his goons, I got angry. I spent the remainder of the day alternating between pacing the floor and trying to nap, with little success. Ganesh returned later that afternoon, and we now sat in the living area of the suite, discussing the next steps in my training.

"Our primary concern now, Colin, is to determine just how much control you currently have over your change. In some cases, 'thropes have difficulty triggering their change, even after passing their trials."

"I honestly have no idea how to trigger my change, Doc," I said with a sigh. "The only times that I've transformed have been when I was about to die, and I don't care to engage in any self-harm at the moment. There has to be an easier way for me to trigger and gain control of my transformation."

Dr. Ganesh smiled and raised one hand in the air, finger extended. "There is, in fact. I was going to suggest..."

A sudden whoosh of air interrupted our conversation as

Maeve stepped into the room through one of her portals. She wore tailored jeans, a fashionably expensive pair of hiking boots, a fitted t-shirt, and a high-tech, weatherproof hooded jacket. As always, Maeve looked to be the epitome of upper-middle-class style. The portal remained open behind her, revealing the dense scrub and harsh, rocky landscape of the Balcones Wildlife Refuge through the opening.

"I hate to interrupt, but it seems that our timetable has moved up. I sincerely hope you've made progress over the last twenty-four hours, because we're out of time."

I stood up. "Out of time? Has something happened to Samson and Fallyn?"

"Not to my knowledge, although I'm as clueless regarding the disposition of Samson's daughter as you." She glanced back and forth between the doctor and me. "Now, have you made any progress in learning to control your ability to shift?"

"Yes, we've made some progress—but I certainly wouldn't say I have complete control yet."

Maeve glanced at Dr. Ganesh, and then back to me. "And just how would you define your current ability to control your transformation?"

Dr. Ganesh and I spoke over each other as we scrambled to respond.

"He has little control..."

"I don't think I'm ready..."

"—which is to say that..."

"—to confront the Pack right now..."

"—he has none at all."

"—because I don't know how to change yet."

Maeve stood with her arms crossed and heels together, tapping her foot as she listened to our babbling. Then she raised one hand and extended it toward us, fingers spread. "We don't have time for this. Colin, whether you are ready or not, the wolves are calling for you to complete your trial immediately. Sonny has forced Samson's hand."

I slumped in my chair. "Oh, holy hell. Dr. Ganesh barely led me through the process of coming to terms with my beast last night. I don't even know if I can change yet or not."

The doctor laid a comforting hand on my forearm. "It'll be fine, Colin, because you won't need to. Remember what I told you about the trial. It's all about self-control. And since you can't force yourself to shift, then you're in no danger of failing the test. All you have to do is spend three days and nights locked up with a baby goat. If anything, Sonny has made a serious misstep by forcing the Pack to move your trial up."

"I'm not so sure," Maeve responded, "but there's no time for speculation. Once the challenge has been made by the Pack, a prospect only has a certain amount of time to appear and start their trial. I was informed a few minutes ago that the orders went out through Pack channels this morning. Colin has until nightfall to show, else the Pack will declare him a failure, and they will hunt him to the ends of the earth."

I reached for my phone out of instinct. Finding it missing, I glanced at the clock on the wall. "Well, there's still plenty of time. You can just portal me in, and bam! I walk into the Shaft, eat some snacks while I hang out with the baby goat, and then walk out three days from now, scot-free. Dr. Ganesh and I will pick up where we left off then. Piece of cake."

Maeve pinched the bridge of her nose with her thumb and forefinger. "My dear boy, why must you always be so short-sighted? If I appear to be assisting you in any way, not only could that be grounds for the Pack to declare your attempt null and void; it will also cast aspersions on Samson's leadership. It's not as though our alliance is out in the open. Many within the Pack would howl in anger if they knew their alpha was working so closely with the local fae queen."

"Still no big deal," I said with a shrug. "Just zap me in a mile or so from the Shaft, and I'll jog the rest of the way."

Maeve gave me a look that said I was about to get the dunce hat. "You obviously do not understand how Pack politics and power struggles work. Colin, have you considered how desperately Sonny wants you to fail? If you do, it will further undermine Samson's position as Pack leader, legitimizing any challenge Sonny makes to his leadership."

"Meaning...?"

"Meaning, he will have the entire area surrounded by wolves that are loyal to him. You are certain to experience great difficulty sneaking past them. If I had known that Sonny planned to have your trial moved up, I would have portaled you in before any of his wolves could have arrived. Hiding you in place would be a trifling thing—but getting you past a cordon of wolves who are actively seeking you out? Well, that's another matter entirely."

I HEARD someone snap their fingers behind me, just as a familiar voice joined our conversation. "I believe I can help the young druid with that," Click said as he walked into view.

"Click, just how long have you been lurking invisibly inside my room? And, how did you know I was even here?"

He polished his fingernails on his t-shirt and examined them with a manicurist's attention. "T'wasn't hard to figure where the queen would stick you, to keep you from the clutches of the big bad wolves. I've been here watching over you since last night."

Dr. Ganesh leaned back in his chair, a wry grin on his face. "You must have an impressive talent for stealth, to escape my notice this entire time. I wonder, what sort of fae can fool the senses of a weretiger?"

I looked to Maeve. Her eyes darkened as she glowered at the new arrival. "Yes, what sort of fae indeed. So, Click, is it? Is that what you're calling yourself these days?"

Click bowed to the queen with all the flourish and grace of a seventeenth-century courtier, then he fixed her with a knowing look. "Just so, milady—and if you're accusing me of subterfuge, well... that would be the pot calling the kettle black."

Maeve's voice took on a dangerous tone. "Enough. If this" — she hesitated, apparently searching for the right words to categorize my mysterious new ally—"this—entity—wants to assist you in sneaking past Sonny's wolves, I'll not be one to stand in his way." She fixed Click with a glare. "But mark my words—should your actions cause the druid harm, I will rescind any promise of safe conduct through my demesne that I've previously extended to you."

Click lit a cigarette with a battered Zippo lighter. He took a drag and blew smoke from the side of his mouth. "Aye, it'll be as you say. But the lad has nothing to fear from me. He's proven his worth, and deserves every bit of assistance I might provide."

Maeve and Click locked eyes for several seconds, then Maeve spoke. "So be it." Without taking her eyes off Click, she beckoned to me with one hand. "Colin, the time has come. I'll get you close enough to the location so you may arrive there on foot before the Pack's deadline. But you'll still need to get past any scouts or sentries Sonny may have posted."

She walked back to the portal. I snatched my Craneskin Bag, shaking hands with Dr. Ganesh before falling in behind her. I jabbed a thumb over my shoulder at Click. "What about him? Isn't he coming with us?"

Maeve frowned. "Oh, he can easily manage to get there on his own."

I looked back, but Click was already gone. I cocked an

eyebrow and winked at Dr. Ganesh. "Curiouser and curiouser. Wish me luck, Doc."

"Luck to you," he said. "But somehow, I doubt you'll need it."

I flashed a parting grin, and walked through the portal.

MAEVE STOOD WAITING on the other side. As I exited the portal, I spared her outfit a quick glance. "By the way, I love the new look. From HGTV to National Geographic—nice."

"One should dress appropriately for every occasion," she stated. "Also, if one of the wolves happened to spot me from a distance, they would mistake me for a hiker or park employee. Now, if you are through commenting on my choice of attire, I suggest that you head to your destination without delay."

I looked around. "Shouldn't I wait for Click?"

"I assure you, he's around here somewhere. Make sure that he disguises the Bag for you—you might need its contents later. They won't allow you to take it inside the mine. I'd hate to think what kind of trouble it may cause if it decides you're in danger and makes an attempt to assist you."

I rested a hand on the Bag as I adjusted the shoulder strap. "Good point. I'll be sure to mention it to Click. Anything else I should know before I leave?"

Maeve looked grim. "Only that you should expect treachery from Sonny and his followers. He knows you're resourceful. He'll have made plans, should you manage to evade his sentries. Do not let your guard down this evening."

I smirked. "Hey, this is me you're talking to."

Maeve's expression remained stern. "I'm fully aware, and that's what concerns me." Without another word, she stepped back through the portal and disappeared.

I got my bearings and headed toward the Shaft. As I rounded

a large oak tree, I found Click sitting on an old stump. "So, you ready to get started?"

"You have to show me how to do that disappearing and reappearing act." I grabbed my Craneskin Bag and hefted it in front of me. "Maeve said you should help me hide this from the wolves."

"The Bag I can help with, but the other thing? You're not ready, lad. Come see me in a decade or so, and we'll negotiate, magic for magic." He hopped down from the stump and brushed off the seat of his jeans. "Now, let's be off. And if you see any of the wolves along the way, pay them no mind. They'll not be able to see us or hear us—not unless I allow them."

Click strolled off into the brush and trees, and I struggled to keep up as the strange fae drifted effortlessly through seemingly impassable undergrowth. Vegetation parted as he approached, and as soon as he passed, the plants and trees closed ranks once more. I stayed close on his heels, fearing that I might be trapped if I strayed too far behind. Click whistled a lively tune as we walked, and I took that as a sign that it was okay to speak.

"What's the deal with you and Maeve?" I whispered.

He glanced over his shoulder at me. "No need to whisper," he whispered, then spoke at a normal level. "We knew each other ages ago, peripherally, and were more or less on friendly terms. But a few centuries back, the balance of power shifted in Annwyn, and I decided that I needed a vacation. So, I parlayed for safe passage through her realm."

Annwyn was the Welsh term for Underhill. I tucked that tidbit away for safe-keeping. "But why is she mad at you?"

He looked back at me and grinned. "The terms of safe passage didn't include how *long* it would take me to pass through her realm. I took a slight detour, as it were, and overstayed my welcome by a few centuries. Could happen to anyone."

I chuckled at the thought that someone had gotten the better of Maeve. "I get the feeling you're no ordinary fae."

"A bright lad, you are. But do you think the queen is any run-of-the-mill faery herself?"

"Maybe I did once. But I've come to the conclusion that Maeve is anything but typical."

Click winked and touched a finger to the side of his nose. "And you'd do well to remember that."

A few yards on, he stopped suddenly. He gestured grandly toward a wall of cedar and brush ahead of us. "Ah, here we are. I believe you'll find your destination just beyond those trees. Now, you keep calm as you enter that circle. The more confident you appear, the less likely they'll be to set upon you and tear you limb from limb."

I twisted my mouth to one side as I considered his advice. "That's... reassuring."

He waved me off. "Ah, don't mention it. Now, go do your thing." He rubbed his hands together, and his eyes sparkled in amusement. "Oh, I can't wait to see how this all turns out."

I laughed, despite myself. "You've been a helpful ally, Click."

He scowled. "Pfft... please. I like you, lad, and that's a fact—but it's not as though I'm doing this for you. Any help I've given is payback for those bastards who took Little Sal. Besides, I prefer to bet on the underdog."

Click reached forward and parted the foliage with a gentle sweep of his arm. "Enough chatter. It's time to show these wolves what you're made of."

I wasn't sure how I felt about having another of the elder fae taking an interest in me. Deciding it was best to avoid looking a gift horse in the mouth, I nodded to him and slipped through the gap.

I EXITED the trees and stepped directly into the crowd of Pack members who had gathered around the entrance to the Shaft. They milled about in small groups, conversing with each other quietly. I could have cut the tension with a knife.

As I made my way through the 'thropes in attendance, the Pack gradually became aware of my presence as I jostled my way through their midst. Nervous conversation turned into a low murmuring, which gradually rose in volume as more wolves noticed my arrival.

Samson stood near the entrance to the Shaft, flanked by Sledge and Trina. On the other side was Sonny, joined by Klaus and Jaeger. Anger flashed across his face as he spotted me, but he quickly masked it with a smart-ass grin.

"Ah, so the druid finally decides to grace us with his presence," he sneered.

Sledge's deep voice rumbled opposite of Sonny's crew. "Not such a coward after all—is he, Sonny?"

"Coward or no, it remains to be seen whether he can pass his trial." Sonny looked past me as his eyes swept across the gathered wolves. "And we all know the penalty for those who can't meet the standard."

I glanced around, searching for some sign of Fallyn, but she was nowhere to be seen. I waited until Samson looked at me and mouthed, "Where's Fallyn?" He shook his head, and the worried look on his face told me all I needed to know. I figured Sonny and his goons were holding her ransom as leverage against Samson.

That pissed me off.

Samson locked eyes with me, holding my gaze for a moment and then nodding. He raised both arms in the air, calling the Pack to silence. "Enough! The druid may have been expelled from the Pack, but he still has the right to complete his trial and prove he's not a liability."

Despite what Maeve had said about Samson's tenuous hold on his position as alpha, he didn't seem to lack any authority with the wolves present. His voice still held the same timbre of command as always, and the gathered 'thropes hushed at the sound of his words. Even Sonny clamped his jaw shut, choosing to remain silent and let events run their course.

Samson continued. "The trial is as it always has been. The Druid must spend three nights in the Shaft, without killing or spilling blood. Should he fail, the Pack will spare him no mercy. Thus wills the Pack."

Every wolf present echoed Samson's words. "Thus wills the Pack."

The alpha spoke again, this time addressing me directly. "Colin McCool, come forward."

I did as he commanded, and approached the door to the Shaft. I stopped in front of Samson, keeping my eyes lowered. I pointedly ignored Sonny as he whispered jokes to his goons, which they answered with barely concealed laughter.

"Survive the trial, shed no blood, and take no life, and you will have proved your right of existence to the Pack."

"Well, let's get this party started," I said with a smirk. I turned and spat at Sonny's feet. "I'll settle up with you when I get out." The beta wolf's face spasmed in anger, and he snarled at me in response.

I cracked my neck, rolled my shoulders out, and strolled calmly into the Shaft. A few yards inside, I paused to listen to the loud, familiar clank of the door being shut and locked behind me.

"Well, I guess it's just me and you, goat," I stated to no one in particular.

That's when I heard the thrum of a bowstring, right before intense pain lanced through my chest. I looked down to where a thick, clothyard shaft had sprouted just to the right of my breastbone. The shaft vibrated before quivering to a stop. I noted the dappled pattern along its length, and the bright spiral fletching at the end.

Fucking fae, I thought. *No one else fletches an arrow like that.*

Blood seeped from around the wound, slowly soaking my shirt. I fell to one knee, barely catching myself with a hand. "Aw, shit," I coughed. "This was a new shirt."

Then I tumbled backward, losing consciousness as my head struck the hard limestone surface of the mine.

"Gotta admit I'm a little disappointed, druid. They told me you were a lot tougher."

As I regained consciousness, I felt someone grab under my armpits and drag me across the floor. My eyes were sticky, the way they might have felt after about four hours of sleep on a twelve-pack hangover. Every movement was agony, and as my mystery companion propped me up against the wall of the mine, I winced at the searing pain in my chest.

I felt weak and dizzy, and it took me a moment to get my bearings when I opened my eyes. The first thing I saw was one of Sonny's goons, Claw, hunched over me with a fae-crafted bow in his hands. He pressed his finger against the end of the arrow in my chest and twirled it in small circles, making me scream.

I reached into my Craneskin Bag, searching for my Glock. I wanted to plant a silver bullet right between his eyes. But then I remembered the rules of the trial. If I drew blood or killed anything, I failed. That would result in permanent enmity between the Pack and me, a literal death sentence. I decided that if Claw wanted me dead, he would have ripped my head off already. For posterity's sake, I kept a firm grip on the pistol, keeping it hidden inside the Bag.

Claw squatted on his heels next to me. "I'm tempted to kill you right now," he sneered. "But Sonny is bound and determined to see you fail your trial and make a fool of Samson. So I'll just leave you here, to either choke on your own blood, or shift and meet the surprise I left for you. Either way, you die. Guess I'll have to settle for that."

He tweaked the tip of the arrow one more time, sending waves of pain through my body. I coughed reflexively, blowing flecks of blood all over Claw's boots and jeans. He stood and spat on me. "I'll be seeing you, druid. Like I said, I left you a little surprise back in the torture chamber. I'm sure you'll find it, just as soon as your beast comes out to play."

A portal opened up behind him, identical to those I had seen Maeve cast many times over the last few weeks. Through the portal, the sun was setting over a field that had been left fallow after the harvest. Claw stepped through, sparing me one last look. I lifted one shaky hand and flipped him off, right before the portal winked out of existence.

I sat against the wall for a few moments, wheezing and choking on my own blood while I took stock of my situation. Things did not look good. It was more than likely that I had a collapsed lung, I was going into shock, and I'd soon lose consciousness again. And the bitch of it was, I didn't even know if my transformation would take over to save me once I hit the brink of death.

Even if it did, I still had no idea if I could control it yet. If not, I'd kill the goat and fail this whole stupid trial. I reflected on what a dumbass idea it was to go to Samson for help in the first place. But there was nothing to do for it now; I had made choices that led to this, and now I had to deal with the consequences.

The way I saw it, I had two options. I could die, and then

hope that my Hyde-side would take over before I bit the big one. Or, I could try to survive the next three days with an arrow in my chest, with only the food and water I kept inside my Craneskin Bag. Either way, I was screwed. It was times like these I wished I was better at healing magic.

I must've drifted off again, because I heard someone's voice calling for me in the dark. "Must be dreaming," I mumbled. Then I heard it again, a bit louder the second time around.

"Colin, can you hear me? Are you there?"

It sounded like Fallyn. And unless I was imagining things, that meant Sonny and his crew had left her in here with me, hoping I'd lose it and kill her. If that happened, Samson would likely kill me, or I him. Either way, Sonny would get rid of two out of three of his strongest adversaries, and gain control of the Pack in one fell swoop.

How they planned on explaining how Fallyn had gotten into the mine shaft was anybody's guess. I suspected they'd say she hid in here to help me with my trial. It wouldn't be much of a leap to claim that her plan had backfired. The Pack would be Sonny's to lead, and his evil alliance with the Rye Mother would continue.

And I simply could not allow that to happen.

———

I ATTEMPTED to stand by getting on my hands and knees, only to find that the arrow shaft got in the way. I bumped the tip against the wall as I turned, and felt the arrowhead scrape bone. The pain was nauseating, and the sensation triggered another coughing fit. I collapsed against the wall and waited for the coughing to subside.

I reached inside the Bag and dug around until I found what I needed. I pulled out a large multi-tool, and began using the wire cutters to snap off the arrow shaft a few inches from my chest. I came close to passing out a few times, but finally managed to complete the task. I tossed the broken shaft away, then returned to the task of pulling myself to my feet.

I dragged myself up the wall on unsteady legs, and began to make my way deeper into the mine. Fallyn kept calling for me, but I was too weak to answer. I stumbled my way down the Shaft, resting every few steps to lean against the cold surface of the mine wall. I was thirsty, dizzy, and weak, and it took some time to reach the room I affectionately referred to as the torture chamber.

I was almost there when Fallyn called again. "Colin, is that you? Please tell me it's you. Say something, dammit!"

My voice was faint and raspy as I replied. "Yeah, it's me. I'm almost there." I dragged myself the last few feet, staggering into the room and collapsing next to the doorway.

Inside, Fallyn hung shackled to the wall, in the same chains they'd used to restrain me during my training. She'd been badly beaten and looked pale as hell. For some reason, her werewolf regeneration hadn't kicked in to heal her.

I held a hand to my chest and coughed up more blood. "You look like shit. Why aren't you healing?" I asked.

She smirked, wincing as she opened a deep cut on her lip. "Gotta say, I think you got me beat. Jaeger and Klaus poisoned me with silver. Pricks injected me with it before they knocked me around." She shook one of her arms and rattled the chains. "Think you can get me out of these things?"

I held up a hand as I fought off another coughing spasm. "Give me a second. With this arrow sticking out of my chest, I'm moving kinda slow."

"Excuses, excuses."

I wiped blood from the corner of my mouth with my sleeve.

"If I don't die before I get over there, I swear I'm going to punch you right in the baby maker."

Fallyn chuckled.

I got to my feet again, and stumbled over to help her. The shackles were locked, but a simple cantrip took care of that. I released her wrists, and then allowed her to do the honors for the ankle shackles.

"I'm gonna sit down for a minute," I mumbled as I slid down the wall.

"I believe I'll join you," Fallyn said as she did the same.

I dug around inside my Craneskin Bag, pulling out two bottles of water and a couple of energy bars. She took one of each, and we both ate and drank quietly for several minutes.

I broke the silence first. "Think you can crawl to the entrance and yell for help?"

She slowly shook her head. "The rules say no one opens the door until midnight of the third day. No matter what."

I took a swig of water. "You werewolves have some messed up traditions, you know that?"

She shrugged. "It is what it is. You know you're gonna have to change, right? Otherwise, we're going to die in this hole."

"The thought had occurred to me," I said as I tilted my head back to rest against the rock wall. "But there are a couple of problems with that." I paused and coughed blood into my palm. "The first problem is that I still don't know if I can control myself after I change. And if I shift, I might Hulk out and rip you into bloody little pieces."

Fallyn arched an eyebrow. "Gonna die anyway if you don't," she said. "And the other problem?"

"Well, the other problem is I don't even know if I can change right now. Dr. Ganesh helped me come to terms with my beast. That's the good news. The bad news is that we never got around to seeing if I can actually change under my own volition."

Fallyn sighed. "You know it's all in your head, right? Your ability to change, to control your beast, everything... it's all a mental thing. Some shifters are naturals at it and get it right away. Others have to learn control. And still others never get a handle on their beast. But when it comes right down to it, it's all just a matter of willpower and self-control."

"That's easy for you to say," I gasped. "You were born into this. I was cursed with it, and I'm still scared to death to change."

Fallyn sat quietly, sipping her water while she considered my words. "The truth is, Colin, almost everyone is afraid of the change at first. I was born a werewolf, but the first time I shifted it scared the hell out of me. After that, I was always worried I'd shift at the wrong time, either at school, or at a friend's house, or in front of a boy I liked.

"Dad kept telling me to stick to my own kind, and then I wouldn't have those concerns. But I wanted to be normal like everyone else. By the time I got older and had full control over my change, I came to hate being a 'thrope. For a very long time, I hated who I was and the life I was born into. Add in the pressure of being one of the few female werewolves in the Pack, a teenage girl who got way too much attention from the grown men in her life. You can see why I was bitter about being a werewolf."

I cleared my throat, coughing up more blood and spitting it off to the side. "I get that. For a long time, I was pissed that I was born a McCool. I just wanted to be left alone, to be normal, instead of having the fae trying to kill me every time I turned around."

Fallyn sniffed and rubbed her nose. "Yeah, I guess that would kinda suck. At least I had everyone in the Pack looking out for me. Even though half the males in the Pack look at me like a piece of meat, I guess it's better than being on every other fae's shit list.

"But you know what I finally figured out? I'm stuck being a

shifter, whether I like it or not. So, I decided to make the best of it. I learned to embrace that side of myself, and made it part of my identity, of who I am. And now? It's the best part of me, and I wouldn't trade it for anything."

I chuckled, triggering another coughing fit. Once it subsided, I wiped a trickle of blood from my mouth and looked at Fallyn. "So what you're saying is, embrace the suck?"

"Yep. That's exactly what I'm saying." She took the last swig of her water, looking at the bottle and then tossing it to the side. "Besides that, I'm dead anyway. Sonny's sidekicks shot me up with enough silver to kill an alpha. If I don't get out of here and get Dad to heal me soon, I'll be taking a dirt nap regardless."

"Point taken. FYI, I'm pretty sure I'm dying too. In a few minutes, I'm either going to kick it, or my Hyde-side is going to come out. So, it'd be a good idea if you chained me up before that happens. After that you need to make yourself scarce, and stay quiet until we know how much control I have over my beast."

"Or until you bite the bullet. Let's not rule out that possibility."

"That's what I like about you, Fallyn. Always looking on the bright side."

She elbowed me in the arm, jostling me and causing another coughing fit. "Yup, that's me. Little Miss Sunshine. Now, get your ass up and shift so you can get us the hell out of here."

HANGING from the shackles by my arms made it that much more difficult to breathe. Soon, I was gasping for breath. I remembered why the Romans had chosen crucifixion as punishment for their worst criminals. Eventually, your arms and legs gave out, and then your whole body hung from your arms. After a while, your shoulders dislocated and your torso sagged forward, making it hellaciously hard to breathe. Once your accessory breathing muscles fatigued, it became nearly impossible to take a breath. Then your lungs filled with fluid. If your heart didn't give out first, you asphyxiated.

Hell of a nasty way to die. After Fallyn chained me up, I collapsed and immediately had difficulty breathing. She realized what was happening and attempted to lift me to ease my breathing.

I shook my head. "No, don't. Just let it happen. Either I die, or I change. You need to go hide, until we know which it'll be."

She lowered me until the chains supported my weight completely. "Alright, it's your call. But if you take the easy way out, and I somehow make it out of here alive, don't think I'm going to tell everyone you were a hero."

I tried to laugh, but I couldn't get enough air. "Bitch... stop making me laugh. Can't... breathe as it is. Now... go."

She grabbed my chin between her thumb and forefinger, lifting my head to look me in the eyes. "Don't die on me, druid. We still have asses to kick and names to take."

I'd begun to nod off, so she slapped me. Hard. "I mean it. Don't you dare die."

"Understood," I gasped. She nodded once and left the room. I listened to her footfalls fade in the distance, struggling to hold myself up. But I was already weak, and my arms and legs fatigued rapidly. Soon, I was unable to hoist my body up to take a breath.

I gasped for air and wheezed, then fluid clogged my airway. The world around me grew dim as I fought to maintain consciousness. Finally, all faded away. As my vision failed, I felt myself falling into a deep dark pit that had no bottom and no end.

"COLIN, GET UP."

I felt someone slapping my face, and made a halfhearted attempt to brush their hand away. "Fallyn, stop already. You made your point."

She slapped me again. "It's not Fallyn, you idiot—it's me."

Jesse? I opened my eyes. Sure enough, there she was. "Jesse, what are you doing here?"

"Duh, you're dying. And I'm a ghost, remember? Do I have to explain how all this works? You get close to death, and I'm able to talk to you. Pretty much standard life-afterlife stuff."

"But if you're a spirit, how can I feel your hand slapping my face?"

"Look, slugger, we don't have time for me to explain deep metaphysical theory and the effect of the id and ego on the astral self. You're about two minutes away from permanent brain death. If you don't shift right now, you're going to end up hanging out in ghost land permanently with yours truly. And that'll royally screw up a whole lot of shit you and I still have to do."

"But I—" She slapped me again, harder. "Ow! Seriously, what's with all the women slapping me today?"

She placed her hands on her hips and narrowed her eyes. "Colin McCool, we do not have time for all your whiny bullshit. You know and I know that we'd both like nothing more than spending a few hundred years together. But unfortunately, that is not going to happen. You need to get up, get your shit together, and find a way to shift. Now."

I laid there for a second looking at her, hoping I'd remember the moment when I awoke.

"Colin—I said now, dammit!"

"Alright, alright... I'm moving. No need to get so bossy about it."

She rolled her eyes. "You don't get to bitch about having bossy women in your life, when you're the one who keeps inviting them in. Now, I have to go. I don't particularly want to be around when that other side of you shows up. You need to figure out how to get in touch with your Hyde-side, shift, heal yourself, and save that girl's life. Got it?"

"Yeah, I got it." I smiled. "I still miss you, every day. You know that, right?"

The lines in her forehead relaxed, and the tightness at the corners of her mouth turned up into a smile. "I told you we didn't have time for this shit. But what the hell—here's a kiss for good luck."

I closed my eyes as our lips met. When I opened them, she was gone.

25

With one foot in the grave, it took me no time at all to reach the Void and summon my Hyde-side. And like all the other times I'd been near death, my alter-ego was more than willing to take over to save our lives. Or rather, to save my life, since we were one and the same being.

After my Fomorian side showed up, we faced off like two gladiators preparing for battle. My counterpart stared me down like a heavyweight prizefighter just before the bell. I knew it was all in my head, but I still felt tense and on guard.

"Aren't we supposed to be working together, now? I mean, you're part of me, right? What's up with the stare down?"

My alter-ego shrugged, a noncommittal answer if there ever was one.

"What, giving me the silent treatment now?"

He flipped me off.

"Well, the feeling's mutual. I'd rather be me without you, believe me."

My Hyde-side continued to glare at me. While he was no longer outright hostile toward me, he was acting like a sullen, angry teen who'd just been grounded for life. The change in his personality told me we were making progress, but we still weren't at a place where I could change at will. I decided to ignore him while I devised a suitable approach to triggering my change.

I wracked my brain, trying to come up with ways to start my shift. I realized that in all the time I had spent with Samson and Dr. Ganesh, I'd never asked them how to shift at will. All this time, I'd been so concerned with preventing the change, that I'd never given much thought to learning how to trigger it. I considered what Fallyn had told me, and decided that I needed to best him in a battle of wills. But precisely how to do that, I hadn't a clue.

I stood up straight and looked the beast in the eye. "Alright, let's give this a shot. Change me into you, now."

The beast crossed his arms and shook his head, like a petulant child refusing to take his medicine. I ran my fingers through my hair, and growled in frustration. "Are you really going to fight me on this? You know we're running out of time, right? In a few seconds, I'll be brain-dead, and that means you'll bite the bullet right along with me. Is that what you want?"

The beast remained silent, observing me with an inscrutable expression that was both quizzical and hostile. Then he smiled smugly, and mimed looking at a watch on his wrist that wasn't there.

"Oh, I get it. You're waiting for me to kick it so you can take over my body and finally be in charge. Um, I hate to tell you this, but I don't think that's the way it works. See, you're a piece of who I am—a magical construct made from my curse and the worst parts of me. But you're still me, and that means if I die, then you go down with me."

The beast rubbed his deformed chin with one massive, calloused hand. Then he scowled, and extended an open hand toward me, as if to call a truce.

"That's it? We go all 'wonder twin powers, activate,' and that triggers the shift? Alrighty then, let's get this show on the road." I reached out and clasped hands with him, expecting to start the shift.

Instead, as soon as we locked hands, he snapped his head forward and headbutted me right in the nose. It might've been all in my head, but it still hurt like hell. The cartilage crunching and blood flowing from my nose felt real enough.

"You dirty son of a bitch! That does it!" I threw a punch and cracked him across the jaw. The blow snapped his head sideways. Then, it was on. In an instant, we were beating the shit out of each other.

I was pretty sure that if I lost this battle, I'd wake up with my Hyde-side in control again. I had to change tactics, because exchanging blows was getting me nowhere. I slipped a punch from his left hand and launched myself in the air. I wrapped one leg across his face while bringing the other across his chest. I arched my back and locked his arm straight, ending a textbook flying armbar with his arm hyperextended across my torso.

If this were real-life fight, someone as strong as my alter ego would pick me up and slam me to the ground, likely knocking me out in the process. But since this was all happening in my mind, there was no ground beneath us to slam me into. Sure, he tried—but it was my dream world, and his attempts to free his arm had no effect.

I cranked his arm until I heard something pop. "Yield!"

The creature shook his head, grimacing in pain despite his superhuman ability to withstand it. I assumed that here in the recesses of my mind, I could hurt him just as much as he could hurt me. So, I cranked harder.

"Yield, or I'll snap it off." The creature grunted one last time, exerting himself in an attempt to bend his arm and relieve the pressure. His was a losing battle, because the fight between us was a figurative one. We were locked in a battle of wills and not strength, and I had more to lose... which meant I would win.

Finally, he dropped his chin to his chest and fell to his knees. "I yield," he growled.

I opened my eyes, awake and chained to the wall in the mine. The only problem was, everything still hurt like hell. I was still wheezing and coughing up blood, and I still had a cut off arrow shaft sticking out of my chest.

"Still human. Great." I released a bloody, gurgling sigh and hung my head, resting my chin on my chest in frustration.

Almost immediately, I felt something happening within my body. First, it was a sort of vibration, like an involuntary muscle twitch. It started in my gut, and then it moved outward, expanding through my torso, down my limbs, and up my neck into my head. As the trembling spread, it turned into full-on spasms. They increased in intensity until my back arched like a contortionist.

The pain was unbearable. All the while, my heart beat faster and faster, thrumming inside my rib cage. I began to shift.

My bones thickened and elongated. It began at my spine and moved outward through my rib cage, down my arms and legs to my fingertips and toes. Unable to stretch enough to match, tendons tore and muscles ripped away from bone. Moments later, my flesh began to catch up, knitting back together and bulging until my skin split in several places and I cried out in tortured agony.

———

FINALLY, my skin knit back together, thickening and hardening. As the pain subsided, I looked down to survey the damage.

Surprisingly, I didn't appear to have grown in size as much as I had on previous occasions. It felt as though I'd shifted into a form that was somewhere between my human body and my full Fomorian self. I wondered how durable this version of me would be, and whether I'd be able to communicate with the Eye in this hybrid human-Fomorian state.

The Eye itself answered my question.

-Colin McCool, it appears you've managed to gain some control over your ability to shift into your Fomorian form. Unfortunately, you'll only have limited access to my powers in your current state.-

"Wonderful." I tugged at the chains, testing my strength in my newfound form. The chains had been designed to hold a fully shifted werewolf, and I was unable to snap them from the wall.

-Sarcasm detected. I recognize the vocal inflections and speech patterns from our previous interactions.-

"Good for you. Any chance you might be able to get me out of these chains?"

-Certainly. Turn your head and focus your vision on the shackles.-

I did as the Eye asked. Red-hot magical energy shot from my eyes, blinding me. The metal shackle on my left wrist was super-heated in an instant, but so were my eyeballs. I shut them and screamed in pain.

"Gah! What the hell? I don't remember it hurting like that before." I opened my eyes. My vision was hazy and filled with white spots.

-It appears your current hybrid human-Fomorian body cannot safely channel my magic. This could be problematic in a battlefield situation.-

"You think?" I asked, my voice dripping with sarcasm. I ripped my left hand out of the shackle before the metal cooled. It had seared my wrist, but the pain paled in comparison to the agony I was currently feeling in my eye sockets. "Let's not do that again anytime soon—at least not until I can figure out how to shift completely."

-Noted. I shall attempt to support and assist you in other ways until we devise a suitable solution to allow you to channel my full power.-

"Fair enough." I continued to blink the spots from my eyes as I fumbled to release the other shackle from my right wrist. As I did, I noticed that the arrow shaft was working its way out of my chest. It still hurt, but it was more of an annoyance now than a debilitating injury. After I'd freed my ankles from the shackles, I grew impatient and yanked the rest of the arrow out of my chest.

"Ow, son of a bitch! I didn't expect that to hurt so bad."

-Your body is not quite as durable or pain resistant in this form. It also seems your ability to heal has been stunted in comparison to that of your full Fomorian body.-

"So, I'm tougher and stronger now, but not nearly as tough and strong as my full Hyde-side is, eh?"

-Correct.-

"Well, it'll have to do. I need to get Fallyn out of here so her dad can heal her."

-If you leave the confines of the mine before your thirty-six hours are up, you will fail your trial.-

"I'm fully aware of that. Fallyn's life is way more important than my status with the Pack. Besides, I have a feeling Samson and his supporters will understand."

I ran through the mine, calling for Fallyn along the way. I located her in a nearby room, curled up under some old tarps. She was unconscious when I found her, so lifted her in my arms and marched to the metal door that locked us in.

I knew no matter how hard I beat on those thick metal doors, there was no way anyone would open them. So, I walked right up and planted a nuclear bomb of a front kick right next to the latch on the door.

My first kick shook the entire doorframe, and metal groaned and twisted with the impact. With the second kick, I created a gap between the door and the frame. And with the third, I snapped the hardened padlock on the outside of the door. It swung open with a crash. On the other side stood a dozen Pack members, some of them already shifting in preparation for a fight.

I stepped through the door, carrying Fallyn's limp form in my arms. About half of the wolves who had been assigned to keep watch were loyal to Samson. Those who were loyal to Sonny scattered as I emerged from the mine. Trina stood among the remaining group, and I addressed her as I spoke.

"I know I'm breaking the rules and failing my trial by busting out. But it was a rigged game from the start." I nodded to draw their attention to Fallyn. "She's been poisoned with silver, and unless we get her to Samson now, she's going to die. So, you can fight me, or you can save the life of your alpha's only child. Your call."

IT DIDN'T TAKE LONG for Trina to jump into action and start giving orders. Samson had left her to keep an eye on things, to make sure there was no funny business while he was gone. Trina explained that he'd been searching for his daughter since she'd disappeared. He was presently running a sweep of the wildlife preserve, on the odd chance she'd been injured or attacked while hunting alone.

Samson wasn't stupid, and he knew chances were good she'd been abducted by Sonny and his crew. But with the current tense situation within the Pack, he had chosen to withhold any accusations. Trina said he had hoped Sonny would screw up and reveal some clue about where he was holding Fallyn. Samson and the other wolves had completed a search of the mine before the trial had begun. They'd found no trace of Fallyn inside, which meant she had arrived there the same way that Claw had left.

It didn't take long for Samson to show up. Even so, his daughter wasn't looking good by the time he arrived. Her breathing was labored, her skin was ashen, and by the looks on the faces of Trina and the other wolves, I figured she was a goner. All I could do was stand by and feel helpless. I hadn't known Fallyn long, but I'd come to respect her for her honesty and loyalty to her father and the Pack. I hoped against hope that I'd gotten her out of the mine in time.

The grizzled old werewolf knelt beside her and placed a scarred, clawed hand on her forehead. He placed his other hand on her stomach and closed his eyes, slowing his breathing as he focused on his task.

As Samson drew on the nearby Pack members' strength to heal Fallyn, several of them staggered with the strain. It appeared that Pack magic didn't extend to excommunicated members, because I didn't feel a thing. I stood by and observed, keeping a silent vigil as the seconds ticked on, while Samson did everything within his power to save his daughter's life.

The healing took a toll on him, and soon he panted with exhaustion. I thought for sure that he'd failed. Fallyn's pulse was thready, and her breathing was so shallow it was almost nonexistent. Just when I was ready to give up, gray beads of sweat began to appear all over her body, sizzling like drops of water on a hot skillet as they ran off her skin. I ripped off a large swatch of my shirt and knelt beside her, mopping the beads of silver away.

Minutes later, it was over. Her heartbeat strengthened, and her breathing grew deeper and steadier. Those Pack members still standing gave a collective sigh of relief. Samson shifted back into his human form and lifted his daughter into his arms.

"Let's take her to the farmhouse," he said to me. "Fallyn will need to rest, and you and I need to discuss what's happened. Trina and Sledge will attend to the other Pack members. Come."

He took off at a jog, so I fell in step behind him, keeping watch as we traveled to the Pack's base nearby. By the time we neared the farmhouse, I'd changed back to my human form. I waited in the kitchen while Samson cleaned his daughter up and helped her into bed.

A few Pack members were already in the kitchen making breakfast for everyone. I helped by putting a pot of coffee on, and then headed to find Samson. I finally found him watching over Fallyn's sleeping form in a back bedroom. He'd obviously dressed in haste, and remained barefooted in jeans that were a few sizes too big and a t-shirt that was one size too small.

I coughed as I entered the room. Samson glanced in my direction and motioned for me to sit. "Looks like you've gained some control over your ability to shift."

"In the nick of time, it seems."

He rubbed the back of his neck and sighed.

"I suppose you're thinking that for an alpha, I don't exactly have my shit together."

I hitched my shoulders in response. "I don't think I have the right to express an opinion about your leadership skills. It's not my place."

"Oh, but you do. Tonight, you proved to everyone that you have what it takes to be a part of this Pack. I know it was never your intention to become one of us, at least not for the long-term—but you've earned your place here. And that means you get a say, just like everyone else."

"But I didn't complete my trial."

He shook his head. "The trial is bullshit anyway. It's an anti-quated custom that I've been trying to get rid of for years. But trying to get my people to accept that we need to bring the Pack into the twenty-first century... well, it hasn't been easy. Some of these wolves are hundreds of years old, and old habits die hard. That's one of the reasons why I brought you into the Pack—to shake things up by introducing an unknown element. I wanted some of the old-timers to question the accepted norms."

"Seems like your plan kind of blew up in your face."

He laughed out loud, causing Fallyn to stir under the covers. "See, that right there is exactly what I'm talking about. Besides my daughter, none of the other Pack members would ever consider speaking to me like that. They're either falling all over themselves to please me, or they're sneaking around behind my back like Sonny.

"But times are changing. Humans are getting smarter, and technology is making it harder and harder for 'thropes to stay in the shadows. Soon, the old ways aren't going to be enough to keep us safe. We need access to magic, the type that can help us keep our true nature hidden to the world at large.

"If we stick to our old-fashioned, insular ways, we'll never create the partnerships and alliances we need to survive in this brave new world."

Finally, it was starting to make sense to me. I could see now why Samson had been so eager to help me learn to control my change. Sure, Finnegas and Maeve had influenced his decision, but ultimately the wily old wolf was fighting to save his people. He needed to open their minds to the possibility that an alliance between the wolves and the fae could be beneficial for the Pack. The fae had glamour, and fixers—magic that could help the Pack keep its secrets from the mundane world. What better way to show them that magic could be a good and useful thing, than to bring a druid into the Pack?

He scratched his head. "But, Sonny made his move too soon. I'd always known he was a little off, and that someday he'd be vying for my position. But I never suspected he was twisted enough to steal kids and sell them for profit."

"Maeve told you?"

He gave a minute nod, and I cleared my throat before continuing. "Samson, all politics aside, I think it's clear that Sonny is a problem that needs to be dealt with immediately. Whether I have the Pack's help or not, I intend to take him and his goons out. I'm not asking your permission—but it sure would be nice to know that I had your approval."

The alpha bared his teeth as he spoke. "You know, there is such a thing as too much candor, druid."

Fallyn's voice cracked as she butted into our conversation. "He's right, Dad. Sonny and his crew are an infection that needs to be cut out of the Pack. And I for one don't intend to let the druid handle this on his own."

Samson sighed. "So be it then." He cocked his head, pointing an ear toward the front door of the house. "Looks like you two won't have to hunt Sonny down. Sounds like he might be coming to us."

26

Soon after Samson had given us the heads up, I heard the rumble of a motorcycle approaching the house. I helped Fallyn out of bed, so she could go with her father to hear whatever challenge or threat was to come. She was healing rapidly, but still weak, and she leaned on me as we followed her father to the front door.

Before we exited the house, she nudged me away, pulling her shoulders back and lifting her chin. We stepped into the drive followed by Sledge and Trina, but found only one Pack member waiting for us. It was Claw, the wolf who'd planted an arrow in my chest.

He sneered at me. "Druid—you're looking well." He crossed his arms and spat at Samson's feet. "He should be dead by now, old wolf."

Samson showed no reaction to Claw's remark, and his face was calm as a Zen master's. "You know as well as I that someone rigged the druid's trial. Yet, he was still able to show control over his change. He gets to live." I opened my mouth to protest the "gets to live" part, but Fallyn stared me into silence. Her father's expression darkened as he continued. "Now, say what you came here to say, and then leave before I lose my patience and kill you where you stand."

Claw didn't exactly tremble in his boots at the threat, but he did take a step back before he replied. "You know why I'm here. Sonny challenges your right to lead the Pack as alpha." He tossed a folded map at Samson's feet. "The time and place are marked. Bring your second and third, and say your goodbyes. By sundown, your corpses will be feeding the coyotes, and the Pack will have a new alpha."

Fallyn growled, but the old alpha looked bored. "We'll see. Now run, cur, before I change my mind about letting you live."

Samson stared the wolf down, and Pack magic made the hairs on my neck stand as the alpha brought his authority to bear. Claw stumbled, then he averted his eyes as he backed up and mounted his Harley. I grabbed the map as the roar of the motorcycle faded into the distance. Fallyn took the arm I proffered with a frown, and we limped over to a nearby picnic table to spread the map out on its surface.

"Looks like they want to meet in the middle of nowhere," I said, pointing at an X on the map. It was far to the north and east of Austin. "If my memory serves correct, there's nothing out there but farms and fields."

"It's remote, so that's good." Fallyn drew a circle with her finger around the X. "Less chance of drawing spectators. And, if I had to guess, I'd bet Sonny owns this land."

"Home turf advantage?" I asked.

"What do you think?" she replied.

I looked up to get the alpha's opinion. Samson was still staring down the driveway. I got the feeling he was regretting his decision to allow Claw to leave in one piece. Finally, he sent Trina and Sledge out to patrol, then he joined us at the table. "He has something planned," the Pack leader rumbled. "Normally, the alpha chooses the field of battle—not the challenger."

"So just any Pack member can challenge the alpha whenever they want?"

Samson arched an eyebrow and smiled ruefully. "Pretty much, although few wolves are stupid enough to do it."

Fallyn slammed a fist on the table. "Sonny didn't even have the balls to deliver his challenge in person, the coward."

"You and I both know that was intentional." Samson crossed his arms and stroked his chin as he looked at the map. "He's sending a message to the Pack that I'm beneath him, not even worth his time. Thing is, he can't take me in a fair fight—and Sonny's not dumb enough to think he can. He's not doing this to try to psych me out or intimidate me, because he knows that won't work. He has something up his sleeve. I'm sure of it."

I cleared my throat. "How does this all work? And what's this about bringing a second and third?"

Fallyn stretched and rubbed her neck. "It's a pretty simple process. Samson chooses two Pack members to show up with him to face down his challenger, and of course Sonny will have two wolves with him as well. The fight is to be between the challenger and the alpha. The other four are only there to make sure it's a fair fight."

"Yeah, but what about the rest of the Pack? Can't they step in if someone cheats?"

Samson scratched his chin. "They can't. Once the challenge begins, Pack magic seals off the area, and only those within can intervene. The rest of the Pack will be watching from a distance, but they'll be unable to act—regardless of what happens."

I yawned; it had been a long night. "What determines the boundaries? Is it like a ward, or more of a compulsion?"

"It works exactly like a ward," Samson grumbled. "And the boundaries are determined by property lines. Don't ask me how the magic knows where they are. It just does. Until either the challenger or the alpha dies, no one can get in or out of the boundary set by the Pack's magic."

I whistled. "Sounds like it could turn into a free-for-all, pretty damn quick."

The grizzled alpha nodded. "And it often does. I attended more than a few challenges before I became an alpha. And I've fielded several since that time. You never can tell how things are going to go down when the stakes are this high. Assume that if they see their boy taking a beating, Sonny's buddies are going to jump in."

"Who are you gonna take with you tonight?"

Samson pursed his lips. "I was kind of hoping you two might have an open schedule this evening. Anyone up for a good old-fashioned rumble?"

Fallyn growled. "Couldn't keep me away. But, Dad, don't you think the druid's a poor choice right now?"

"Trust me, he's the right choice." She began to protest, but the alpha waved a finger at her. "Uh-uh, I don't want to hear it." He looked at me. "So, druid, you up for it?"

"I have unfinished business with Sonny and his crew, so you can count me in. But I also kind of agree with Fallyn. You trying to stir up more controversy?"

Samson grinned ear to ear. "Most definitely. That's *one* of the reasons why I want you there." He strode toward the house whistling a tune, then paused as he spoke to his daughter over his shoulder. "Fallyn, make sure the druid can shift on cue before tonight. I don't want him getting eaten before he can be of use to me."

Fallyn waited until her father had entered the house before she spoke. She narrowed her eyes and stared at the map. "Dad's right. Sonny's up to something." She lifted her gaze to meet mine, concern evident on her face. "Rules say no magic during the fight—unless the other side cheats, then all bets are off.

Means you'll have to be in your shifted form if things go south. That gives us about twelve hours to get you up to speed."

I sighed and ran a hand through my hair. "Looks like it's going to be a Red Bull kind of day." I stood, and extended a hand to help her up. "I'm not about to do this on an empty stomach. Let's see if there's any food left, then we can get started."

WE SPENT hours working to give me some semblance of control over my ability to shift. By mid-afternoon, I still wasn't able to shift at will. But by using the techniques that Finnegas and Dr. Ganesh had taught me, I found I could enter a trance on command and then battle my alter ego into submission. At that point, I could shift into my hybrid human-Fomorian form— provided I didn't lose the battle of wills that preceded each shift.

I made another crucial discovery over the course of the day. I could only remain in my shifted form for short time; fifteen to twenty minutes seemed to be my max. So, there were several limiting factors in my ability to shift. The first factor was the time and concentration it took to shift. The second was the finite period I could remain in my shifted form. And the third was that each mental battle with my Hyde-side took a lot out of me. By the time late afternoon came, I felt spent, and I was still unsure of my ability to shift. Unfortunately, it was the best we could do on short notice.

The location Sonny had chosen was along Texas Highway 95 between the tiny towns of Granger and Bartlett. In late summer and early fall, the area produced thousands of acres of corn, soybeans, and cotton. This late in the season, the fields would already be harvested, and the ground would likely be tilled to prepare for the next planting season.

That meant our footing would be uneven. It also meant we'd

be fighting in a large open area, with nowhere to hide and no place for an ambush. I still couldn't figure out what Sonny's angle was in making us fight there. Other than the possibility that he might be familiar with the area, I couldn't think of anything that would provide him with an edge in the coming battle.

Even so, something gnawed at the back of my mind, some detail from my investigation that I couldn't quite put my finger on. I spent the better part of the day trying to figure out what was nagging at me. But practicing my shift took precedence, and I still hadn't figured it out before we left the farmhouse. I decided to think it through on the way to the fight.

Samson and Fallyn made the trip on their bikes, and I followed in the Gremlin. My uncle still hadn't finished tooling around with the Harley he'd gotten me, and I doubted he would anytime soon. The last I'd seen it, he'd reduced the motorcycle to a pile of parts so he could rebuild it piece-by-piece. Too bad. It would've been cool to ride up on a Harley with Samson, Fallyn, and the others.

Then again, being cool wasn't really my thing.

It took the better part of an hour to make the trip. I spent most of the drive slamming energy drinks, trying to stay alert. The location was a nondescript field on a dirt road off Highway 95. By the time we arrived, most of the Pack was already there. Motorcycles lined both sides of the road, and loyal Pack members milled about, drinking beer and bullshitting to pass the time. Sonny and his faction held court a short ways up the road.

I pulled in behind Fallyn and Samson and opened the car door. Hiding behind the door, I grabbed my Bag and slung it over my shoulder, then pulled it flat against the small of my back and pulled my coat over it. I hoped no one would notice it or protest the fact that I had it. Something told me that I needed to have some tricks in reserve, in case my hunch about Sonny was right.

"Don't worry, I'll make sure no one notices." I yelped, surprised by Click's sudden appearance in the passenger seat.

"Shit, Click, what the hell? Trying to give a guy a heart attack?"

He chuckled and pulled a cigarette from behind his ear. "Maybe if you'd lay off the caffeine, you wouldn't be so jumpy."

I reached in the car and snagged the cigarette from his fingers. "Not in the Gremlin." He frowned and rolled his eyes. "Now, you sure you can hide this thing from everyone?"

"Was Lleu of the Skillful Hand hard to kill?" He produced another cigarette from thin air and lit it with a snap of his fingers. "No need to worry. You just focus on putting a proper beating on those 'rotten wolves.'"

The way he'd emphasized "rotten" led me to believe he was hinting at something important. But I knew asking what would only result in ambiguity, or a request for something in return. I liked Click, but I had no delusions about the fact that he was powerful and dangerous. I decided to leave well enough alone, and hoped that once we killed Sonny and his crew, he'd do the same in kind.

"Just don't burn the seats," I grumbled as I stood and slammed the door.

I leaned against the car, scanning the area where the fight was to happen. Surprisingly, the site wasn't barren at all. Instead, a short growth of winter wheat covered a good acre of land before us. This, combined with Click's remark, made my mind race. I gnawed at my thumbnail to trigger the magic of the Salmon of Knowledge as I followed Fallyn and Samson.

A hush fell over the Pack as we walked past. Then, Trina broke the silence with a raucous yell.

"Kick his ass, Samson!" she hollered. Soon others joined in, with similar shouts of support and enmity toward Sonny and his faction.

Sonny and his goons walked out to meet us, and Samson raised a hand to silence the crowd as they approached. I was still chewing my thumbnail, trying to figure out what Sonny's game was in choosing this location. Klaus noticed I had my thumb in my mouth and sneered.

"You always suck your thumb when you're scared?" He turned to his friends and snickered. "Looks to me like the druid's about to piss his pants." They responded with a round of laughter, and I waited for it to die down before I spoke.

"You know what, Klaus? When this shit goes sideways, I'm going to kill you first."

That caused quite a bit of grumbling and yelling from Sonny's followers, and a cacophony of catcalls and taunts from the wolves behind us. Before things could escalate into an all-out brawl, Samson's voice rumbled a command.

"Enough." His power fell over them like a father's hand clamping down on a child's shoulder. Samson waited for complete silence, then he spoke once more. "It's your show, Sonny," he chided. "Are you going to fish, or cut bait?"

Sonny ignored Samson's comment. He turned to his supporters and spread his hands wide, lifting them up to the sky like an old-time preacher at a tentpole revival. "Members of the Pack! You know why we're gathered—and why I've challenged our current leader."

He glanced over his shoulder and gestured at Samson, then turned his attention back to his audience. "We all know he's been slipping for some time now, cozying up to the fae and bringing their freakish experiments into our midst." At that, he pointed a finger at me while still addressing the crowd.

"But now, Samson's time has ended. Today, a new era will begin. It's time for the Pack to return to the old ways, the right ways. It's time for us to stand together again, apart from other factions in the world beneath."

Sonny supporters responded with yells and cheers. Those wolves who remained loyal to Samson shouted epithets and insults. Sonny turned and faced Samson again.

"You ready to die, old wolf?"

Samson looked almost regretful as he spoke. "Last chance, Sonny. No one has to die today."

"No one but you, old wolf," Sonny replied. "Your time is over."

Samson nodded once. "Then the time for talk has passed. Let's get this shit show over with. I have a Pack to run." Without another word, Samson strolled toward the middle of the field. Fallyn and I shared a look, then followed him.

I HAD no doubt that Samson could take Sonny in a fair fight. Samson was older and more experienced, and frankly he came across as a much tougher wolf. But the circumstances still rankled me, so I chewed furiously at my thumbnail in hopes the magic might reveal Sonny's plan.

Fallyn elbowed me, snapping me out of my thoughts. "Don't you think it's time you shifted? We won't have to fight just yet, but once Samson starts whipping Sonny's ass, his sidekicks are totally going to jump in to save him."

I mumbled around my thumb. "I will in a minute. I just have to..." I froze in midsentence as the Salmon's magic finally made things clear. "Oh, shit. I know exactly what's going on."

Samson turned his head and whispered as we marched to the center of the field, about thirty yards away from Sonny. "What is it? And keep your voice down—I don't want them to know that we've figured it out."

I jogged up to Samson's side and spoke in a low voice as Fallyn joined us. "When we found the kids at the warehouse, I questioned one of them about what he'd heard and observed during his time there. He said the fae who were running the place kept calling Sonny and his goons 'rotten wolves.' But I think he misinterpreted their relationship. In fact, I believe they've been working for the Rye Mother and those fae from the very beginning."

"So what?" Fallyn asked. "We already knew that, right?"

"Yeah, but listen... in German, 'Rye Mother' is *Roggenmutter*. In German, 'roggen' means rye, like the grain." I glanced at the short plant growth around us. "I'm pretty sure this is winter rye we're standing in."

Fallyn's eyes grew wide. "Shit, he didn't mean rotten wolves—"

"Nope," I replied. "He meant *roggenwölfe*—the Rye Mother's children."

Samson stared across the field, where Sonny and his chosen companions were taking their places. "Well, it's too late to do anything about it now."

Fallyn slammed her fist into her palm. "Those lying cheats. If they're feldgeister, then they'll have the advantage out here."

Samson looked at me and rubbed his chin. "Good catch, kid. I didn't know what he had planned, but I figured Sonny would use magic to tip the scales in his favor." He turned to his daughter and grinned. "I guess it's a good thing I decided to bring the druid, huh?"

He placed a hand on my shoulder and looked me in the eye. "Colin, you're to stay out of the fight at first, even if the others jump in. Once I start laying a beat down on all three of them, Sonny will have to cheat. Make sure you wait until his treachery is good and clear to the rest of the Pack. Then, you have my permission to rain hell down on their heads. Got it?"

I cracked my neck and rolled out my shoulders. "Clear as a bell. Now, if you two don't mind, I think I'll start shifting, before shit gets serious."

Fallyn glared across the field, clenching her fists. "I'll keep an eye on Dad until you're ready." She turned to address her father. "Daddy, don't hold anything back."

Samson slapped a mosquito feeding from his forearm. He flashed his daughter a Han Solo smile and laughed. "Don't worry, I don't intend to."

The alpha leapt a dozen feet or more in the air, shifting into his werewolf form and shredding his clothing in an instant. He landed in a crouch, slamming his fist into the ground and creating a magical shock wave. Pack magic expanded out from where the alpha had landed. It spread through the field until it hit an invisible boundary, then the ward locked into place.

Samson stood in his werewolf form and made a very "come at me, bro" gesture as his voice bellowed across the field.

"Let it begin!"

And at that, Sonny ran toward him, shifting into his werewolf form and clashing with the alpha mid-field. I closed my eyes and began to center myself, hoping I could tap into the magic that would allow me to survive the coming battle.

27

The fight started off bloody, and it only got bloodier with each passing second. Neither Samson nor Sonny were large men. Since their werewolf forms reflected their human bodies, each was lithe, quick, and deadly. It was clear that the fight's outcome would hinge on speed and skill, not brawn and size.

I found it hard to concentrate, because I kept peeking to see how the fight was going. I'd meditate for a few seconds, until I heard the Pack react to something that Samson or Sonny did to one another. Then I would open my eyes, just to make sure Samson wasn't losing. He wasn't, but Sonny was doing a damned good job of holding his own against the alpha.

That spoke volumes about the fact that Sonny wasn't your run-of-the-mill werewolf. From what I understood, Samson had been around much longer than any of the other wolves in the Pack. I guessed that meant he could be a thousand years old or more. Even the werewolves in the Pack who were a few centuries old would have had a difficult time lasting more than a few minutes against the grizzled alpha. Sonny was definitely something other than a werewolf, that was plain to see.

They ripped and tore at each other with claw and tooth, shredding flesh and skin with lightning speed and laser precision. Yet, each healed just as quickly as the other. Only a truly debilitating injury would decide the battle. The winner would be the one who severed an artery, shattered bone, or secured their jaws around the other's neck or throat. Once that happened, it would be over in an instant.

I'd only watched the battle for a few seconds before deciding that both combatants were far too wily to make such a mistake. Most of the attacks they landed resulted in superficial injuries, and each was careful to avoid leaving their vital areas open. But Samson appeared to be the more skilled fighter, and I guessed it would only be a matter of time until he found an opening in Sonny's defenses.

Sure enough, I was right. Samson left his lead leg exposed a split second too long, and Sonny opened a cut across the alpha's quadriceps. The alpha stumbled back, dropping to one knee. His challenger saw an opportunity to turn the tables in his favor, and leapt forward to finish his former boss off.

And that was exactly what Samson wanted.

Once Sonny was airborne, he'd committed to his attack. Although he dove with arms extended and claws spread, he left his vital organs open to an attack from below. Samson preyed on this opening by diving into a forward roll, clawing across Sonny's pectoral muscles down to his pelvis with his uninjured leg.

Samson continued his roll and bounced to his feet, neatly pivoting to land in a crouch facing his challenger. Sonny crumpled to a heap several yards away, his innards trailing behind him. The injury was a fight-ender, since it would be impossible for Sonny to heal until he stuffed his intestines back into his gut. The beta wolf scrambled backwards to gain space, dragging at least ten feet of his guts with him.

Then he did something unexpected. Sonny grabbed the length of intestine hanging from his torso and brought it to his jaws. With one snap of his teeth, he severed the ropy mass from his body, tossing it away like a butcher discarding offal. He rolled to his feet, and motioned for Samson to attack.

Rather than jump in to finish him off, Samson stalked him in slow circles. He was looking for an opening, a lapse in Sonny's attention. Like any hunter, he knew that his prey was most dangerous when it was most vulnerable. So, he paced around his quarry, waiting for the right moment to end the battle.

Unfortunately, that moment never came. Rather than leaving an opening, Sonny wiped both of his hands across his abdomen, covering them in his own blood. Then he drove his claws deep into the earth beneath him.

"Fuck this fair play shit," Sonny snarled. "It's time to show you what I can really do, old wolf."

A powerful wind blew from behind Sonny, flattening the rye stalks as it passed. The wind tore into the alpha, causing him to crouch and lean against it while digging the claws of both feet and one hand into the soil to remain upright. Next, the ground began to rumble beneath Sonny and Samson. Seconds later, thick vines grew from the ground, securely entwining the alpha's legs within the span of a few heartbeats.

As soon as Samson saw what was happening, he attempted to escape. The alpha ripped and tore at the vegetation that trapped him, but nothing worked. Sonny's magic was obviously at its peak here; as a feldgeister, he was in his element. If Samson ripped away a half-dozen tendrils, a dozen more took their place.

Soon the plants had wrapped around him completely, and they began pulling him to the ground. His challenger shoved the remaining length of his intestines into the rapidly-closing hole in his stomach as he stood watch. Then he smiled at Samson, displaying a mouth that now bore way too many teeth, even for werewolf.

He beckoned to Jaeger and Klaus. "Come on, boys. Let's show these shifters they're not the biggest, baddest wolves in the forest." His companions grinned in response, and the three of them began to morph into something other than a werewolf or human.

Each dropped to all fours, then their bodies blurred and twisted as their flesh melted and formed itself anew. As their glamour dissolved, we saw that they were not and never had been anything close to human or werewolf. Instead, they were completely and fully made of plant matter, like some kind of grotesque topiary. They reminded me of a museum display of cadavers, with their skins peeled away to reveal the muscle and sinew beneath. But rather than muscle and bone, vines, twigs, leaves, and sticks formed the rye wolves.

They were revolting to behold, but I couldn't tear my eyes from their transformation if I tried. Within seconds, the three had transformed into pony-sized wolves made from a hodge-podge of vegetation and plant growth. Sonny, the largest of the three, panted as his corn leaf tongue lolled from his mouth around bramble-thorn teeth. And though his jaws never moved, his voice boomed all around as he commanded the others to attack.

"Boys, show the bitch and the druid what Mother thinks of their meddling."

With that, the other two rye wolves loped across the field toward us.

THIS WASN'T SUPPOSED to happen. Samson was supposed to take the piss out of Sonny and his boys, well before I got involved. It all happened so fast, that for a split-second I sat stunned at the rapid reversal of fortune that had occurred. Fallyn's voice cut through my disbelief, growling at me as she shifted and ran to meet one of the rye wolves.

"Colin, snap out of it!"

I kept an eye on the advancing rye wolves as I replied. Thankfully, they knew they had the upper hand, and were in no hurry to attack. "Um, Fallyn? I think I'm going to need a little more time to shift!"

She yelled over her shoulder as she moved to cut off Klaus and Jaeger before they reached me. "I'll buy you as much time as I can, but you'd better shift or come up with a plan B, fast."

"Right, plan B it is then... only problem is, I don't have one," I muttered. I'd wasted my opportunity to shift, spending it on watching the fight between Samson and Sonny unfold. It looked as though I would pay the price for not staying on task. Fallyn was already locked in combat with one of the wolves, and the other was steadily closing in on my position.

At a loss for a better strategy, I stood and reached into my Craneskin Bag for my sword, pulling it out as I backpedaled in a panic. "Shit, shit, shit—think, Colin, before you get eaten and shat out as fertilizer."

Before I could come up with a solution, the feldgeister was on me, snapping his blackened briar teeth and slashing at me with his thorny claws. Based on how Fallyn's fight was going, I wouldn't withstand a single blow from these creatures; one hit and I'd be out. So, I went batshit on it, cutting and slicing, then dancing out of the way before he could land a counterattack.

But the rye wolf was fast, and he soon landed a blow on my arm. I counterattacked, landing a cut that sliced off half his paw, making him limp out of my reach. Two things happened then that told me this fight would likely end in the rye wolf's favor. First, the wolf regrew his missing digits and claws before my eyes. And second, the arm he had scratched began to feel numb and leaden.

"Poison? Are you kidding me?"

The rye wolf stalked in a slow circle. His weird, raspy voice echoed around me. "Like that, punk? Oh, we're full of tricks. Admit it, you're out of your league. You may as well just lay down and die. I promise to make it quick."

Before the arm became completely useless, I switched my sword to my other hand and reached into my Craneskin Bag to grab an equalizer. I kept the wolf talking while I searched for what I needed with rapidly numbing fingers.

"Which one of Sonny's flunkies are you? Jaeger? Klaus? I keep getting you confused. I'm just going to call you Sprout. So, tell me, Sprout, what's your watering cycle like? And would you consider yourself to be an annual or a perennial species?"

The roggenwolf growled. "You won't be laughing for long. After I turn your flesh into fertilizer, I'll crack your bones to suck the marrow dry. Then I'll go after that little hunter girl you've been banging. Maybe I'll even show her a good time before I kill her. Wouldn't be the first bitch I roofied with poison."

I backed away as it circled me, threatening him with my blade as I stalled for time. Inside the Bag, my numb fingers landed on the object I needed. At least, I hoped it was. I'd only get one shot, so I decided to taunt the wolf to get him to drop his guard.

"Sprout, please. You'd be biting off more than you can chew with Belladonna. Trust me, you're better off sticking with druids and werewolves. Now, not to change the subject, but I'm curious —do you prefer plant food stakes, or liquid food? I'm betting on stakes. Do you shove them up your ass like suppositories, or swallow them whole?"

"That's it," he rasped. "I'm killing you slow and painful." The rye wolf leapt at me with murder in his glowing green eyes.

I yanked a glass bottle filled with clear liquid from the Bag, with a rag dangling from its neck. With no time to light it, I threw it overhand with all my might, striking the rye wolf on the snout as I dove out of the way. The bottle shattered and splashed its contents all over his face and upper body. Temporarily blinded, the wolf landed awkwardly, shaking his head and blinking to clear his vision.

Before it could recover, I mumbled a spell and gestured, throwing a spark from my hand at the rye wolf's face. The spark ignited the grain alcohol, gasoline, and dish soap mixture with a whoosh, and the rye wolf howled in fear and pain.

"Like that, Sprout? It's a magically enhanced Molotov cocktail. Gnaw on that, you piece of shit."

The feldgeister went up like a match as the fire spread over his body. He screamed and wailed in response, rolling around in the dirt and batting his paws at the flames. As the fire did its work, the wolf's movements slowed and his howls and screams grew weaker. Within seconds, only a charred husk remained.

I walked up and kicked it lightly a few times, just to see if it was really dead. "Huh. Smells like burnt popcorn."

A desperate howl from Fallyn cut my victory celebration short. Across the field, she fought against tendrils of vegetation that wrapped her legs and body, dragging her down to the earth. Several yards beyond, Sonny was busy ripping and tearing at Samson's torso, devouring his organs as he remained pinned and trapped. Despite the fact he was being eaten alive, he still struggled and strained to free himself.

My sword arm was now nearly useless, completely numb from the forearm down. I could barely move my hand, much less fight with it, so I dropped my sword and reached into my Bag for another Molotov cocktail.

Sonny glanced up at me from where he fed. "Ah, ah, ah. I don't think so, druid."

Thick vines sprang from the ground to trap my feet, just as they had trapped Samson and Fallyn. I pulled my skinning knife from the small of my back and slashed at the vines and stalks that held me. But even Samson had been unable to fight free from Sonny's feldgeister tricks, and I was no alpha werewolf.

The vines and stalks wrapped around my body, encircling my neck and pinching my windpipe shut. I dropped my knife and reached up, tugging at the vines in a vain attempt to free my airway. As I fought, they constricted further, cutting off the blood to my brain.

Seconds passed, yet my efforts to escape proved fruitless. And the bitch of it was, I couldn't even utter a smart-ass retort. I blacked out hoping that I'd be able to shift in time to save us all.

IMMEDIATELY, the Eye's voice filled my mind.

-*The vines have crushed your larynx. Your airway is compromised. You must change forms immediately, or you will die.*-

"Yeah, I kind of figured that out already. You get an 'A' for effort, though."

-*I fail to comprehend your meaning.*-

"Forget it. Give me some quiet so I can concentrate."

I mentally prepared myself for the prolonged struggle about to take place between my alter-ego and my conscious self. Yet, that fight never came. Instead, my Hyde-side came barreling out of the nothingness and dove at me like a lion taking down a gazelle. Rather than tackling me, he sort of dove into my chest and disappeared.

"Well, that was new," I said to no one in particular.

The next instant I awoke, still fighting for air but already changing into my more durable, hybrid human-Fomorian body.

But I was still trapped and unable to breathe. I assumed that in this form, my body could last much longer without oxygen, but for how long, I had no idea. I looked across the field and saw that Samson had almost stopped struggling. On the other hand, Fallyn's adversary was toying with her, making shallow cuts on various parts of her body. Soon he would tire of the game, and she would be a goner too.

The Eye spoke inside my head. *-You must allow me to burn the vines away.-*

But that'll leave me blind and defenseless, I replied wordlessly.

-Blind and defenseless would seem to be preferable to being dead.-

I couldn't argue with that logic. *Do it,* I replied.

I struggled to crane my neck so I could look down at my body, where the plant life had grown thick around my feet and abdomen. The Eye's magic blasted from my eye sockets the second I brought the lower half of my body into my field of vision. The blast incinerated the vines, as well as what remained of my clothing below my chest.

Was that really necessary? It's not like I have a huge wardrobe, you know.

-Perhaps this presents an opportunity to expand your clothing choices for a change. Now, your lower body is free. I suggest you escape immediately before you become trapped again.-

The blast had blinded me, but I could feel that my legs and torso were indeed loose. I dropped into a squat, then leapt from the ground to pull free from the rest of the vines that trapped me. As my upper limbs tore from their bonds, I immediately reached up and ripped the remaining tendrils from my neck.

I landed and stumbled, finally able to breathe but unable to see anything around me. My eyes burned with a searing pain, and I snapped them shut reflexively.

"I'm flying blind here, Eye! Help me out!"

-Lift your head forty-five degrees, turn it ninety degrees to the right, then open your eyes.-

I did exactly as the Eye requested. Once more, the Eye's power burst forth in a rush, causing me even greater pain. The blast was followed by a howl of agony from one of the rye wolves that quickly faded into nothing.

I looked around and blinked impotently. Blindness was disorienting and frightening, and I fought to avoid panicking. "What happened?"

-We struck one of the rye wolves dead center, incinerating him on the spot. Now we must free the female werewolf. She is in much better shape to assist you in surviving this battle than the alpha.-

"Well, hell, tell me where to go." I blinked my eyes out of reflex, still hoping to be able to see, or at least to ease the pain. I got neither result, and panic began to set in.

"Eye, tell me what to do!"

-Turn your head fifteen degrees left and open your eyes, now.-

Again, I did as I was told. Once more, my eye sockets felt like they were on fire—which they were. The burning flesh I smelled confirmed it. I heard a yelp, followed by the sounds of something big crashing away from me to my left.

-Sonny has stopped feeding on the alpha. I believe he now sees you as the greatest threat on the battlefield.-

"Well, that's just flipping great. Where's Fallyn?"

-Five degrees right and forty-seven feet ahead. Move now, before the rye wolf recovers.-

I ran, weaving like a drunk as I closed the distance with Fallyn. I stumbled over her supine form, and scrambled around until I felt plant matter and fur. I immediately began ripping and tearing at the vegetation to release her. Within seconds, she was partially free and helping with the task.

"Colin, look out!" she screamed. I felt two large clawed hands strike me in the chest as something snapped just in front of my face. I flew several feet backwards, until I finally skidded and tumbled to a stop.

"What the hell was that?"

-*The she-wolf saved your life.*-

"Then I'll owe her one—now tell me where to aim."

-*Forty degrees right and ten degrees down.*-

I turned my head and opened my eyes. Again, I smelled burning flesh and felt agonizing pain as the magic was released.

"Did we get a hit?"

-*No, the creature dove out of the way.*-

"Shit, time for a new tactic." I yelled as loud as I could. "Fallyn, can you hear me?"

Her voice replied next to my ear. "I'm right here, you moron. Did you go deaf, too?"

"How did you know I was blind?"

"Your eyes are kind of crispy and smoking right now. Sort of gives it away. Shit, we gotta move." Her furry arms grabbed me and threw me over her shoulder. I bounced around in her grasp, and felt the sensation of moving at speed.

"Well, I guess that explains the searing pain in my eyes and smell of burned bacon."

"Yeah, but the bright side is that you're hung like a bear in this form. If we live though this, something tells me you're going to be popular with all the back-warmers and hardbellies around the clubhouse."

I did my best to cover my nads while bouncing like a tennis ball in a laundromat clothes dryer. "Please tell me no one is filming this on their cell phone," I muttered.

I felt Fallyn's head swivel about. "Um, sure—of course they're not." She paused, then turned on a dime to sprint in a different direction. "So, druid, what's your plan? Dad's out of commission, and I can't dodge Sonny the freak forever—especially not while my body is healing and fighting that thing's poison."

"I don't want you to. In fact, I need you to take me to him."

I'd begun to slip off her shoulder, so she hitched me higher again before responding. "You crazy? You can't see, which means you can't fight. He'll rip you to shreds as soon as he gets hold of you."

"I only need a second. Toss me at him."

Fallyn pivoted and sprinted in yet another direction as she replied. "You want me to do what? Like, a fastball special or something?"

"Exactly. Just make sure we're close enough so he doesn't see it coming and he can't dodge out of the way."

"You're crazy, you know that?" she growled. "I guess at the very least, you can tangle him up for me while I get Dad free. Maybe together we'll have a chance at killing Sonny."

"If this works out, hopefully you won't need to."

"Alright, then hang on." She swung me off her shoulder and cradled me in her arms. Fallyn zig-zagged left, then right, then she spun in a tight circle, releasing me at speed while tossing me like a sack of grain. I flew in a shallow arc through the air with my arms and legs flailing.

"Holy shit!" I yelled, or at least I started to. My scream cut short as I collided with something that felt like a bale of hay wrapped around a stack of cordwood. "Got you," I exclaimed, wrapping my arms and legs around Sonny's body as we tumbled in a heap.

"I'm going to tear you limb from limb, then I'm going to eat your guts and shit you out for fertilizer," he growled.

"Yeah, I don't think that's gonna happen," I said as I pulled him tighter. "Eye, blast this fucker now!"

I opened my eyes, and the mother of all energy beams flew out of my eye sockets. Sonny had just enough time to yelp, and then I was holding nothing more than charred wood, cinders, and embers in my arms.

I coughed and spat ash from my mouth, then felt and heard the tatters of clothing on my upper body burning. I rolled over several times, recalling the "stop, drop, and roll" training I'd received in grade school. I came to a stop on my back, eyes closed.

After a few moments, I gently probed my eye sockets with my fingertips. They were hot and blistered. Underneath my eyelids, my eyes felt mushy and not entirely intact.

"Eye, please tell me that my eyes are going to heal."

-I estimate that some of your eyesight will return before you shift back into your human form. However, at that point the pain may very well cause you to pass out. I would suggest finding a magical healer immediately.-

"You know what, Eye? Next time, you can just shoot flames out my asshole—you have my permission."

-A revolting proposition, but one that might have certain tactical applications.-

"On second thought, forget I mentioned it. I'm going to pass out now."

-As you wish.-

28

J ust as the Eye had predicted, the pain caused me to lose consciousness after I shifted back into my human form. Were I able to stay in my Fomorian form longer, eventually I would have healed, but my human form offered no such advantages. Thankfully, Samson quickly recovered and used the Pack's magic to restore my eyesight.

After getting dressed, I walked around the area to survey the aftermath of the battle. The only traces of Sonny, Klaus, and Jaeger were piles of ash and cinder on the ground. Whether or not they'd ever return was anyone's guess; so-called "primaries" in the supernatural and fae world were known to regenerate over decades and centuries. Just to be sure they wouldn't come back anytime soon, I dug out more of my magic Molotovs, and burned their remains to dust.

A quick count of the wolves who were left told me that about half the Pack was missing. I presumed most of Sonny's people had beat feet after the fight. When I asked Samson what he intended to do about the mutineers, he shrugged.

"If an alpha decides to kill half his Pack every time some pup decides they have what it takes to take him out, he won't have a

Pack for long. I'll put the word out that all is forgiven, especially considering the extenuating circumstances. But, just in case, stay on your toes and keep one eye over your shoulder for a few weeks—just until we can track Claw down."

"Something tells me he's running back to the Rye Mother right now," I said with a frown. It irked me that he'd gotten away, but I was certain I'd catch up with him soon. In fact, he might even lead me directly to the Rye Mother. *Small comfort, but it'll have to do. Job's still not finished though,* I mused. Fallyn's chiding voice and uncharacteristically bright smile broke me out of my brooding mood.

"Well, druid, I guess I had you pegged wrong. You're actually pretty handy to have in a fight. Plus, you're surprisingly well-endowed when you shift. So, bonus on that count."

I covered my face with my hands. "Please tell me there are no pictures."

"What? Of course there are photos. In fact, you'll be the first male Pack member to grace our annual club calendar. All proceeds go to the children's hospital, so it's for a good cause. You should be honored."

I groaned and rubbed my hands down my now flushed face. "Samson, please pinch me so this nightmare can end."

Fallyn slugged me on the shoulder, probably harder than was necessary. "Relax, you baby. No one took any photos. Too risky. Imagine if that fight got out on the Internet? You can rest easy knowing your secret will be safely kept within the four dozen or so members of the Pack."

"Kill me now," I muttered.

Samson rubbed his mouth with one hand as he graced each of us with an amused look. "Well, look at the bright side. If things don't work out with that cute little hunter, you'll be hella popular with the back-warmers at the clubhouse." He slapped me on the shoulder with a chuckle, then turned on his heel and walked off.

Fallyn giggled and punched me on the same shoulder, even harder this time. I rubbed it and scowled at her. "Hey, chill out already." I pointed at her, then back at me. "Werewolf strength, human body. Remember?"

"Meh, don't be such a pussy. You're part of the Pack now, so you have to represent."

"Yeah, about that..."

She briefly closed her eyes and shook her head gently. "Uh-uh, nope. You don't get to ghost on us now. If you don't want to spend all your spare time at the clubhouse, I get it. I mean, you're not exactly the biker type. But as far as I'm concerned, once you're family, you're family. Pack for life. That's the way it works."

"Alright, I can live with that. But I'm going to stick with my Gremlin, if that's all right. Besides, last I checked, my uncle stripped my hog down to the frame. I doubt I'll see that thing back in one piece anytime soon."

She frowned at me. "Shit, son, I've been turning a wrench since I was a pup. You ever want to get it running again, just give me a call. As long as you provide the beer, I'll help you get that thing back together in no time."

I extended my hand, and we bro shook. "I'd hate to deny Uncle Ed the pleasure, but if worse comes to worst, I'll hold you to that."

At that moment, Sledge, Trina, and a few other loyal wolves walked up to congratulate us. Someone produced a cooler full of cheap beer, and an impromptu party began. I stayed well into the night, drinking at a leisurely pace and enjoying my newfound acceptance in the Pack. What I really wanted was a soft bed and a warm Belladonna at my side... but that could wait. For now, I needed to solidify my bond with the Pack, however tenuous it might be.

Speaking of which, I still got a few sideways glances from members of the Pack—but that was just to be expected. Sure, I had their acceptance, but I'd never truly be one of them. I was a druid, and the product of a fae curse. That made me an oddity and an unknown factor to many of the wolves. Still, I couldn't help but feel a small bit of pride at the fact that I'd stuck it out to the end.

Maybe I was just being macho, but it felt right.

SOON AFTER THE FIGHT, I texted Hemi and Bells to let them know what had happened. Hemi expressed relief that things had turned out okay with the Pack. Of course, Bells was pissed that I hadn't invited her to a good brawl.

Detective Klein was all over the news for weeks, which wasn't surprising considering that she'd been credited with cracking over a dozen missing kids cases. The Circle and Maeve's fixers had ensured that the evidence lined up with her story, and she got fast-tracked for promotion to sergeant. Thankfully, her superiors chose to overlook her apparent investigative breaches of protocol, as the positive PR for the department was worth far more to them than enforcing procedure. We buried the hatchet for good, and I agreed to be her go-to consultant on all things occult and unexplained from then on out.

Truth was, I needed to keep an eye on her, both for her own safety and to make sure she didn't reveal any secrets about the world beneath. I knew from experience that it was a hell of a burden to bear, knowing that monsters lurked all around, and not being able to tell anyone. Klein had been tossed right into the deep end, and she'd need someone to guide her through the minefield that was the supernatural world.

I just hoped it hadn't been a mistake to clue her in, but only time would tell.

Unfortunately, Hemi had been deeply affected by what we'd seen at the warehouse, and he was uncharacteristically melancholy for days after. He dropped out of sight for a while, then a few weeks later he showed up at the junkyard in his rice rod, excited as all hell for no apparent reason.

"Hey, Colin—guess what I did?" he yelled out the window as he honked his horn.

I walked over to greet him, wiping grease on a rag before leaning on his car door. "I dunno, what did you do? Wait, let me guess. You decided to become a polygamist and married those cute Hawaiian triplets that are always hanging around at the club."

"Naw—although, that's not a bad idea. My mum would kill me though, eh? Have a wedding and not invite her—shit, that would be the end of me." He tapped a rhythm on his steering wheel in time with the heavy bassline that thrummed from inside his vehicle. I stood silent just to mess with him, and finally he scowled. "Oh come on, you're not even gonna take a second guess? You're no fun, bruh."

I chuckled. "Dude, just tell me already."

His eyes lit up as he flashed me a movie star grin. "I became a big brother, eh? Turns out a couple of those kids that got abducted come from a bad home, yeah? So, I got Luther to pull some strings for me, and now I'm their mentor. Pretty cool, right?"

"Yeah, man, that is pretty cool. I'm sure you'll be great at it."

"Yup. I already have plans to take them to the gym to teach them MMA. Betcha they'll be going to tournaments and winning trophies in no time."

I cocked my head sideways. "You sure they're going to like that—the organization, I mean? I don't know if it's going to go over so well, you teaching those kids rear naked chokes and armbars."

He dismissed my concerns with a wave of his hand. "Nah, I already asked them if it would be okay. Turns out, they really don't care what you do with the kids, as long as it's safe and you're willing to spend plenty of time with them. Of course, I have to help them with their homework and stuff like that too. But it's going to be a lot of fun, regardless."

I looked him in the eye and raised my chin in a show of respect. "You know what, Hemi? I'm really proud of you. It takes a lot of guts to make a commitment like that—not a lot of guys our age would do it."

He twisted his mouth into a mock frown and gave me the eyebrow. "Yeah, well—maybe you should consider doing it too."

I became very interested in wiping grease from my hands. The truth was, I was spending all my time trying to locate Claw —but I didn't want to spoil his mood. "I would, but I have a lot of stuff to take care of right now. Have a feeling it's going to eat up a lot of my time, and I don't know if it'd be right to commit to something like that."

"I understand. But I think you could do more good spending time with these kids, than trying to get revenge for what happened to them."

I hung my head and stared off in the distance. "Somebody has to stop them, Hemi."

"True. But it doesn't necessarily have to be you."

I squeezed the door frame so hard it hurt. "Yeah, Hemi— yeah, it does."

I HAD LIKED the presidential suite at Maeve's lodge so much, I'd managed to finagle her into letting me use it for a weekend. The plan was to treat Bells to a romantic getaway, in a last-ditch attempt to keep her from leaving me and heading back to Spain.

But as it turned out, I didn't need to give her the full court press. After the events at the warehouse, she'd decided on her own that she wanted to stay—both to keep me out of trouble and to help me squash the Rye Mother's operations in Texas and along the Gulf Coast. Also, she'd expressed a strong desire to escape from under her mother's thumb.

After that, I'd deal with Fuamnach and the Dark Druid. All things in due time.

We were in bed, entwined skin to skin after a marathon love-making session. It was our second night at the lake retreat. After spending the day canoeing and hiking the many trails surrounding the hotel, we had retired back to the room, ordered room service and a couple of bottles of wine, and engaged in all manner of adult diversions.

To this point, I hadn't pressed Bells to share any of her family's history with me. However, she chose to fill me in on what might happen after she ignored her mother's summons.

"Chances are good she'll come for me, and she won't come alone. Colin, my mother is a dangerous woman. I hail from a long line of powerful women who dedicate their lives to a very specific cause."

"And I take it that you're expected to pick up that cause as well."

She brushed a strand of hair away from her face. "I am, but the responsibility goes far beyond simple family expectations. Colin, have you ever heard the stories of the *moura encantada*?"

"The enchanted Moorish girl? Did I get that right?" She held a hand up and wobbled it back and forth. "No, I don't believe I've ever heard of that particular story."

"*Mouros* are like our version of the fae. In Portuguese and Galician folklore, *mouras encantadas* are female spirits who guard the passageways to the Underrealms. The stories are just that—a myth—but they are based in truth. Many centuries ago, the town where my ancestors lived was plagued by attacks from supernatural creatures who came from the Underrealms. The men who went out from the village to fight these creatures all died, and none ever returned.

"Eventually, no one was left to protect the village but the women. A very brave young woman by the name of Vitoria sought help from a wise woman who lived in the hills. This wise woman turned out to be a very powerful witch, and she made a deal with Vitoria. In exchange for her service, and the service of her female descendants, she would give Vitoria and her female offspring the ability to fight the fae and close off the paths, so they could never return."

I sat up, leaning against the headboard and wrapping an arm around her. "That's your family, then? You're one of her descendants?"

"I am, as well as being my mother's only daughter. I chose to rebel by coming to the United States to work for the Circle. Actually, I tricked my mother by convincing her I had entered a study abroad program. She didn't even know I was working for the Circle until the hospital contacted her when I was injured fighting the Dark Druid."

"No wonder she was so pissed. Wow... so what are you going to do?"

She looked up at me and tweaked my nose. "I'm going to stay here with you, silly. What do you think?"

"And if she refuses to go along with your plans?"

She closed her eyes and laid her head against my bare chest, sighing dreamily. "Then I'll just tell her no—forcefully, if necessary."

I didn't think it would be that simple. But I kept my opinion to myself, for fear of ruining the moment. Bells was a grown woman, and she could make her own decisions regarding her family and the direction of her life. Her decision made me happy, because I certainly didn't want to lose her.

But the question was, how wise was it for me to get involved in a spat between Bells and her mother? I resolved instead to try to act as referee between them, should it come to that. Somehow, I had a feeling it would end badly, no matter what I did. But if it came down to it, I'd fight for Bells. Of that, there was no doubt.

MUCH LATER THAT EVENING, I awoke with the feeling that someone had entered the suite. I gently disentangled myself from Belladonna's arms, slipped on some boxers and a pair of jeans, grabbed my sword from the Bag, and quietly exited the bedroom.

The balcony door was open. I found Maeve sitting outside, sipping a cup of tea and staring at the stars. I grabbed my coat and draped it across my shoulders, then walked out to join her. She continued to look up at the night sky as I sat next to her, and we shared a few moments in silence as I joined her in admiring the view.

"This was the reason why I purchased this property. I wanted a place where I could enjoy the night sky, and admire the stars in peace. We don't have stars in Underhill, you know—not sun, either."

"I didn't know that," I replied softly. "Truth is, I don't know much about the Underrealms. Just what Finnegas told me. I get the feeling he spent a lot of time there over the centuries."

She closed her eyes and inhaled deeply, then spoke in a

quiet voice. "This air—I believe it's one of the things I will miss the most about your world." Her voice rose to a conversational volume as she continued. "Yes, Finnegas has spent much time in the Underrealms. In fact, that's where he is now—investigating rumors of an invasion."

I sat up straighter in my chair. "An invasion? Where?"

She opened her eyes and turned to look at me. "For one so intelligent, you do so often insist on being dense. Where else would the fae choose to invade, but here?"

"But why? I thought all your power derived from Underhill? And, I also got the impression it was some sort of paradise—that you could have anything you wanted there, with a snap of your fingers. Why trade that for our world? I don't get it."

"Because, Colin—the Underrealms are nothing more than a pocket dimension, created by the sum total of the magic the fae commanded, back when they were driven from the earth by man. We could no longer return to the place from whence we came. So, we were forced to create Underhill in order to retreat there and allow the age of man to commence.

"And now, the Underrealms are dying. It takes a tremendous amount of magic to fend off the entropy that is the Void that surrounds Underhill. It constantly eats at the edges of those worlds. By its very nature, the Void is driven to destroy the Underrealms, because they're an unnatural construct that does not belong there. Whether in centuries, or in millennia—eventually, Underhill will be destroyed."

I shook my head. "It still sounds like it's pretty far off. Why would your people be in such a rush to get back here now?"

She smoothed her pants self-consciously in the darkness. "My kind are not immortal, no matter what they might lead you to believe. However, we do live for thousands, and in some cases tens of thousands, of years. Centuries pass as years to us, and millennia, as decades. An event that might seem incredibly far in the future to you, would appear to us as an impending disaster."

"So why are you telling me this? Why confide in me, Maeve? Why betray your kind?"

She glanced down and closed her eyes again, placing one hand over the other in her lap. "For several reasons. One, because long ago I decided that this world and your race held far more virtue than the Underrealms and my people ever had. I once fell in love with one of your kind, and that experience changed me forevermore."

I cocked an eyebrow at her, still unconvinced. "And the second reason?"

She opened her eyes and looked at me, gracing me with a smile that was not altogether unkind. "Also because I've chosen you to be my champion. I've selected you over my own subjects, because they're not human, and they do not share your many virtues—selflessness being chief among those."

"Yeah, I figured as much. Not about your reasons why—they've always been a mystery to me—but that you'd chosen me to be your representative. To be honest, though, I don't buy it. Not completely. The way your kind thinks, humans are merely tools to be used and disposed of at your whim. And a tool doesn't need to understand why it's being used to be wielded effectively. So, I'm asking you, Maeve: why tell me this? Why expose your secrets to me?"

She leaned in, clasping one of my hands in her own, and looked me in the eye as she replied. "Over the centuries, I have watched over and observed many of my offspring and their descendants. I have seen them live, grow old, and die—all while I've remained relatively ageless and lived on. And yet, among all the offspring who've come and gone, you alone have reminded me why I chose to side with the human race."

I snatched my hand away and stood quickly, knocking over my chair. "Maeve, what are you saying?"

She withdrew her hands and sat up. "I thought I spoke plainly. My dear boy, you are my descendant."

This concludes the fourth volume in the Colin McCool Junkyard Druid series. Colin's story continues in the next novel in the series, Underground Druid. Subscribe to my newsletter at http://MDMassey.com now for free books, announcements on upcoming releases, and to be notified about future book promotions!

IRL RESOURCES

Modern-day slavery exists, and it often hides in plain sight. Learn more at https://polarisproject.org.

The effects of physical and sexual abuse may be experienced for months or even years after the event. If you are in crisis, call the Mental Health America hotline at 1-800-273-TALK.

Want to do more? Consider donating to or volunteering with Operation Underground Railroad. Find out more at https://ourrescue.org.

Made in the USA
Middletown, DE
02 February 2021